ALSO BY

SANDRINE COLLETTE

Nothing but Dust

JUST AFTER THE WAVE

Sandrine Collette

JUST AFTER THE WAVE

*Translated from the French
by Alison Anderson*

Europa
editions

Europa Editions
214 West 29th Street
New York, N.Y. 10001
www.europaeditions.com
info@europaeditions.com

Copyright © Éditions Denoël, 2018
First Publication 2020 by Europa Editions

Translation by Alison Anderson
Original title: *Juste après la vague*
Translation copyright © 2020 by Europa Editions

Library of Congress Cataloging in Publication Data is available
ISBN 978-1-60945-567-5

Collette, Sandrine
Just after the Wave

Book design by Emanuele Ragnisco
www.mekkanografici.com

Cover image: detail from a photo by Pexels, Pixabay

Prepress by Grafica Punto Print – Rome

Printed in the USA

CONTENTS

To Anne-Marie,

Fairies do exist.
I know one.

JUST AFTER
THE WAVE

L ouie bent down to pick up the little wet thing the sea had brought to the shore. It lay there motionless, scarcely touched by the water, inching forward onto the earth. It was a blue tit, one of those they'd been trying to protect, before, because they were becoming rare. He picked it up and handed it to his father.

"Here, Pata. Another one."

His father nodded and held it close. The others looked on in silence. They would go and bury it later, in the place where they had put the dead birds. This was number one hundred and thirty-four: Louie knew the tally by heart.

And like the others, he went back to staring at the raging sea.

* * *

They were like drowned kittens in the rain, clinging to each other with their stunned gazes, their eyes blinking in the gusting wind and the warm downpours. That was the sea there before them, but not only before them. Behind them, to the left and to the right, there was also the sea. They hadn't had time, in six days, to become accustomed, but they'd understood that the world would never be the same. They did not speak. They just held hands, all eleven of them, father, mother, and the nine children, their faces lashed by the demented weather, the near-constant deluge that obliged them to stay close to the house.

Six days since the wave.

The tidal wave had come and no one had heard it.

Or if someone had heard it, it was already too late.

Should they have expected it? *What's the point of torment-ing ourselves*, the father whispered, *now that it's done.*

Since then they had not seen a single soul; Pata had said they might well be the only survivors, because of that damned hill, which used to scratch the little ones' feet on their way home from school at the end of the day, yes that hill had saved their lives because it was set too high and rose too steeply. The village was down below, in the valley, where there was nothing left to see. And still, at that moment they turned as one toward the village, as if they'd all had the same thought at once: there in the valley, it was all sea, again.

The wave had swept over the world and taken everything with it: houses, cars, animals, and human beings by the thou-sands, trapping flesh and concrete walls alike to bury them beneath the swell and the terrifying currents, to crush them and swallow them wholeheartedly—and if the waters had receded, they would have left behind mangled fields, littered with dead bodies and the debris of bones, metal, and glass, but the waters had not receded, they had settled there, invasive and lethal, and for six days they had been transporting fallen trees, broken beams, and corpses with swollen bellies that the little ones watched drift by, trying to recognize them.

And yet, for months the old folk had voiced their warnings. Even though they sensed that something was about to happen, they'd also gotten it wrong, and with a vengeance. But they were no longer here to talk about it, or shout about who was right and who was wrong, because they were all as dead as the next one, and their straw hats floated on the surface of the water, following the currents and meanders of this new ocean. But in all fairness it must be said they'd been only too aware of how the climate was playing up. They had been the first to stare at the heavens and gently nod their heads while frowning and muttering under furrowed brows. This wasn't normal, they murmured, first among themselves, then before long to anyone who would listen. No, these winds whirling in circles, constantly returning to damage the crops and the houses, these air pockets that upset the animals and painted the sunsets yellow and purple, nothing good would come of it all, nothing anyone knew, and they nodded again, and waited, certain that some day *it would come to pass.*

That other lot—the governments, the politicians—for sure they knew just as well. But not a squeak. No one spoke about it, other than a handful of nutcases doom-mongering on internet sites, and who were instantly taken for heretics and evil prophets, hauled before the judge or discredited by a dozen studies that had been signed, certified, and validated. The previous winter a few hundred inhabitants had left the region without saying a word—mustn't cause the real estate market to crash and end up leaving empty-handed. People remembered them with a scornful sneer: *Oh, you mean those scaredy cats?* And now look.

In short, the old folk had been right, because the heavens and the seasons had gone all out of whack, and an era of storms and small hurricanes had begun. It churned up the sea below them, and every time, the trees lost their branches, like scarecrows amputated first of one arm then the other, and the branches, the trees, crashing and rolling, had killed a few people and quite a few animals, the winds had lopped the roofs off the houses and the waves had dug holes and planted geysers in the sand by that ocean that no longer knew what was going on.

But what the old folk had not foreseen was that the disaster—the real one, the enormous one, the one that had caused thousands or millions of deaths—there was no way of knowing, now—had come from somewhere else altogether: on the sunken island in the sea across from them, the volcano had collapsed, causing a gigantic tidal wave that had swallowed half the planet.

According to the father, who was interested in geology, it was the northern flank of the volcano that had slid into the water with a colossal crash, one hundred million tons of rock, Pata figured, and this had caused the first wave, which was approximately three hundred feet tall; if he had to put a number on it, even a rough estimate, the wave must have shot forward at a speed of two hundred and fifty or three hundred miles an hour. The only thing in their favor was that the groundswell had headed out to the Atlantic; along the coast, they'd only suffered the fallout—a meager consolation when they gazed out at the drowned world around them: the floodwaters had spread over the entire hinterland, and on this too Pata had thought long, concluding gravely that the sea had surely moved three hundred miles inland. Everyone here knew that the same disaster had already occurred a very long time ago, and back then it was the western flank of the volcano that collapsed and produced a groundswell which, despite the distance, went all the way to America, devastating the coasts.

Louie was the only one who saw the wave.

Since then he had been crying at night, and his mother stayed with him until he fell back asleep.

He had seen the wave because he was the one who tended the hens; at seven p.m. precisely, when they had all finished their homework, taken their shower and put on their pajamas, at seven p.m., before supper, it was Louie's job to check one last time that the chicken coop was properly closed; six months earlier a stone marten, must have been, or a fox, had killed half their poultry, getting in through a loose wire fence, and Louie had sworn never, ever again. He had reinforced all the gates, and kept a close watch. But that night, it wasn't the hens he'd been looking at, eyes wide, so wide you'd think they'd never close again, it wasn't the hens that had caused the earth to tremble and his guts with it, sending him to his knees. The wave, towering like some watery monster, made him cry out in terror. It had darkened the sky for miles around him, like a yawning mouth, and had launched its attack on the world, on man and beast.

Louie had run like hell, barricading the front door behind him, screaming, panting, stammering, his mother thought he'd gone mad, he didn't know how to explain, not until the shock of the tidal wave caused the ground to tremble and the walls to shake, and the waves broke all the windowpanes.

They wished they could forget that night, all of them, from the parents down to the baby, that night that had left the house streaming with water and their minds full of an inextinguishable terror, the sea slithering everywhere, its tongue lapping up everything in its way, everything it could rip off and tear and take with it to the deep heart of the water, whence nothing would ever return. By the following dawn, wherever they cast their gaze it fell upon a gray, blue, or green expanse, tufts of grass breaking through when the depth must have been only a foot or two—but nothing anywhere else. So much water you thought you were in the middle of the ocean, for indeed it had become an ocean, with a few rare islands emerging in places where, a few hours earlier, there had been a world.

Rocky ground, and the collapsed volcano.

They had all known, since that dawn, that the house was barely standing. The constant wind made it creak day and night. For a day or two they had hoped they'd spot someone on the sea, encounter a poor soul so they could convince themselves that there was still something alive on this earth turned ocean; they could not conceive of the fact that everything might have perished, even if the sea never stopped its constant careless hustling of lifeless bodies, *They look like little boats*, murmured Noah as he watched them go by, and Madie and Pata didn't scold him because in fact that was what they looked like, like when you put empty walnut shells on a stream to watch the current catch them, and they dance and shudder and capsize.

So there it was, they had waited and nothing had appeared, other than three or four small boats they had seen in the distance, but which never came any closer, boats fleeing in haste, toward higher ground, said Pata, and no matter how they shouted their lungs out and waved their arms, the boats had gone far away, turning their backs on the volcano, returning to the drowned countryside where only two days earlier cars had been speeding by.

Yes, they knew that they had to leave. Despite Pata's reassuring words, by the sixth day the waters had not subsided. The sea level rose, and he kept saying: it will go down. The little ones had stared at the ocean, sure that at any moment it would drain away, like a siphon swallowing the contents of a sink. But the sea was doing just as it pleased and it stayed there, maybe slightly lower than on the day after the cataclysm, but there it remained, and there was still too much of it. So of course there was no other option than to leave, to abandon land's end to the wind and tide, to leave behind forty years of one's life, or fifteen, or one, for all of them it was wrenching, and as the days went by departure became ever more imperative. But they were rooted there by disbelief, by their sense of panic that had not yet yielded to calm but rather turned their legs to jelly, and the only thing they could do, in the end, was hold hands, all eleven of them, on the shore, and look out at the sea and the volcano that had been the source of so much pain, the sea that never stopped rising and the volcano: there was no guarantee that a third flank was not about to slide into the sea and drive the waves out to conquer the hills.

Leave, they murmured in the void.

Pata had to finish repairing the boat that they moored all the way at the bottom of the steep path, in the inlet where they went fishing when there was no school; it had been damaged by an uprooted tree, gored on one side, and the wave had deposited it at the top of the garden with immeasurable force.

But every morning they had to find food and drink, too, and enough for the twelve days the voyage would last if they wanted to reach terra firma. Madie and Pata had studied the maps and planted their fingers on the same spot at the same time, and they'd said, *There*, and there, we'd be safe—but the thing was, to begin with, if no rescuers came to find them they would have to sail for twelve days, maybe twelve days of complete solitude, they couldn't just go off like that as if it were some picnic.

"Yes, a picnic!" exclaimed Sidonie and Emily, clapping their hands.

So whenever the weather allowed, Liam and Matteo, the two eldest, took the big rubber raft that they used to play with in the sea, and with Pata at their side they went to search over by the nearest houses, yesterday's neighbors, the ones they used to say hello to on their way home from school or work; but there were no more neighbors, and the houses had vanished under the water. The only thing they found, and which brought them some small consolation, was another little hill twenty minutes from the island, a hill that had been spared and where a field of potatoes was growing, and they'd gone back there to pull up a few spuds, *This will give us something in reserve*, said Pata, spreading his arms, *months to live on.* The second time, Louie wanted to go with them, but the older boys pushed him away.

"You're only eleven, you're no use."

And they were fifteen and thirteen, almost little men, with their smiles full of delight, for them the tidal wave meant adventure, no more school, and they didn't care about the rest—they were bound to be rescued someday.

"Beat it, with your gimpy leg," growled Matteo, pushing Louie aside when he did not move.

And Louie lowered his eyes to look at his leg that earned him the nickname Limpy when his brothers were angry, this damned crooked leg he'd been born with God knows why, and which his parents only discovered when he was old enough to start walking. The nearby bonesetter had told them it would mend itself. He had manipulated the little boy's leg, recited prayers. *It will be fine*, he'd concluded with a nod, and nothing had changed. Louie had his game leg and his older brothers knew only too well how to remind him of it when he started clinging to them or pestering them, *tattletale*, they said, so he went off to see Perrine and Noah, who'd been born just after him and before the babies; the babies were all the ones who were not yet seven, which was the age of reason: Emily was six, Sidonie, five, Lotte, three, and Marion, just one year old.

When they were in a neat little row on the shore looking at the angry sea, holding hands—except for Marion, tight in Madie's arms—Louie wondered what had happened in the middle.

The middle being the three of them: Louie, Perrine, and Noah.

In the middle, something had gone wrong.

Louie had a twisted leg, Perrine was blind in one eye, and Noah, at the age of eight, was no taller than a five-year-old. Before them, Liam and Matteo were handsome and well-built; after them, the four little sisters had not the slightest flaw. So what had happened to them?

Three rejects. Maybe there was no explanation.

It just landed on them, that was all.

So because there was no answer, Louie squeezed the hands of the dwarf and the one-eyed girl, as the older brothers called them when their parents were out of earshot, and the little ones smiled, never taking their eyes off the ocean, squeezing their fingers even harder, and that was enough, Louie held his leg very straight, blinking in the gusts, while inside, he was singing.

* * *

What on earth were they going to do now.

The boat was almost completely repaired, but that wasn't what worried them: Pata had predicted that the waves would subside, but they were getting more skeptical by the day, and couldn't help but check the water level in the basement or on the flagstones in the garden. Madie was the only one who'd had her doubts ever since the first morning. And yet she could have succumbed to the ease of believing what Pata said; it would have been comforting, the thought that everything would revert to the way it had always been, that the sea was bound to go back where it belonged, and that underneath, they would find the swing, and the blue pebbles surrounding the flower beds, and the green bench—and further down, the village in the valley. Yes, if she listened to the father of her nine children, she would be convinced through and through that the sea would give them back their land, the grass, the trees. She would even have conceded that the more time went by, the greater their own chances of seeing the gray waters ebb away, because who had ever heard of a flood that stayed forever, the world was in perpetual motion and would force the waters to recede, it couldn't all just stay like that, motionless, such things didn't happen.

But Madie didn't believe it, she really didn't, and there was no comfort for her. She refrained from saying how, on the contrary, years ago, on the other end of the planet, there was land that had been devoured by the desert, and all the people had fled, and the rain never ever fell again, and no plants ever grew again, to bring the people back. Those lands had died under the sun, for good, the same way that now their own fields had been drowned, forever, six days earlier. The waters were no longer rising, but they weren't receding, either, as if the ground had been covered with an impermeable web, and nothing could budge. Everything was frozen. There was no end to Madie's worry.

But she pretended everything was all right, and went on smiling. She didn't really have to try very hard, to be honest: she loved her little children, and even her idiot of a husband who so stubbornly hoped the water level would drop. She looked at them and knew that her life had meaning because she was there with them all, and that they had miraculously survived the huge tidal wave. Her kids were laughing in the morning sunlight, holding hands as they ran outside before scattering over the three and half thousand square yards which were, henceforth, nothing less than their entire world—they were right when they said as much, at that moment their mother was redrawing the horizon, there were eleven of them, just eleven in the whole world. And all at once she forgot her anxiety, she forgot nostalgia. Her entire body trembled for them alone, the nine little children she'd brought into the world, and with their father she had laughed for joy every time it happened, she mustn't give up, ever, for every single one of her children justified her efforts, her fatigue, her constant readiness.

When Madie's thoughts took this turn, she would begin to hum, overcome with joy. The kids came to listen and she sang nursery rhymes, and they joined in, they knew them all, sang them in the evening to fall asleep in their bedrooms, where they left the doors open so that light, sounds, and life itself would move around them, never mind if they were late to bed. Their father would come closer, too, drawn by their joyful cries, and he'd lead their mother in a farandole, and they'd instantly do likewise, in such a way that all together they performed a strange disorderly dance. From a distance it might have looked like some shamanic rite or a slightly demented procession, when it was nothing more or less than a very short and very wonderful moment of happiness.

* * *

And so, to prove the mother right, and destroy all their hopes, on the seventh day the waters began to rise.

* * *

It began with the look in the father's eyes.

Just one look, and Madie knew. She closed her eyes, he didn't need to say anything.

Because on that seventh morning, when she looked outside, the rock she used as a landmark had vanished. She didn't want to believe it. She didn't want to look again, either, she preferred doubt and anxiety to any terrible certainty. That would come soon enough.

It would come from the father: she knew that, too.

Just a murmur, maybe because things seem less terrifying in a hushed voice:

"Oh, bother."

And even though Madie knew, she couldn't help but repeat what he'd said, also in a murmur, *Oh, bother, what?*

Looking out at the dawn that day, Pata had felt the shock right to his heart. He had come away pale, his legs trembling: of course he had to tell the mother.

And she went and repeated it, because he was being so stubbornly silent:

"Oh, bother, what?"

"The water."

He didn't say anything more. He placed his hand thigh-high

to show her the water level and Madie stared eyes bulging at his hand. She put her own hand on his to lower it, to conjure fate, in a way, as if the waters might subside at the same time as the father's hand, if there was a god, if only.

The father lowered his hand and nothing else happened.

And so they kept an eye on the sea's advance. On the ninth day, the big boulder at the bottom of the garden vanished. The tenth day, the twenty-eight hens and the rooster that had survived the tidal wave awoke with their legs in water, the chicken coop flooded. Louie opened the gate to let them roam free across the island; in any case, the foxes had died long ago.

On the eleventh day the weather began to change. The August heat was stifling, but finally relented during a storm. When they saw the first lightning bolts, and the thunder rumbled far on the horizon with sinister crackling, the children cried for joy. Louie and Perrine, however, glanced at each other, then looked at their father, who was sniffing the air.

"The clouds are yellow," said Louie.

Pata replied, *I know*, and the two children knew they had to keep quiet, that the sky was abnormally heavy and the clouds were a threatening ochre: things were not as they should be. Louie dared to ask:

"What shall we do?"

"Get inside the house, all of you. There's a storm coming."

"Liam and Matteo aren't here. They went with the raft to see if the Turpins' house was underwater, you know, they live on a little hill, too."

Liam and Matteo: their father was searching for them on the horizon. He had let them go on their own, without telling Madie, the sea was choppy, but they were used to it. And besides, the Turpins' place wasn't far. But they must have gone a bit further, to look for the corner of a roof, or a chimney-top, or to play. Teeth clenched, and angry with himself, Pata muttered, *Damn kids*. But they'd be back. Maybe they'd seen how the sky had filled and were right nearby, hidden by a treetop still piercing the surface, their raft was about to appear—yes, God, make sure they had see the sky.

But the father had every reason to believe that Liam and Matteo were still far away when the clouds gathered and the rumbling of thunder startled him, because the storm arrived in no time at all; from where he stood he could see gray whirlwinds of crazed wind and torrential rain. Ten minutes more and the gusts would arrive at their hill. Pata could already feel his hair clinging to his face, and he parted it with both hands to try to make out something on the surface of the water, hatched with black waves. He had to keep wiping his eyes because of the spray.

Then he saw them.

At first, for a second or two, he hoped it wasn't them. But who else could be afloat in a rubber raft, when they had not seen a soul since the tidal wave—and the father let out a long cry which Madie and the children heard through the closed shutters in the house, despite the roaring wind, and it made them cluster together at the paneless windows and look through the cracks. *It's them, it's them*, shouted Noah.

The rubber raft was dancing on the waves. Liam didn't know what to do, with the paddles that no longer obeyed, the waves pounding against them, and the hill just there, out of reach, the water was playing with them, the raft was nearly taking flight, too light, too much wind.

Onshore the father began to bellow.

"Hang on behind, and swim! Swim, otherwise you'll never get back!"

But neither Liam nor Matteo could hear him. They could hardly make out their father's figure one hundred yards from there, his eyes full of tears and rain, his figure shouting something else in vain, then spinning round and running.

The father yanked the ropes from their hook on the side of the house.

When he came back to the edge of the water, the raft was almost vertical on the raging sea.

"This way!" shouted Pata at the top of his voice. "Liam, this way!"

He threw the ropes as far as he could across the water. He didn't know if he'd managed to fling them far enough, but clearly he hadn't, and Liam couldn't even see them, and he shouted again, waving his arms, because the kids had to understand.

"Go over to the rope! The rope!"

This time the elder boy must have seen him because he waved to signal to him, and the father's heart sank. It wasn't a sign that the boy had understood; and if the father could have heard Liam, he would have faltered at his words, *Pata, help, Papa, we're going to die*—and instead he went on shouting for all he was worth, *The rope, the rope, over here!*

And when at last he had to accept the boys were doomed, that they would never manage to find the ends of the rope, too far away, that the wind was scattering his useless cries, he moored the rope to a tree on the shore and flung himself into the water, following the rope.

It took considerable energy to fight his way through the waves. Fairly quickly he was in over his head and he fought the current, his terror, too, a little voice in his head whining, *What are you doing, you are going to die, all three of you*, and he thought of the mother who must have seen him from the window and repressed a cry of horror as he dove in, and of the seven children still in the house and who needed him, the rope was getting in his way, tangling in his legs, ten times over the waves submerged him and he thought he wouldn't make it, then he struggled upward yet again and just had time to raise his arms to protect himself from the raft which loomed like a black orca above him then slapped down on the water, knocking him on the shoulder.

The father clung on, found a handhold. Liam and Matteo were hanging onto the raft, almost upright with the storm-shrieking wind. For a moment time was suspended and all the father could see was the boys, and behind them the black and yellow sky, this was how he had pictured the end of everything, the roaring hurricane, the furious, yawning waves, all of it in a strange muffled sensation devoid of sound; then the fracas came to strike him head on, he nearly lost the rope, and coiled it around his wrist.

"Liam!"

He gave an almighty shove to hoist himself on the raft with them.

At that very moment a wave knocked them all over, Liam, Matteo, the raft, and the father. With a burst of energy Pata grabbed his sons, swallowed water with them, and brought them back to the surface, spitting and coughing. The raft bounded on the sea like a mad horse. The father reached for it, even though it was already beyond his grasp, he didn't think he'd catch it, it was just a reflex, panic, too.

"Hang onto my back!" he shouted to Liam. "And you, Matteo, hang onto Liam. And don't let go. Don't ever let go!"

He tightened his grip on the rope, still fastened to the tree. His head was roaring: *We are going to make our way along this rope.* The moment Liam and Matteo fastened themselves to his shoulders, he felt their fingernails on his skin, the resistance of the current and their weight dragging him ever lower into the water, obliging him to make a colossal effort. And he began to doubt.

But it was not far to land, he could see the hill beyond the curtains of rain, a black shape rising up to the house, his island, his refuge—the waves buffeting him, furiously, his arms burning in the water, making hardly any progress. Suddenly he knew he wouldn't make it, his strength would give way before he reached the shore, even if he let go of one of his boys, or both of them, half strangling him as they clung on. He was swimming, on the verge of collapse, gripping the rope inch by inch to help himself, but the tension was exhausting, he was sinking, so that was what it was, he was drowning, gradually, and with him his sons who were panicking and could not help him, he was foundering, he could no longer move forward along the rope and it was dropping deeper into the water, he would have to go faster, have to pull hard, as he used to say to the boys when he was teaching them how to row, but his arms were no longer moving, he had nothing left. Still full of rage at how weak he was he struggled for a last burst of energy, but all he could do was hang onto the rope, and yet what was the point of clinging to it for dear life if they were all going to drown, Liam, Matteo, and him; despair tightened his throat, there he'd gone and rushed into the water, so sure he'd be able to bring his boys back safe and sound, so smug, and the storm was coming down on him even harder, a fraction more and it would tear his arms from his body, something inside him was surrendering, shouting for mercy.

Then for a second the rope went taut and he thought he'd caught it on a tree trunk that would take them back out to sea. He struggled for a few seconds, already vanquished, the line wrapped around his wrist. And he felt that they were moving forward.

At first he thought it was an illusion, dizziness taking over, his head knocked about in the cold waves. But it wasn't: the rope was pulling him toward the hill. The current pounded at him, furiously, eager to pull him back, hurling pieces of wood and lumps of turf at him, but he was slowly progressing toward the house, which he could now see a bit more clearly. He didn't try to understand. He let himself slip through the water, Liam and Matteo still on his back, half drowning him, it was enough to make him weep, but he had no strength left to say anything to them—just stay afloat, on the surface despite these waves coiling around them and the wind driving them back, the rope was holding, and when the father had one last hope that they might make it after all he raised his head and, ravaged and incredulous, he saw them.

They were there on the shore, a hundred feet away, except for Lotte and Marion, whom the mother must have left shut in the house. His mouth open in a cry of panic, the father murmured their names in his head: Madie, Louie, Perrine, Noah, Emily, Sidonie. All pulling on the rope, even his one-eyed daughter, even his stunted son, pulling in time to the steady, formidable call of *Heave!* coming from the mother's throat, crushing the roar of the wind, all of them breathing hard to pull the three drowning figures toward them, they didn't falter, despite the gusts, the rain, the thunder, despite the waves' attempts to make them stumble, they helped each other up, they went on winching, rolling the rope around the tree. And the terrified father watched them struggling against the storm and the sea, so tiny on their little wind-lashed patch of earth, heads down, backs rounded like animals huddled against bad weather, not one of them would yield, not even Sidonie who was not really much use but who gripped the rope as well, constantly slipping, what if she fell, and rolled down to the water—and the father murmured her name in a sob, prayed the mother would make them go back to the house, all it would take was one broken tree, one slab of earth breaking off and they would all be washed away. But they stood there shouting together for courage and to curse the heavens, the rope pulling constantly against the current, and suddenly the father felt the sludge beneath his feet, a few pebbles, and land, yes, it was land.

The mother stopped the children from running toward them as they stumbled onto the shore: the storm was too violent to go near the edge of the water. Pata fell to his knees, his heart pounding, Liam still on his back, letting Matteo slip off behind him. The father took them by the hand, stood up, and with a superhuman effort walked the few steps that separated him from the others. The mother spread her arms. The father let go of the boys' hands and embraced her, sobbing; then they all ran up in a clamor that for a few seconds silenced the wind, the little ones, the older ones, and they all held each other so tight they couldn't breathe, a dense, drenched huddle in the midst of the storm, a warm, powerful heart throbbing with the children's laughter, defying the waves, until at last the mother stood up straight, her eyes wide in the pouring rain, and she said, as if they had won a war:

"We can go in, now."

* * *

Go in, and flee. There could no longer be any doubt. This land—or what was left of it: they didn't want it anymore; it terrified them. The father looked out the window. It wasn't really a land, to speak of: a little island in the middle of the water, a rock condemned to vanish. There was an urgency, now. Madie had put the children to bed after making them some crepes with the hens' eggs, and now she was on the sofa, waiting silently.

Pata didn't speak; he was gazing out at the night.

Of course he couldn't see anything. It was just so it wouldn't show. So that he wouldn't worry the mother, or pass his fear onto her, because she would have been upset to learn that he felt this bad, and besides it was stupid, she'd find out soon enough, he was going to tell her. He had to. This evening, the storm that had nearly cost them their lives had brought the water level up to the threshold of the house. And even if this storm, which had taken the raft from them, suddenly brought it back, tossing it onto the shore in a furious gust of wind, this was of no consolation to anyone, because no one would ever have the courage to head out onto the sea in such a flimsy vessel again; they'd put it away in the back of the barn, where you could hardly see it.

Madie had been saying, from the very morning after the tidal wave, that they had to get ready to leave; Pata had sworn they wouldn't need to, all they had to do was wait for the waters to recede. She'd been right, and he'd been wrong.

Which meant that the time had come.

Only problem was.

How to tell her.

She could see, just as he could, she must have figured it out. Why didn't she bring it up first, ordinarily she had a ready tongue, why didn't she open her bloody chatterbox mouth, for once he wouldn't have minded. She wanted him to get bogged down, that was it, and she wouldn't mind shouting that it was all his fault, he was the one who'd decided to stay, he'd sworn to her that the waters would depart as surely as they had come, that they'd do better to hang onto their land. And she, the bird of ill omen, who looked at him askance with doubt in her eyes: she should be jubilant now, and yet.

Pata let out a long sigh. Yes, it was all his fault, Madie was right. He'd been stubborn, he hadn't wanted to listen, to see the obvious signs. Hadn't been afraid. The imbecile.

And now?

The mother was still silent, and all of a sudden the father could no longer stand her silence. He would have preferred a good fight, in the end, a shouting match, like when he was convinced he was right. But now . . . He didn't even dare look up at her. And it was as he turned his head one more time toward the window with its broken panes, toward the darkness that showed him nothing, that he murmured, "We will have to leave."

Madie didn't answer. So he added:

"We will have to leave the island, and soon. The water is going to flood everything."

And because she still did not whisper even half a word, he let his wretched gaze slip toward her, in vain, because she would not forgive him, ever, and in her eyes when they met his he saw her answer.

Leave.

Yes, but.

"I know," he stammered.

He didn't say, *It will be fine.* This time he couldn't.

It would be a long trip, they had to gather supplies. Nearly two weeks' worth.

No, that wasn't what was worrying him. The fact that it would be a long trip, they'd get used to that. They'd hardly eat, they'd ration themselves. The little ones would understand.

Maybe if Liam and the father rowed hard, they could make it in twelve days. But twelve days still wouldn't solve the problem. The problem was something the father couldn't bring himself to say and it was tearing his throat out: they had only one boat.

And the mother grasped it immediately, as he had known she would, because just then she looked at him with fire and hatred and despair all at the same time, a look that condemned him now and forever—and she murmured, as if it was because of him, just him, as if it were all his fault, the sea, the storm, and misfortune:

"Who are you going to leave behind?"

ON THE ISLAND
The morning of August 19

There was always noise in the big house, and it woke them at dawn, one after the other, with a smile. There were good, warm, toasted smells. Madie, since the tidal wave, had been making French toast in the morning with the stale loaves they had put aside. Of course she was parsimonious as she sprinkled the bread with sugar, because she didn't know how long they would be there on that stump of earth without any help. The children didn't mind, they realized the situation was exceptional and when it wasn't raining too hard they made their own fun baking rolls with flour and water on a fire outside, stuffing a square of chocolate into the middle to make them less insipid. Then Madie had decreed that they had to save on the food, and on the wood she was keeping for the old stove they'd retrieved in haste from the barn where it had been languishing, and by the third day they were no longer allowed to cook their soft, sweet pastry. As it happened, it was on that third day that the restrictions began. Madie was getting organized, it was a siege, she said, the sea had surrounded them, they had to resist. Pata and the older children had already started putting aside the cans, jars, and bottles they found in every nook of the most hidden cupboards—but how long would they be on the island? The rough seas meant flight was impossible, or only at great risk, they didn't dare think of it, there was only the need to survive on their hill from one day to the next and hope the house would stand. The sea is getting calmer, murmured Pata, and Madie wondered what her man had between his ears, because with the naked eye you couldn't see it getting any calmer, not as far as she could tell, not according to the children, either; she could do nothing but shrug in response to their questioning looks.

But the fact remained that in spite of the mother's decision to ration everything it still smelled good when they woke up in the morning. When Madie didn't feel like using up her vanilla and sugar anymore, all she had to do was fry her pancakes, which they used as bread; even the slightest burning on the stove and the smell filled the room, wove its way down the corridor, up the stairs, and into the bedrooms.

Yes, Louie would recall those mornings for a long time, those dawns that had enchanted his taste buds and lured him spellbound into the kitchen.

Until the thirteenth day.

He would never forget that, either.

It had started the same as any ordinary morning. But it wasn't a morning like the others: there was no smell in the house.

At first he didn't really notice, it took him a few seconds to emerge from sleep, feeling calm, drowsy. In the bedroom, Perrine and Noah were still asleep. For a few seconds he listened to their breathing, watched their blankets rising and falling rhythmically. He pushed back his sheets.

He wasn't thinking about anything just then. Or maybe only that it was hot. He could leave his shirt off. Open the door, quietly.

And finally: no smells, no coffee or toast, nothing, just the smell of the void.

* * *

Outside, the water hasn't moved. Or surely it has risen a bit, but you can't see it, either in Louie's eyes, or Noah's, or in Perrine's one eye. No room.

They stand looking out to sea.

They have seen the footprints around the jetty and they know it is true. And anyway, the boat is gone. Afterward, they'll go back into the house and reread ten times over the note that Madie left on the table. For now they are staring out at the horizon as hard as they can. If they could spot the boat somewhere, even at the farthest point, they would throw themselves in the water to swim to it. But all they can see are the usual reeds and scattered shrubs, and their vision blurs.

With tears, naturally.

Noah is the first to fall to his knees. He calls to their mother. Perrine sits next to him, takes him in her arms. Louie joins them. All three cling to each other, their hands squeezed, white with the energy they put into silently promising not to leave one another. Three little creatures, their wet cheeks pressed together, sobbing words which the wind sweeps away.

They're afraid.

They don't know who will say it first: why have their parents abandoned them? Actually, they understood why when they read the letter that crumpled their faces and stopped their hearts—but there is something else they can't stop thinking about, nor find the means to express: why them?

Why them and not the others.

Noah was the one who asked.

"I don't know," murmurs Louie to start with.

Perrine snivels, still looking out at the horizon as if she might miss seeing her parents on their boat, out there on the water. Her clear little voice, just the same. *I don't know.*

"Because we were naughty?"

Silence. Maybe they are thinking. Noah continues.

"Because I'm too small, Louie has a sick leg, and Perrine's only got one eye, is that why they left us? Because they didn't love us?"

At the same time, they reply in one breath.

"No," says Perrine.
"Yes," says Louie.

* * *

That their parents didn't love them; and if they knew, those little children left behind on the island, how their mother is sobbing in silence on the boat, just as they are crying alone on the damp earth, the mother who is holding Lotte and Marion tight, inconsolable. Emily and Sidonie are curled up next to Matteo. In the middle, Liam and his father are rowing. Because of the mounds of supplies, lashed in place with criss-crossing straps, they don't have an inch to move, crowded fore and aft on their small craft. The father has installed ropes all around the gunwale, as a precaution.

Madie doesn't know how the little ones will manage to sit still for twelve or fourteen days. *We'll stop*, said Pata. But she silenced him with a look. No, they won't stop. They will keep going until they reach higher ground and he will go back for the other three right away. He promised.

The night before their departure he was also the one who decided which children would stay behind on the hill. The mother didn't want it, she was set on one impossible idea: take them all.

"We won't last three days without supplies or water," said the father. "We can't be sure we'll find any other people to help us. There might be nothing more until we reach the mountains. No people. No islands."

Madie repeated, *No more love. No more honor. We're like animals.* And she fell silent, because her gaze had met Pata's, no need of words to pierce soul and flesh, is there, silence is enough, when it is so heavy with meaning, and it was the father who took a breath and started speaking after that silence; the harm was done. Nothing would ever erase the mother's silence, nothing would ever prevent the words she had not uttered from going through Pata's head over and over again, and every day he'd wonder if there was not some truth in them, and yet no, God, he swore that when, sick at heart, he had picked the names of the three little ones who'd stay behind, not once had it occurred to him, it was Madie who thought it must have, Madie who eventually came out with it, because it was too much to bear.

"The lame one, the half-blind one, the dwarf. So, we'll leave them behind, the most damaged. We'll finish what nature began."

But the father saw things differently. He needed Liam and even Matteo to row, and they couldn't abandon the little girls: they would never survive on the hill. Louie, Perrine, and Noah slept in the same room. It would be easier not to wake them when they left. Louie and Perrine were very resourceful. They would manage, they'll surprise us, hey, don't you think, implored the father. The mother wasn't listening, she was blocking her ears. She didn't want to hear his pathetic arguments. She simply murmured, "Suit yourself."

"You'll blame me."

"I'll blame you for everything, anyway."

Because earlier that evening, when he had decided they must flee, she had tried. Oh, yes, she had tried to make him change his mind, and she'd hit him in the chest ten times, until he took her in his arms to stop her, until he murmured that they had no choice, and with all the spite she'd accumulated she snarled how unthinking he was, how stubborn, how criminally stupid, *You see where it's gotten you, your stubborn pride? You think I brought children into the world so that you can go and kill them?*

The father had wept, too, but he'd held his ground. This time he was right, he was sure of it. He didn't tell the mother but he felt they had to start by saving some of the children;

deep inside, a little voice echoed, *That's already something.* And when the mother swore she would stay on the hill to give her place on the boat to one more child, he refused point blank. She had to go with them. To watch over the children, to keep them calm. To look after them once they landed and the father went back for the others. He wouldn't let her discuss it: she would be the mother of the six children on the boat.

But God, the other three!

"We could at least explain to them," she begged.

But the children would scream and weep and cling to them when it came time to leave, thought the father. Neither one of them, neither he nor the mother, would have the courage to pry their little fingers from the ropes on the boat; neither one of them would be able to shove them away with the blades of the oars when they flung themselves into the water to follow them like little abandoned dogs about to drown. Their cries would stay with them all through the crossing: shrill at first, then more and more distant. No, it was unbearable.

The mother begged him to think about it.

"Can't we find something to put them in—a tub, a feed trough. We could tow them behind the boat."

The father shook his head: every solution was futile. There was nothing left on the hill. Nor any time left. The sea was still threatening, it would already be hard enough with one boat. So they gathered the necessary supplies, hiding them in a corner of the barn; they threw together a few belongings, blankets, tarps, when the children wouldn't see them, most often in the middle of the night. Madie helped, weeping, sick with shame. *Hiding from my own children*, she sobbed. *It's as if I were preparing their coffin.* Pata took her by the shoulders and shook her.

"Will you stop?"

He had repaired the boat without a word, as the children cried for joy. When he first launched it, Noah wanted to go with him to check that it was watertight, sliding his little hands over the repair, looking for any signs of a drop seeping through.

"Not a thing," he concluded, delighted. "Pata, you're great."

And the father had given him an odd look, you'd think he wasn't all that happy to have such a seaworthy boat after all. Noah went on smiling, calling to the others onshore, who called back, somewhat envious.

And so Madie and Pata left at dawn on the thirteenth day, rousing six of their nine children without a sound, piling their belongings wet with their mother's tears there among them, while Liam and Matteo, whom the father had ordered to keep quiet, whispered together, wide-eyed.

"Where are Louie, Perrine, and Noah? Where are we going?"

* * *

But of course this is of no consolation to the children on the island. The only thing they can see is the deserted land around them.

"There's nobody left," cried Noah, after running around the house.

Louie and Perrine did not protest: the three of them are nobody. They don't really exist anymore.

All that's left is the rising sea.

D ay one of wandering.

Stupor keeps them riveted to the hill. One thing makes Louie fly off the handle: the hens squawking to be fed. He eventually kicks them away.

"Shut up! Shut up!"

All they had ever wanted was more time to play, but now they don't know how to fill the hours. There is a terrifying void inside which prevents them from thinking, moving, even talking sometimes. Never has their land been so silent.

They don't dare get separated. They follow each other for everything, they walk together around their plot of land as if the parents might be hiding somewhere, they keep close together to go back to the house to eat a pancake, tidy the kitchen, turn their sheets back at night.

They constantly return to the shore, to the water's edge, where they sit side by side. A part of them has not yet understood, not yet accepted. Noah asks:

"When are they coming back?"

Louie's furious gaze: *They're not coming back.*

"Yes they are," says Perrine. "Madie said so in her letter."

Louie stamps his foot on the ground.

"They're not coming back."

"They said they would."

"They're liars."

Noah starts crying again. *Don't worry,* whispers Perrine, *it's not true, what he said, he's the liar.* But her eyes are stinging, little Perrine, she's not all that sure what the letter has promised. That they've gone away, yes, the mother does say that. That there wasn't room enough on one boat. As soon as they've found higher ground, the father will come back— "which means he'll come and get us, you see, Louie, you're full of nonsense."

Noah looks his sister right in the eye.

"Are we going to die?"

At the bottom of the letter the mother wrote that they have to keep adding wood so the fire in the stove won't go out. And that they have to eat the hens. That she has left enough food, if they share it every day, and that she loves them all, Perrine, Louie, and Noah: those were her last words. But whether they're going to die or not, she doesn't say. Perrine turns the paper over. There's nothing written on the back. So she repeats it to herself: "Die?"

She doesn't really know what it means, or how it happens. Neither does Noah, actually, he's heard his parents say the word but he's hardly seen anything more than fish or poultry lifeless in the kitchen sink, and that is how he pictures death, in fact: when you don't move anymore but your eyes are open. And sometimes there's some blood on your body.

"No," says Perrine after a long pause.

Not that she's completely sure: she answered on principle.

"And what about them," continues Noah, "Pata, Madie, and the others, are they dead?"

"I don't think so."

"I wish they were dead."

Louie looks up. *Me, too.* Perrine frowns.

"You mustn't say that."

Noah shakes his head. *I wish they were. They shouldn't have left us.*

Later, all three of them lie down on the shore, they stop moving, stop speaking. They keep their eyes open, blinking as little as possible. They want to know what it's like to be dead, they wait a few seconds, a few minutes. Noah gets impatient and wiggles, Louie scolds him.

"This is stupid," says the little boy, sitting up.

And then:

"I'm hungry."

Perrine glances over at Louie, who hasn't reacted. She too is finding this immobility difficult, so the thought of eating something brings her to her feet. She's used to helping her mother in the kitchen; what she likes best is making cakes.

"Noah, go get a log."

The little boy runs off.

Louie's stomach is rumbling. They have lost track of time. Does it matter? He grumbles.

"I'm not hungry."

But Perrine is not their mother. She doesn't insist, doesn't ruffle his hair and ask him what's wrong. Doesn't shrug or pull him along behind her. She walks back up to the house next to Noah, he carries his log, out of breath. So Louie stops being dead and catches up with them.

"What are we going to eat?"

Perrine doesn't know. It's one thing to help out in the kitchen, another thing to come up with a meal. She thinks about the days gone by, what her mother used to make. She'll do the same. And like it said in the letter, make portions for each day. On a sheet of paper she writes down what they will eat. At the same time she sets the food out in little piles on the table: one for the first Wednesday, one for the first Thursday, and so on. This reassures her. If they stick to her list, they'll easily have enough. She nods: "That's it, then."

Noah smiles: *They're pretty, those little piles.*

In the afternoon they wander around the hill. Louie stares at the hens pecking at the close-cropped grass; he gathered their eggs, laid them carefully side by side in a basket. They return to sit at water's edge, tirelessly, even if the chances of seeing the boat now are nonexistent. The rain stopped that morning, the sun is baking. They lie on the ground, facing the horizon, exhausted by emotion. With their half-open eyes they keep watch on the expanse of water. The hope that their parents will return has not totally disappeared. They fall asleep, unawares, and when they wake they are sunburnt. Noah has a headache and cries.

"I want Mommy."

Perrine and Louie try to console him, in vain. His sobs turn to moans, he would like to stifle them but cannot, he begins to tremble, his hands stretched toward the open ocean, he stammers, *Mommy, Mommy* . . .

It's silly, but what can they do, anyway, when they see him so unhappy the two older children begin to cry, too. And besides, they're not the eldest; they feel tiny on this planet which, for the first time, is hostile toward them—tiny and lost, they don't know what to do, they no longer know how to live, or why. Two weeks is too long. One day, yes, that they could understand, or even two or three. But now it's getting all muddled in their heads. Two weeks is infinity, something unimaginable and terribly impossible. They miss their parents, and this hollows out their bellies, leaves a lump in their throats. Abandonment has begun.

Only exhaustion restores calm.

On her sheet of paper that evening Perrine crosses off the day and all three of them look at the number of days remaining. It's huge. Not one of them has any idea what their life will be like during this endless period that lies ahead.

"I wish the planet would sink tonight," says Louie.

Noah frowns.

"Planets don't sink."

Sitting on their beds, they stay up late, exchanging a few meager words to fill the silence and, once anxiety returns, to forget the sound outside of the rising wind and the shutter hooks banging against the walls. To drift off without noticing into an unquiet rest, broken by tears, all three of them in the same bed, otherwise it's too scary. And to dream of Madie, of her warm arms, her lovely smile when she kisses them in the evening before they go to sleep—Madie who is no longer there except in the space of a dream, she left without them, they sob in their sleep, they're almost dead.

B y the second morning, they are already little animals, pale and hairy, wordless creatures who rub their eyes as they look at each other, grumpily, as if each one of them was guilty for the terrible abandonment, as if anger had grown during the night and all it would take was one misstep, one word, one gesture too many, a sneeze. They get dressed without washing, without combing their hair—in fact they don't get dressed, they simply put trousers over their pajamas and go barefoot to the kitchen where there is no smell, no movement. Then they look at each other and remember; until now it was only a dream. Noah sits on the floor. They wait.

How long?

To see if their mother is simply late. If she's going to get up.

A quarter of an hour, a bit more. In silence. If their mother hums behind the door, they'll hear her.

But there is no one humming.

Reality takes hold of them again: their parents are gone. There is no more dream. They wander aimlessly, empty of all desire, sitting at the table the way they did when their mother was still there to give them breakfast, pancakes and tea, hot chocolate, or hot water with a few grains of coffee just to give it some taste, sometimes fruit or a crêpe, or bread and honey. They look at each other. Who is going to make breakfast? Louie slips off his chair and opens the cupboards. He knows that in one cupboard there are cookies and candy, at the very top; he knows, too, that Madie must have taken them with her, but he tries all the same, and lets out a shout. The shelf is nearly full, the candy is there, all the ones they're only allowed to have from time to time, green, red, blue, pink, or yellow, it's junk, says Madie, Pata buys it to keep the children happy, what's the point if we can't eat it?

Louie takes everything down and puts it in the middle of the table, next to Noah, who bursts out laughing and holds out his hand. Louie crushes his hand with his.

"Just one. Otherwise we'll be sick."

They tear the packets open, furiously. In the beginning they count them, because Perrine told Louie that they could have three each, but those three go too quickly, they'll stop at five, six, eight, and then they forget, the sugar sticks to their gums and saliva whenever they stuff their mouths with a licorice or a marshmallow gummy bear, and they laugh. Of course they don't leave a single one, and they already feel sick to their stomachs, but in defiance, vengefully, they will devour every last one, right down to the grains of sugar that fell on the floor, until they put their hands on their tummies, hesitant, and Noah murmurs, "I'm gonna puke."

They scatter, prey to the strange experience of making themselves sick with no one there to scold them, no one there to hand them a basin or a damp cloth, afterwards, when they've run outside bent double and stayed on their knees in the grass for a long time, one after the other, each one in their own little spot, they come back together hanging their heads, eyes red, mouths still grimy, *We shouldn't have eaten everything*, whispers Louie.

The morning goes by in a sort of semiconsciousness between disgust and sorrow, a time in between where nothing gets done, where they wander absently and shuffle along until they end up on the shore, overwhelmed, distraught. They forget to have lunch, the candy has upset their stomachs. In the house they take out a game, then another one, and spread them across the floor. They don't begin to play. Don't feel like it. Don't have the energy. They go on sitting on the old parquet floor, heads to one side, gazing at the cards spread before them, the dice, the pieces, and they don't touch them, they're not interested. They sigh, frequently. *I'm bored*, says Noah. The others shrug.

Melancholy, at a loss, they eventually fall asleep. Something inside them has realized that sadness fades during sleep, that many hours gone by, stolen hours during which they don't need to live, are tiny, vital moments of respite. If they could they would sleep for two weeks. But the wind and sun and hens wake them. They go on lying on the floor—why should they get up? Eyes floor level, they glance at their abandoned games, not seeing them. From time to time one of them cries for a spell. Then it passes.

To rebuild a world, they hang sheets between the upturned beds in their room and make forts: closed at the top and on all four sides, cocoon-like tents where they can find refuge. They have taken the mattresses off the beds. They tell each other stories in a hushed voice. Memories, made-up things, quiet laughter.

They doze. They only go out to use the toilet or bring some food and drink back. They stay there for hours. At the end of the corridor the door is still open and the hens have wandered into the house; they hear them cackling, ferreting, pecking at things; they don't care. Their food is hidden in the cupboards. The chickens bring some life, they listen to them and say nothing. Louie decides he won't shut them inside the flooded chicken coop ever again. He wonders if the cage is big enough for them to take the hens along when their father comes back, or if any of them are missing, although he doesn't know where they could get to. He'll count them, later on. And if any are missing: so what.

But when night begins to fall, the children haven't moved,

and Louie hasn't counted the hens. They find some candles which they place on saucers in the middle of their tents.

"Careful," says Louie. "Not to start a fire."

They burn little pieces of paper to make long flames. Perrine has tied her hair back with a blue rubber band. Before long the heat bothers them, so they open the sheets to let the air through and snuff out all the candles but one, and they lean around it on their elbows, close together.

"We should close the door," says Perrine. "It's nighttime."

Louie smiles. *There's no one here.*

"Still."

He slips out of the tent, making fun of her. As he walks along the corridor, glancing at the stairs that lead down to the ground floor and to the cellar, off-limits because of the flood, he notices that the water level has risen a little more and is covering the third step. At the moment, he doesn't really pay it much attention. Tomorrow, or maybe the day after, once he's decided to brave the sea again, he'll go down for their half-submerged fishing rods, and then he'll have a look. And he'll number the steps with chalk, from four to thirteen, so he'll have a gauge, so he can keep an eye on it—whether there's any point, he has no idea.

* * *

Too much sun, too much heat: when there were birds, Louie, Perrine, and Noah thought the birds went quiet when they were overcome by the heat, that they went to cluster in the tree branches, sheltered from the burning rays; but they haven't heard any birds for days. Only insects have survived the invasion of water, they cling and whirr, little brown or yellow flies that buzz in their ears and stick relentlessly to their sweaty skin, impervious to being flicked off, immediately returning, pests, pains in the butt—that's what Louie cries, beside himself, in the heat of the third day.

JUST AFTER THE WAVE · 51

"What shall we do?" asks Noah with a sigh.

Too much freedom, too much indolence. The other two are sitting on the grass, silent.

They are waiting. That's all.

They could stay there for two weeks, until their father comes back. As if they were afraid of missing him or that Pata might not recognize the island, might sail by without stopping, of course that's impossible, but the fear of it has them in its grip.

"We have to keep watch," murmurs Louie.

Noah looks around him.

"Over what?"

"The sea."

Perrine nods: *You think Pata might already be on his way back?*

"You never know."

"I can't see anything," grumbles Noah.

Louie gets annoyed. *You're just way too little.*

Then thinks.

"We'll build a watchtower."

They rummage in the barn and find cinder blocks and an old worm-eaten wooden door, and drag them to the shore, huffing and puffing.

"No," says Perrine. "It's too close. What if there's a wave."

Louie agrees.

"Further back, then."

"It's heavy," says Noah.

Halfway between the sea and the house they slowly build a platform and place the door on it horizontally, then lean a stool against it to climb up. Louie with his bad leg slips on the aluminum rungs, catches himself just in time, gets annoyed; Noah pushes behind him. And then there they are, all three of them, and to be honest it doesn't put them much higher up, but the impression they get as their gazes sweep the horizon is enthralling. Louie goes back down to hand up the last of the cinder blocks for a sort of guardrail which makes them feel safer. They plant a wooden pole in each corner and hang a big sheet as best they can over them to serve as a roof. They decide to have their snack in their new refuge once they've consolidated it with a pile of stones all around; now when they climb up it doesn't wobble at all. Sitting overlooking the ocean, nibbling the last of the pancakes Madie left for them, they are silent for a long time. Until Perrine says, "Is that the way they left?"

"That's where the boat was," Noah points out.

"Yes, but maybe they turned."

"I don't know," says Louie, because they were asking him.

How many times since the parents left has he had to say this. *I don't know.* He feels his helplessness right down to the stinging in his fingertips.

"But then," says Perrine, "can we be sure Pata will come back this way? What if he goes past the other side of the island?"

Louie freezes for a moment. He hadn't thought of that. For him there is only one place where the boat can land, and the watchtower is right opposite that place. He frowns: *No.*

Perrine insists.

"But still, if he—"

"No!"

Louie stands up on the platform and stamps his foot.

"And anyway, he would go around the island to come and get us. He'll call out to us."

"So we shouldn't sleep, then," says Noah gravely. "Otherwise we won't hear him."

"That's why we built the tower."

"So we'll be here even at night?"

"We'll take turns, yes."

The little boy's eyes gradually open wider, and he purses his lips. The tower all on his own, in the middle of the night; that's not how he had envisaged things.

"Even me?"

There's a tremor in his voice. Louie shrugs his shoulders:

"Are you scared?"

"Like I would be."

"So what is it, then?"

"It's just, uh, if it starts to rain, you know. This—" he points to the sheet roof—"this won't keep the rain out, will it?"

Louie shrugs.

"We'll see."

* * *

First night on watch. The weather has stayed warm and Louie can see the stars scattered across the sky. He hears the sea lapping regularly against the shore, *shlap shlap*, a sort of calm, repetitive lullaby. He listens to the sounds all around, and has trouble identifying them: tiny cries, rustling, animal sounds—and yet everything was drowned two weeks ago, there's nothing left, he pricks up his ears to see if he can recognize something.

The hens? Or a surviving bird, lost in the night.

The sea lapsing onto a leaping fish.

Something else?

He thinks of Perrine and Noah back at the house asleep. With these boards beneath his back, hard despite the blankets, too much darkness, too much light, he cannot sleep. When the sounds vanish, the silence makes him sit up. He wishes dawn would come. In the end, it's pointless keeping watch at night.

Will Pata come back? If the sea doesn't carry them away first. The water around him is oppressive, a sort of living creature looking for cracks to slip through, to gnaw at the foundations of the house, and of the tower, to dig in silence until everything collapses all of a sudden. For three days Louie hasn't said anything, but he's afraid.

He kneels on the board. He does so without thinking, the way he used to. For two years he hasn't been doing it anymore because it's for little kids—Madie tried to persuade him to, in the beginning. Tonight it has come back to him. With his eyes closed before the immense ocean, his hands joined in mute supplication, Louie prays, as hard as he can.

Perrine wakes him in the morning, calling his name. Louie? He struggles to rouse himself. A sort of titanic fatigue; he's not sure he has the strength to stand up or even open his eyes.

"Louie?"

He has to answer, he knows. A grunt at best.

"Are you asleep?"

"Mmm."

"It's nine o'clock."

Nine o'clock. Louie sits up all of a sudden, his heart pounding, sweat on his brow.

"Really?"

"Yes, that's what it says on the kitchen clock. Were you asleep?"

"No. No, no. Or maybe a little . . . "

"So you didn't see anything?"

Louie rubs his face, haggard. Morning moodiness: he must have fallen asleep in the middle of the night and didn't realize when day was breaking. He was supposed to be watching the horizon for the last three hours.

"Oh."

Perrine presses her hands on her T-shirt.

"What if Pata went by?"

"He wouldn't have, not yet. This is just practice, you know."

Tears in the girl's eyes.

"But you said—"

"It's no big deal, Perrine, he didn't go by, I promise. The sound of the boat would have woken me up for sure. Come on, let's go get breakfast."

The hens welcome them with a loud cackling, running to meet them at the door of the house as if the children's arms were full of seed and salad leaves and worms. Louie holds out his hand and doesn't flinch when they peck at his palm.

"What can we give them to eat? There's not much on the island."

But Perrine shakes her head:

"We don't have anything for them, they'll just have to manage. We don't have enough. And anyway in the letter Mommy said we have to eat them if we're hungry."

Louie scowls. He's attached to his hens. He's the only one who knows them by name, all twenty-eight of them, even the rooster: before the tidal wave there were fifty of them and it was no different. He could tell you the name of every one that drowned, too, the ones he called by their size and their color, Little Black, Big Black, Big White Feather, Old Black. The ones he liked best and which had real names, like Peanut or Sulky, or the names of his classmates when he'd run out of ideas, Caroline and Sophie and the others. The only one he doesn't really like is the rooster, he has no idea why, he's more arrogant, stupider, or maybe it's his color, but the thing is you have to have a rooster, if you want chicks who'll turn into young hens, that's the way it goes.

In the beginning, Pata had taught them that you had to keep them in separate groups so that the rooster wouldn't go messing around—that's what he'd said, *messing around*—and that they would wait for a second little rooster to be born and then make two little harems, so there wouldn't be too much consanguinity. But when they had two roosters, and the time came to move the hens from one group to the other, the father got muddled, and didn't know which hens were supposed to go with which rooster. All the children down to Sidonie had given their opinion: this rooster with these hens, and it was by no means certain that the yowling of the somewhat panic-stricken farmyard animals was any worse than that of the children who were choosing them, and the father couldn't identify any of them anymore, he gave a good shout so that at least the kids would shut up, but there was nothing for it, he couldn't make head nor tail of it all. After that, several hens got loose and the groups got mixed up; the father listened to his older boys telling him which hens to put back with which rooster— until he realized that the kids were grouping the fowl by color and it was all a hopeless mess. In the end the father had taken one of the roosters and wrung its neck just so they'd have some peace and quiet. They'd figure out later what to do. And in fact it went no further, there was just one rooster and the hens didn't seem to mind at all.

Why don't we eat the rooster? says Louie.

But Perrine doesn't want to: she knows that hens are much tastier.

"No," says Louie.

His little sister begs him: *Just one.*

"No, we're not hungry yet, not really, and besides, we have the eggs."

"Yes, we are hungry."

"We are," adds Noah, holding his tummy.

Louie looks at the sky, the low gray clouds, the wind hustling them along. Maybe today he can: he is thinking of the island where the potatoes grow. With the swim ring they hid in the barn he can bring back enough to make a gratin, or mashed potatoes, an entire potful. But the waves will have to behave, the gusts have to stay calm so as not to tip him over, he remembers how Liam and Matteo nearly drowned a few days ago.

"Potatoes!" shouts Noah when he tells them.

Noah's eyes are shining, and he gazes out at the horizon,

where the other island is, he wants his brother to leave right away. Louie looks at him out of the corner of his eye then, no, don't look it him, don't feel your heart sinking when you see this little boy with his scrawny arms, already out of breath from running to the shore—what did they do to him, the parents, the air, the earth; where did they fail, what did they forget?

Noah sits by the sea.

"Is that it, out there? The island? Can I come with you?"

"No. It's dangerous."

"And what if you sink?" asks Perrine.

Louie laughs, showing off a little. *Course I won't sink.* Deep down, he's not so sure.

"If there's blue sky, I'll go this afternoon."

The little girl turns to look up with her good eye.

"For the time being it's all gray."

She stands with her head tilted, her nose up to the clouds. Sometimes Louie puts his hand in front of one eye, too, to be like her. With only one eye he can still see, of course, but it bothers him. To the left there is a big black shadow, he waves his other hand, cannot see it, yet he knows it is there. After a few minutes his right eye gets tired and his vision blurs. He closes his eyelids, rubs them, opens then again. He doesn't say anything, so as not to make Perrine sad. She is surely used to it.

She was born with two big blue eyes. But one day the accident happened. Louie doesn't remember, because he was taking his nap just then, and afterwards no one talked about it. No one ever talks about it. It's like a closed metal shutter; the eldest ones keep the secret. Louie knows instinctively that the guilty party is among them, that it is either Pata or Madie, Liam or Matteo, but who, and how, the words have never been said. What sort of error, or negligence, or misplaced gesture. Perrine has a blind eye, and no one will ever restore the sight in that eye to her: he has stopped wondering.

But she can see, all the same, both the gray sky and the blue sky that slowly arrive over the course of the morning and make her happy: they will have potatoes, Louie promised. She loves them sautéed; she explains to Noah, as he stares at the empty frying pan, how to peel them, and how to let the oil get hot; she sends him to fetch two little logs so that the stove won't go out, it mustn't, they can make an omelet as well, but they've been eating omelets for four days. Just potatoes, nicely browned but not burned, soft but not crumbly, with salt and pepper—they have run out of butter or cheese to melt, never mind, they'll add a bit more oil. Noah smells the herbs and spices left in the kitchen: rosemary, curry, basil. He wrinkles his nose. Thyme. He hands the jar to Perrine: this should do. *All right*, she says.

Louie is on the watch tower, still looking out at the horizon, studying the sky as it continues to turn blue. For a long time he hoped the weather wouldn't improve, that the waves would stay black until evening; but now. He knows his siblings will come to him and ask. And he swore he wasn't even afraid; from where he stands, he can see the little mound straight ahead, twenty minutes if he swims hard, forty minutes there and back, plus the time it will take to dig up a dozen plants, he is breathing hard as if he were already swimming, yes he's scared. So he makes up his mind, without waiting for Perrine and Noah to pester him. He jumps down from the tower and runs up to the house:

"I'm on my way. Noah, you're on watch."

* * *

And it's not the sky that betrays Louie that day, not at all, even if it is the sky the boy keeps looking at as he swims, then as he digs frenetically to unearth the potatoes, a strange late afternoon impression, time to go home, but there's only blue up there and the clouds have headed north; were it not for that strange alarm ringing in his mind Louie would just think that it has suddenly gotten too hot. He tries to keep calm as he counts the potatoes he has thrown into the bag. When he reaches forty he wipes his hands on his shorts, ties the bag with the string, and fastens it to the swim ring, his feet already in the water.

That's when it begins.

With a sudden little noise: *psssshhhh.*

Louie freezes, refuses to believe it, finally gives a start, *No, no.* He listens. His fingers tighten on the swim ring, and it seems to him to be getting softer. With an extreme effort, he turns it over: the roots of bushes growing on the shore, laid bare by the waves, have made a hole. Now he shouts: "No!"

A reflex. He slams his hand over the leak. Without thinking, he begins kicking his feet. He can see his island, their island, just over there. Twenty minutes with his hand over the hole. It has to work. In haste, he considers untying the bag on his right, to rid himself of the weight, but he would need both hands.

Never mind.

Swimming fit to burst his legs and his heart. After a few minutes he has to stop, breathless. He rests his chin on the swim ring: it deflates slightly. He wants to get going again, he can't, he's out of breath, mouth open, gasping for air. Putting one arm around the air pump, he waits. He can hear the faint sound of air escaping under his hand.

He thinks, *easy now.*

He looks at the sky as if it were the horizon: there, it's over there. He mustn't look for his island, it will seem too far away, and make him want to cry.

Then he sets off again.

Feet kicking rhythmically, slowly, his legs burning inside.

And the swim ring.

When he is fifty yards from the shore he knows he will make it, even if the swim ring sinks.

It doesn't sink.

Out of breath, he steps on the island, collapses to his knees. And he immediately notices that there is something wrong. Before the words even take shape in his mind, it surges through his body, a discharge of shock and fear. He leaves the punctured swim ring to the waves, the sack of potatoes on the shore, and leaps to his feet.

For a start, there is no one on the watchtower.

And there is blood on the ground.

His breathing, hoarse and heavy, at the foot of the deserted tower. Louie puts one hand on the cinder blocks to support himself. He can see the blood ten yards away.

The blood, but not only: the lump of flesh next to it.

He knows what it is. He recognizes it. That's why he's holding on to the tower. Once again he is gasping for breath, in shock, he ought to sit down but there's nothing, so he collapses on the ground and is afraid he won't be able to get up. His nails scratch the warm cinder block, and gradually he gets his breath back.

At the same time, tears. The only thought he has is, *I'll kill them*.

A manner of speaking. But those really are the only words that spring to mind at that moment.

One step, then another. He glances around furtively, then turns away without stopping: yes, it is indeed one of the hens lying there. Well, its head. He imagines that the rest of it is in the pot.

I'll kill them.

The fact they took advantage of his absence, when he was going to get potatoes in order to feed *them*, to make *them* happy, to be able to spare his hens. He had told them he didn't want to. They weren't hungry enough, not yet. He can't help but see the image of the severed head again: which one did they take? Chosen at random, of course. The one that was easiest to catch. A black one. He goes through their names in his mind.

Rage.

Which hampers his breathing, enough to cause the walls to tremble when he goes into the house and roars:

"What have you done, *shit!*"

Bent over a body of feathers, Perrine and Noah give a start. Noah begins screaming, jumping from one foot to the other, "It wasn't me, it wasn't me!"

And Louie: *So what are you doing?*

Perrine is trembling and sniveling; she lets go of the hen and it falls to the ground.

"I can't get rid of the feathers."

Oh, what a sight. They have been trying to pluck the feathers just like that, because they didn't know you're supposed to scald the hen to make it easier to pluck. In the end they took scissors to shear the bird, and Louie is horrified by the sight of blood on Perrine's hands and on the hen's neck, this hen that looks like a strange hedgehog, pricked with hastily pruned stalks, a battlefield, a massacre. For a few seconds he stands with his mouth open on a word that won't come out. The two children watch him, paralyzed.

"It was to have with the potatoes," sobs Perrine.

"I told you," Louie begins. "I really told you . . . "

So this is how it starts, first with disbelief, and then he sees it's true, the hen is there on the floor before him, half torn apart, and suddenly he explodes with rage, grabs Perrine and pulls her down onto the tiled floor, his hands raised, slapping her relentlessly, Noah screaming, pulling him back, blows, tears, all three of them in a fury. For several minutes they fight and scratch and bite, they shout. Their hearts are racing, their voices turn husky, their pleading, too.

"Stop, I'm bleeding, I'm bleeding!" says Noah as he crawls away.

For the first time there is no one to pull them apart, no Madie or Pata, no voices to contain them, no arms to send them to their bedrooms, what could possibly stop them—fatigue, it is fatigue which suddenly leaves them sitting on the floor in the kitchen, heads lowered, faces scratched, Noah is holding a handkerchief over his wounded nose, no other sound but that of tears and sniffles.

Louie's rage has yielded to a huge sadness, the one he has been hiding for days, and he looks at his little brother and sister and frowns, serves them right, and between two sobs he shouts:

"And anyway, we're all going to die!"

But dying doesn't mean anything to them just then, nothing more, nothing worse then the crushed hen in the middle of the kitchen. They sit around her in a circle, legs outstretched and spotted with blood. Die? So what. For all the difference it would make.

"I don't care!" shouts Noah.

Louie slides across the floor toward him and kicks him; the little boy whimpers, shrinks. Then there is silence. Perrine is hiding her face in her hands. They look at one another on the sly, watchful, gradually their tears dry as time passes. Before long their cheeks are dry, they have wiped them on their sleeves. All that remains is rancor, and shame, they don't want to forgive. Noah is the first to stand up, head high, acting the grown-up, doesn't even hurt, not even afraid, he motions to the hen with his chin.

"So, what are we going to do? Are we going to eat it or not?"

Now Louie is on his feet, so close to hitting him that the little boy can sense it, and backs up to the wall, glaring at him, he doesn't want to let go, after all. Perrine reacts:

"No, no. We're not going to eat it. And anyway, we don't know how."

Noah stamps his foot. *What the . . .*

"We're going to bury it," Louie interrupts. "*You* are going to bury it, since *you* killed it."

Perrine nods. She knows it's better to be reconciled with her older brother, and that they were wrong to decapitate the hen, she tries not to think about it anymore—the terrified squawking, they had to start again four times over, she and Noah, before they managed to chop off its head, she almost gave up; but once you've made the first gash, you can't let the creature die in agony, can you. She wanted to throw up. Then those damned feathers clinging to its flesh as if they were embedded in cement; how did Madie manage to bring out those platters of chicken with that smooth and crispy brown skin?

So little Perrine goes out to the barn and takes the shovel. Louie follows her and Noah stays ten yards behind them to signal his discontent. She places the hen's body in a basket, along with its head, which she went outside to fetch where the ants were already beginning to lurk around it.

"Here," she says to Noah, handing him the basket.

He slowly steps closer, then balks. Perrine raises her voice. *Go on!* He obeys reluctantly, watching Louie and his hands that are only too ready to strike. He sulks. Not a word. Perrine has gone down to the lower part of the island, where the earth will be softer, she thinks. In silence, she digs a little hole, glancing at Louie for his approval.

As for Louie, he is staring at the basket containing the hen. He is eager to get her buried. Not a pretty sight, a skinned creature, with the flies arriving in droves, drawn to the metallic smell of blood. He waves them away. After a while he looks up, because of the silence: still no one has said a word, and Perrine has stopped digging. He can see that she is waiting. Gazing into the hole. He too waits, perhaps a minute. The only sound the buzzing of insects. And then he says, "All right."

He takes the basket and lays the hen on the black earth,

arranging her head so that it will look as if it is attached to the rest of her body. He mutters a few words in a low voice, ending with a murmured *Amen*, he remembers that's how you end prayers, then he gestures to Noah.

"You can fill it in again."

The boy reaches for the shovel.

Afterwards, all three of them stand there unspeaking in the waning daylight, hesitant, should they leave, should they wait some more. Perrine and Noah don't dare move, but they sway from side to side. Finally, Louie sighs and walks away.

"Now what do we do?" shouts Noah.

The older boy doesn't answer. Perrine has gone to fetch the bag of potatoes and is dragging it behind her.

"We're going to cook the potatoes," she says. "I know how to do that."

During dinner they do not say much. Louie has locked the hens in one of the bedrooms and will keep the key on him at night and whenever he's got his back turned. He'll let them out during the day. Neither Perrine nor Noah complain about the squawking from the other side of the wall.

"It was Little Black," murmurs Louie suddenly.

Silence.

"You made such a mess of her I didn't recognize her. So I counted them when we got back tonight. It was Little Black."

The two siblings bite their lips, bent over their plates, and they plant their forks in the overcooked potatoes. Louie looks at them.

"I liked her."

And then:

"You really are assholes."

* * *

In the night, Noah shivers. Not from cold, he's scared.

Punishment.

Louie said: *Tonight you're on watch.* No point looking for support from Perrine, she has turned her head not to see her little brother's wide open eyes.

Nothing for it.

There are sounds out there, all the time, sounds and mosquitos. Noah wraps himself in the sheet, then immediately tears it off—it's too hot. He looks constantly toward the house behind him. There's no light, they blew out the candles a long time ago. But the sky is clear, and there's a moon; Noah gazes at the sea, darkness engulfing everything twenty or thirty yards from there. Even if a boat went by just then, he wouldn't see it.

A rustling sound, he jumps.

Louie?

He listens: nothing. He feels for the stick he put down next to him for reassurance. Earlier, he said to Perrine:

"If there's a thief, I'll split him open."

A thief?

Perrine said: *There's no one here.* But just in case. Louie heard him, and he snickered.

"With your shitty stick, sure. He'll have a knife. Or even a rifle."

Noah trembles.

Still not from cold; he wipes the sweat from his brow.

Could Pata be on his way back already? He spreads his fingers one by one to count, gets a little mixed up. Five days? Six? In any case, he can't keep watch on the sea, with his head constantly swinging left to right because of the sounds. What could still be on the island? What creatures, what monsters? Noah sits down, his heart pounding.

He looks at the house. He looks at the sea.

House. Sea.

Which way lies the greatest fear?

In the early morning, on leaving his bedroom Louie almost

trips over the little boy. Noah is sleeping across the threshold, curled up in a ball, his head on a blanket. He is snoring gently—or has a draft given him a cold? Louie prods him with his toe the way you turn over a dead fish on the shore.

Then leaves him.

What's the point.

Noah lingers behind. From where he is, he knows he can run away if Louie tries to catch him. Run away, how far would he get, on this island which the sea is nibbling at a little bit more every day—but it comforts him to know that he can run a few dozen yards away. He watches for the older boy's reactions, he and Perrine are by the shore, bending over, looking at something. He thinks: *I don't want to go there ever again, not ever, ever.*

Deep inside he feels a certain pride, in spite of his fear that Louie will beat him. It took him a while, last night, with his scrawny arms and little legs, to drag all those cinder blocks into the ocean.

Destroy the tower: yes. So that he wouldn't be sent there anymore. A once and forever solution. If he'd just taken it apart, the others would have told him to build it again. But this way. He threw the rubble in from the promontory, where the boat used to be moored. Where the water is six or eight feet deep.

He left the door there: too heavy. And besides, what would they do with the door all on its own?

So Noah is watching his siblings, who are looking in the water to see if they can fish out the cinder blocks. He is humming to himself, his voice inaudible, *You can't, you can't.* He feels all the tension in his body, because he knows he's done something wrong. To break the silence he shouts, legs spread, ready to hightail it:

"And anyway, it was no use!"

No reply. Louie and Perrine are sitting facing out to sea, their backs to him. After a moment, Noah goes over to them, impatient—*What are you doing?*

"Go away," says Louie.

"But what are you doing?"

"None of your business."

"Come on."

"Scram."

The older boy starts to get up, and Noah backs away, goes to sit a bit further away. He hopes he'll be able to hear what they are saying, but the wind prevents him.

"Are you going to go and get some more potatoes?"

"There's no more raft, you idiot!"

"I'm hungry!"

That morning, Perrine made a batter with fresh eggs, and cooked up twenty or thirty pancakes on the still-warm stove so they'd have a supply. Louie made a list of what they had left to eat, and it didn't match the list Madie had left them, there is much less than they expected, even though Perrine had divided it all up into little piles; he doesn't get it. His sister confesses: she had to take from a pile here and there because they didn't have enough.

How will they manage now, for the last days?

With tears in her eyes Perrine says she doesn't know. They were hungry, that was all.

"Let's do the piles again," murmurs Louie. "But no changing them this time, you hear?"

In the house, once again they make piles of cans, potatoes, eggs. Behind them Noah empties the cupboards to hand them the food, copying them, mute and conciliatory. So he is startled when Louie grabs a can of raviolis from him and growls:

"You're pleased with yourself, because of the tower, aren't you, blockhead."

Noah cringes, makes himself small, maybe hoping for pity, for sure to become invisible. He looks down, hands him another can.

"Blockhead," says Louie again.

In the end, they have enough food for six days.

"It's not a lot," says Perrine.

Noah points to the cans: *I don't like green beans or broccoli.*

"We'll eat eggs," says Louie. "The hens lay every day. And with milk and flour we can make pancakes."

"Every day?"

"Every day."

Noah's eyes are shining.

* * *

Sitting close to the house to avoid the first drops of rain, they are eating pancakes with jam. Perrine fills their glasses with orange juice; they have enough bottles of water and soda to last for weeks. Liam and Matteo brought back entire packs from the neighbors'. Farther away, the sea still shifts its cargo of bits of wood, floating objects, plastic. Maybe there are still bodies, too, but they've stopped looking, they've become accustomed, to be honest, in the beginning it was exciting, the thought that those were dead bodies going by, but now. They're afraid it might be Madie or Pata, or their big brothers, or their little sisters. What if they capsized, and the sea brought them all the way back to the place they were hoping to get away from? And it's not so much the burden of sorrow that would be hard to bear, but knowing that now no one will be coming to get them.

"It's getting higher, isn't it?"

Perrine didn't move her head when she asked. She doesn't need to say what she's referring to, and Louie gazes at the gray sea, waves just starting to toss with bad weather.

"Yes, I think so."

No, he doesn't think so: he knows so. Every morning, the way Pata did before him, he checks the water level on the stairs to the basement. When the parents left, he had marked the third step; now the sea is attacking the sixth one. That means they need boots to go to the ground floor. The previous day they saw that the sea was gradually eating its way across the living room floor and into the kitchen, so they sweated blood to drag the old stove up the stairs. Too exhausted to drag it any further, they left it in the corridor by the stairs. At the bottom of the garden, they will soon be sitting on the pontoon with their bottom in the water. Every evening for the last four days, Louie has been planting a stake precisely where, on the terrain, the water has reached. Every morning, he measures the distance the sea has advanced during the night. Twelve, sixteen inches. One day there was nothing, and he hoped this meant the drop in the water level Pata had spoken about so often—but it was probably only because it had been a very sunny day, because the following day, the water was rising again.

What a strange climate the great tidal wave has imposed on them, with these constant storms, this inconstant, spinning sky. They have learned how to read the portents of storms—sudden choppy water, initially just splashing onto the shore, then proper waves washing onto the land. At the same time the wind rises, whistling and gyrating, intoxicating the sky, filling it with shadows. The veiled sun gives off a terrifying yellow light, that is what they remember above all, the world gone yellow right down to their own faces when they look at each other, anxiously, the sickly reflection of a world that has yet to finish dying. The surface of the water looks as if it has been ploughed full of holes, black eddies, and wherever they turn the sea seems to be gathering in upon itself, growling, towering in turbulent rollers that have formed out to sea, that charge through the spray and make the children recoil. In the house they yank the shutters closed and take refuge upstairs. Perrine throws floorcloths down against the doors to block the gaps, with Noah's help, running crazily here and there.

And then, they wait.

But before, too: it's a game, a challenge. Seek the shelter of the house as late as possible, don't give in right away, not completely, like now as they are finishing their pancakes, the fine rain already wetting their legs. With the hot, damp air, they enjoy the wind on their cheeks and in their hair, for these few minutes, sometimes ten, sometimes thirty, until the storm breaks, it's like an airlock, a time in-between, the sharp lurch of coming danger they feel deep in their gut. Right up to the last minute they stay there, backs against the wall, clothes clinging in the gusts, soaked, to savor the moment when they will go and find shelter, get changed, drink a glass of lemonade. Sometimes the house adds to the terror. Creaking, cracking, a shutter banging, a tile falling. They observe it with a curious sentiment of helplessness, as if it were some sort of giant gradually losing a finger or an eye, now with one knee to the ground—Pata has to come back before everything falls to pieces. And while they might forget their situation when the sun is blazing, forget the fear and abandonment, the storm, every time, brings them back to their terrifying reality: they are lost, all three, in the middle of the ocean.

Louie cannot help but imagine the day the house falls down. What will they have left to cling to, so that the sea does not come after them, bearing them away to a place where everything drowns, so that they won't each become one of those floating bodies, tossed here and there by the waves—to end up sinking in some forsaken corner of the world, once the fish have eaten half their flesh? So he counts the trees still standing, their roots laid bare by the sea; he knows the salt will get the better of them. But for the time being they are still there.

"Look," says Noah.

He points through the window to the pile of stones left at the foot of the ruined tower: the ocean is already washing against them.

"It didn't last long."

At the other end of the room Perrine crushes a spider with her broom.

"There are loads of them," she grumbles.

They're like us, thinks Louie: they're seeking shelter. Refuge. We should leave them, this could be our own ark, there are so many animals missing but at least we have spiders.

Perrine doesn't like spiders. She's always afraid she'll swallow one at night, every since Liam read that every human being consumes seven or eight spiders in a lifetime of sleeping. When he told them, the others had shuddered and cried out.

Bet it's not even true, said Noah.

Bet I'm not even afraid, laughed Matteo—and he'd grabbed a daddy longlegs to show them, a little one, granted, the size of a coin, but it was a daddy longlegs all the same, and he swallowed it right there before them. The girls had screamed. For two or three days they kept a safe distance, convinced that at some point the spider would come back out. Out of his mouth or ears—or eyes, promised Matteo, running after them, and they scattered, shrieking in horror.

Noah watches as Perrine sweeps up the dead spider with the tip of her dust broom.

"If we end up with nothing left, do you think we'll have to eat them?"

The days last forever, as if time were moving in slow motion. If it were winter, it would be dark at five o'clock and they would sleep half the day, but the sun is in the sky from seven in the morning to nine at night, and wakes them, gets them up, they open the shutters, the summer crushes them with heat and the storms come and go, wedged between two expanses of blue sky. Twice, five times a day, they can feel the wind coming from the south, dragging with it those big black clouds which, they know, are harbingers of the storms to which they are gradually getting accustomed. It doesn't bother them: the variations of weather don't interrupt anything, there is no work or play, harvests or picnics, no game of croquet—to be honest, by mid-morning they are already sighing, eager for evening so they can lie down and doze, incapable as they are of filling the absence of their parents and brothers and sisters, gone across the water. This, along with food and weather, makes up the essence of their conversations: do they believe their parents have reached the high ground, or have they been shipwrecked? Are they all dead; and are the three of them the sole survivors? What if even the high ground has been engulfed? And then always, at the end: what if Pata doesn't come back?

They have faces grown weary with anxiety, features drawn with the fear they may have to stay there forever. The night before, Perrine murmured:

"Maybe we'll be here until we're old."

Old, for them, means twenty, thirty years of age: as soon as you're an adult, you're old. Once you're old, you die. There it is. Die on the island.

"Oh, no," protested Noah. "You're crazy."

As if it depended on them.

To conjure fate, Louie bursts out laughing.

"What I want, when Pata comes back, is for him to take me to the car race we were supposed to go to before the storms."

Perrine thought, then said, "What I want is a kitten."

Noah trumpeted: "And I want an ATV!"

For a moment they smiled, the way they used to when Madie had them write their letters to Santa Claus, when they still really believed in him. To start by saying they'd been good, and provide examples to prove it: this was exasperating. *Of course, Madie, Santa Claus already knows that, we don't need to write it, he can see us, can't he? He's kind of like God.*

Making their list, on the other hand, immersed them in frenetic excitement: they would fight over the round-ended scissors to cut out pictures from the toy catalogs so there'd be no mistakes, adding arrows and descriptive notes, using colored felt-tips and little hearts to show how *those* were the presents they absolutely had to have. Afterwards, they had to choose. Two presents each, said Madie, because they were far too numerous to ask Santa Claus for more, he only had two arms, after all (and a sack, ventured Louie). So they would frown at one another, they wished they were fewer in number, even though it wasn't something you could change. At first, Liam and Matteo resorted to the argument about the sheep and the crèche, because that was the rule: every evening during Advent Madie and Pata asked them if they'd been good, or kind, or generous. They'd been allotted one sheep each, and depending on how they'd behaved that day, they had the right to move one length closer to the little terra-cotta structure where Joseph and Mary were hovering, for the moment, over nothing at all, since Jesus wasn't born yet. But if they'd been naughty, their sheep would just stay where it was, or even move back. This was what the older boys were trying to point out: that the first sheep to reach the crèche would be entitled to an extra present. As a result, squabbles broke out, provocations, fights, cheating, too, because Madie discovered that her little ones would sneak in, when she was busy elsewhere, and move their sheep forward a few inches. In the evening, cries came thick and fast:

"But I was ahead of Louie, there, I wasn't there!"

"My sheep has gone backwards!"

"Get out of the way, I'll put it back."

"You weren't there!"

"Yes I was!"

"Cheater!"

Madie eventually raised her voice one day, and ferociously. She picked up all the sheep, despite the wailing, and put them away in a box at the very top of the cupboard.

"There," she said. "And anyway, with all those sheep, it was looking like a racetrack, not a crèche."

Ever since, the lists for Santa Claus were all pretty much the same, and anyway, Liam and Matteo, and then Louie, and then Perrine stopped making them. Noah stoutly maintained that he still believed, and that it was his right; everyone knew he was lying, but Madie let it go, and he would sit next to Emily and Sidonie to pick out toys from the magazines.

"Madie doesn't want you to have an ATV," says Louie. "It's too dangerous."

Noah shrugs.

"I'll get it all the same."

"Oh, yeah? And why's that?"

"Because . . . they're gonna give it to me because . . . they left us here, that's why."

Louie turns to Perrine.

"And you, do you think you'll get your kitten?"

"Oh, yes."

He scratches his cheek; his trip to the racetrack doesn't seem like much in comparison to what the others are asking for, so he tries to come up with a better idea. A new bike? A dog? A game console. Or nothing at all, if they are stuck on this island the way Perrine said, until they're old.

"We'll have beards," he murmured to Noah.

"And we'll walk with a cane."

They giggle and look at each other out of the corner of their eye. In the end they know perfectly well that it isn't funny.

Boredom. Never before have they sat for so long doing nothing. No inspiration, no desire: when one of them suggests something, the other two sigh and shake their heads. It's driving Noah crazy. He jumps to his feet.

"Okay, what do we do now?"

"Stop saying that all the time!"

"Yes but we're not doing anything. I'm bored."

"There's nothing to do," says Louie, spreading his arms to encompass the house and the island. "Where do you want to go?"

"I'm sick of being here."

The little boy goes out to walk along the shore; initially Louie and Perrine can see him, then he vanishes from their field of vision. They go back to gazing at the sea, hoping to see Pata arrive.

"How many days has it been?" asks Louie.

Perrine, who crossed off a Thursday on the sheet, replies without hesitating.

"Seven."

"That's all?"

"Yes."

"You're sure?"

"Yes."

Louie raises his eyebrows and suddenly stifles a laugh.

"What is it?" says Perrine.

"So that means we haven't had a wash in seven days."

The little girl smiles in turn: *It's not as if we were really clean, after the storm.*

"It stinks," adds Louie, sniffing his T-shirt, which he hasn't changed, either.

And then:

"Shall we go for a swim?"

"In the sea?"

"Well sure, it's nice weather, there's no waves."

"Somewhere where we can touch bottom?"

"All right."

They call Noah and he comes running. In the beginning they probe cautiously for the bottom. And yet they know this spot at the end of the garden, not even a week ago it was still grass, and they can feel it tickling their ankles; a gentle slope, and they move fifteen yards or so before they're able to let themselves go into the water and swim and splash. Before long they're shouting and splashing one another, they forget that initially they swore to keep an eye on the horizon, on the sky and the sea. They stay there for maybe two hours, not a cloud, no fear, no twinge in their bellies. Sometimes they spot an object the sea has brought to the shore and they pull it up, shouting. They have found a ball, and pieces of wood, and a plastic chair. When they're not interested they toss the item back into the sea.

"And what's that!" screams Noah, pointing.

A thick tarp floating a few yards away. Louie dives in to retrieve it.

"There's something inside it!"

"Treasure!"

"It's heavy. Come and help me."

The three of them tow the tarp until it beaches on the shore. Impossible to pull it any further.

"Shall we look?" says Louie.

Noah is jumping up and down: *Go on, go on!* Wading by the water's edge, they struggle over the rolled tarp, in vain, it's stuck. Perrine runs to fetch a pair of scissors and hands them to Louie.

"I'm sure it's a safe!" says Noah, fidgeting as he tears off the bits of plastic his older brother has cut away.

Then all of a sudden they recoil.

The smell.

"Yuck," says Perrine. "What is it?"

"Dunno."

Louie cautiously removes the tarp, keeping an arm's length.

"Well?" asks Noah.

"I can't tell but I don't want to go on."

He wrinkles his nose. Noah tries: *One last time.* Leaning forward, he yanks at the plastic.

"Oh!"

All three of them leap away.

"What is it, what is it?" cries Perrine, who knows but—

"Oh, shit!" exclaims Louie.

"It's a dead body!" screams Noah.

At first they thought of pushing it back into the sea. But without touching it, now that they knew. Louie sent Noah to get a long stick so they could shove it in. Impossible. Too heavy, high and dry. They are shivering all over, as if the corpse might infect them, or the island, along with the air and the sea around them.

"We have to make it go away!" cries Noah, stamping his feet.

"I'm going to be sick," gasps Louie, turning away and vomiting the entire contents of his stomach.

Afterwards they give up. They managed to roll the body over once or twice, and the ocean has half covered it.

"The sea will take it away," murmurs Louie, wiping his mouth. "With the tide it will go away again. Let's just not stay here."

Because they feel even dirtier now than when they first went into the water, when they go back up the house they rinse off with a bottle of fresh water; they have a big enough supply, and tonight they'll drink orange juice.

"Yuck, yuck," says Perrine, over and over.

"It was disgusting," whispers Louie, remembering the swollen skin he saw briefly under the tarp.

They haven't stopped shaking, although they are standing by the walls of the house, away from the sea—but still too near, and they'd rather be where it's safe, as if the corpse might suddenly pop up next to them otherwise.

"Who was it?" asks Noah. "Was it Liam?"

"Of course not, don't say such a thing."

The little boy shrugs.

"Well, it could have been."

"Stop talking nonsense."

"It wasn't someone we know, then?"

"Of course not."

"So they're not dead."

"I don't think so, no."

* * *

Louie was right: by morning, the body has disappeared. They walk around the island to make sure the tarp didn't get caught on a root or in an eddy, and they sigh with relief when they come back. They feel as if the smell is still there with them, in their noses, as if it is firmly planted inside them. They rub their noses, blow them. Even while they're drinking their cold chocolate at breakfast and eating their melba toast, the memory of the smell is disturbing.

The weather has turned drizzly, and they look out the windows at the sullen sky, and the sea they cannot imagine swimming in and that is beginning to turn rough. In addition, the hens they let out early that morning have come back, a sure sign the day is turning stormy. At the end of the corridor they're squawking, each one louder than the other. In the room where Louie locks his birds the children find eggs laid in odd little places, as if the hens were trying to hide them, thinks Noah; for the children every day is like a treasure hunt. It reminds them how at Easter Madie and Pata hid eggs in the garden, in the grass, under rocks, behind trees, for whoever could find the most—but those eggs were hard-boiled, painted all sorts of colors, decorated with drawings and stickers, not the white or brown eggs that break if you squeeze them too tight when you pick them up and which leave big gooey driblets all down your fingers.

Perrine makes a new pancake batter. Their eyes no longer glow with delight: eggs, pancakes, noodles, they've had their fill already for eight days. Even this is boring. They dream of grilled meat, the smell of rosemary and thyme, red peppers roasted on the barbecue. Noah nibbles on a potato left over from Louie's escapade and grumbles, "I like sautéed potatoes better."

"There aren't any left," says Louie.

"There isn't anything left, here. It's stupid."

Again they let their gazes drift to the horizon—or to where they suppose it must be, they can't see very far for the curtains of fine rain, that faint drizzle you don't think will get you very wet which gradually soaks you to the bone, freezing your skin and your clothes. Wind, clouds, rain. Noah shouts, clenching his fists as he leans toward the window.

"Wind, clouds, rain! I'm sick of it!"

And that shape all the way at the end of what is visible out there on the ocean, a black mass half hidden by sudden cascading downpours, Noah frowns, stiffens. Takes a step back and looks anxiously at the others.

"I think there's another dead body."

"A what?" asks Perrine.

"A dead body like yesterday. Only it's far away."

Louie shoves the little boy aside and takes his place at the window.

"How can you see that from here?"

And then:

"Oh!"

"What?" says Perrine.

"Is that what it is?" says Noah.

Louie turns to them, frenetic.

"No! It's a boat!"

All three of them cluster suddenly at the window, squint, shout.

"Yes, it's a boat!" exclaims Noah.

"We have to call them!" says Perrine, fidgeting with impatience.

They run out of the house, mindless of the rain, scramble down to the shore and wave their arms.

"Hey!" they cry, sweeping their arms over their heads and jumping up and down.

"Over here!"

"Here, here!"

Perrine sobs:

"They can't see us."

Now and again it looks as if the vessel has disappeared behind the clouds and is going away, and then it reappears for a few seconds, at the mercy of the waves and the spray; they wait for the square shape to turn and head toward them, to come closer, but it doesn't.

"A fire!" cries Louie. "We have to build a fire!"

"But it's raining," says Perrine.

"We have to try! Noah, you and Perrine go and get some kindling in the barn."

"And you?"

"I'm going to take a burning log from the stove. That way it will work."

He rushes to the house, lifts some brands with the tongs and drops them into a metal bucket, slips a box of matches in his pocket. When he comes back, Perrine and Noah are there with wood and pieces of cardboard; Noah gushes, *Cardboard will burn really well!*

Louie tips the bucket out on the ground. The embers hiss in the rain, it makes a funny sound, some are going out already.

"Give me the cardboard!" shouts Louie, tearing it up to get

the fire started again. "Stand around it to shelter it from the wind!"

They kneel on the ground, still watching the shadow in the far corner of the sea as it sails in a disorderly dance, they go on screaming, one after the other, so that the boat will hear them, until Louie gives up: *No point shouting, we have to make the fire, just the fire.* A few flames rise, licking the cardboard. Noah yells.

"It's started, it's started!"

Louie adds some wood, a little bit, not too much, leans closer to listen to the tiny fire, wishes it would crackle; for the time being only the cardboard is burning.

"Come on," he says, urging it on.

"There's smoke!" says Noah, clapping his hands.

"But this is nothing, they won't see it, it's not big enough. If we don't have big flames it won't work."

Perrine leans down, blows on the embers to kindle them. The boys do likewise, hair sticking to their brow. Louie has tears in his eyes, he remembers how he helped Pata burn branches over the years; Pata would grumble, *Fire never starts the way you want it to. Either it's hot, and it burns too quickly, or it's cloudy and you can't get it going.*

Smoke rises from the embers as they die one by one. Louie hears the hissing sound, carefully watches the pieces of cardboard that are still burning. He cups his hands around the twigs that don't want to catch, the rain snuffing the sparks the moment they appear. Noah has already given up, he stands up straight and turns to the sea. He goes on shouting, his little voice covered by gusts of wind and the roaring of the sea, there's nothing else to do, so he tries. Louie cannot even feel the warmth of the flames on his hands anymore, cupped over the brands. He won't give up. He shouts again.

"Come on!"

Suddenly an idea flashes through him: the lawnmower fuel,

in the jerry can. Pata used to take a little to get a fire started, when he'd been struggling for half an hour with his leaves and his green branches and nothing happened. Louie leaps to his feet, runs to the barn, returns quickly, the jerrycan banging against his legs. He remembers it's dangerous. He steps back, removes the cap to pour out a little fuel, holding the can at arm's length.

Nothing.

So he takes two matches from the box in his pocket.

Scratch.

He tosses them onto the fire. The whoosh surprises both him and Perrine, who has already stepped back: they give a start.

"It's beautiful!" says Noah, his arms lowered, as he watches.

A flame three feet high.

Then a foot and a half.

Then, after only five or six seconds, less than a foot, six inches.

And it goes out.

"Put some more," shouts Noah.

Louie tries again. And again the scary sound of the puff of fuel catching fire, the flames eager for sustenance. Louie steps back, stumbles. From a distance he watches the flame rise, orange against the gray sky, then immediately subside. The embers remain red for a few seconds, he hopes the wood will catch.

Nothing.

Soon there is a fine column of smoke, like when you blow out a candle.

"Again!" shouts Noah.

Louie shakes his head. Looks out to sea.

No more boat.

"It's gone," murmurs Noah.

The rain hammers down on their shoulders, icy. *Let's go in,* says Perrine. Louie doesn't answer. Facing the ocean, he waits for the boat to come back.

It doesn't come back.

After a few minutes, Perrine takes him by the hand. *Come*, she says quietly. She squeezes his fingers. Not saying a word, head down, he lets her lead him away.

B y the next day the rain has stopped. In the house, the children's clothes are spread over the backs of chairs, still wet from the day before. The two younger children sleep late, exhausted by their dashed hopes, by their determination to keep watch on the sea through the window, what if the boat came back. They ate pancakes by candlelight, and went to bed with their eyes sticky from tears.

Fatigue keeps them sprawled in their beds, arms outspread, crucified. Only their open eyes are proof they are still alive, and their hoarse voices, which gradually regain their usual timbre, once the words are ready to be spoken.

"Maybe it wasn't a boat," whispers Noah.

Perrine shrugs.

"What was it, then?"

"A whale?"

"There aren't any whales, here," says Louie.

After a halfhearted breakfast, they open the front door with the strange impression of another world, when what is left of the garden lies between lingering dew and the first warm rays of the sun. They can tell it is going to be a fine, hot day. Perrine tilts her head to one side, thoughtful. Yesterday's bad weather, the almost surreal vision of the boat on the horizon, the crushing return to the house after they gave up on the fire: it all seems too distant, too unreal.

Maybe they dreamt it?

The little pile of dead embers, somewhere on the shore,

slowly restores things to her mind. Louie squats down and scratches at the ashes with his fingertips.

"Is it cold?" asks Noah.

"Of course."

The little boy touches the ashes.

A bit further along, the sea has scattered pieces of wood; they nudge against the shore.

"Look," says Perrine.

Boards. They go closer and Noah leans down to pick one up.

"Is it the boat?"

Without a word, they study the broken plank, and reach for a few other laths and lengths of wood.

"It looks like it," nods Louie.

"We were lucky, then," murmurs Perrine.

They don't add anything: they prefer to believe it. That the boat was shipwrecked: it's a consolation. They feel almost happy, suddenly. And so, silently to themselves, they decide that yes, the boat capsized the day before, once it had sailed past their island. They even hope that everyone on board died: it is Noah who says this. Louie puts his hands on his hips, watching the sea.

"For sure they're dead. They all drowned."

He doesn't add, *Serves them right*. But the faint smile in their eyes indicates there's no need to say it.

They don't think about the fact that this is cruel. When your parents abandon you, you have every right. And it really does cheer them up, they run to the house, laughing, because they're hungry again—not the kind of hunger that wracks your belly because there's so much you've been missing, but a proper hunger, voracious and joyful, which makes them grab one pancake after another from the plate, smearing them with honey and jam, swallowing the whole lot with that sensation of power; they are alive, the three of them, the only ones who are alive, without a doubt, and they are celebrating. In the end they open a bottle of soda and the bubbles sting their noses.

* * *

The heat catches them unawares: by ten o'clock, they're sweating, the excitement has passed, boredom is already catching up with them. When Noah opens his mouth, Louie raises a finger in warning.

"If you say, 'What are we going to do,' I'll wallop you."

Noah stands there, mouth agape. Then he closes it.

"Yes, but—"

"Did you hear me?"

So the little boy keeps silent. He wanders off in the house, from room to room, opening doors and closing them again noisily, to the last one.

"Can I open this one?"

"Why shouldn't you?" says Louie, exasperated.

"It's the one to the stairs."

"So?"

"Well, there's the sea down there, isn't there?"

"Not all the way up."

"Are you sure?"

"Just have a look."

Noah decides to laugh it off: *I'm scared.* Louie glances at Perrine, mocking. Walks over.

"Okay, let's check it out."

He puts his hand on the door handle. Noah is standing a few yards behind him, leaning forward to see. They haven't opened it for days, this door leading to the basement, doomed by the rising sea. Last time, they were in water up to their ankles, it felt strange to be walking on flooded tiles.

"Are you coming?"

Noah hesitates. Wipes his hand cautiously over the walls.

"There's no light."

"There's been no electricity since the storm," Louie reminds him.

They go slowly down the steps. Very quickly their feet are in water.

"It's risen," says Louie, stopping when he's in up to his knees.

"Have we reached the bottom of the stairs?"

"Not yet."

"Look, over there, the fishing rods. They're not far."

Louie reaches for them, hands them to his little brother behind him.

"Here, we can go fishing."

"Are we going to keep going down?"

"I don't think so. We'll be in up to our waists, and besides there's nothing left down here."

The bottom of the house is dark and wet, it smells of things rotting—old furniture, cloth, carpets. Louie can make out objects floating, caught prisoner in the room; a dull fear overcomes him, that the sea might rise all of a sudden, and they'll be trapped inside. So he stays on the stairs, clinging to the banister. Noah wrinkles his nose.

"It's kinda gross."

"Yeah."

"Do you think the sea will go all the way upstairs?"

"I don't know."

"What will we do if it does?"

"I don't know."

"Will we drown?"

"Why don't we go fishing?" says Louie, to shut Noah up, so that the fear around his throat will finally loosen its grip.

And so, heedless of the sun and the heat, the three of them go down to the shore. They have dug for worms in the earth and put them in a bucket which they keep in the shade of a tall hazel bush. Motionless and silent—Louie has forbidden them from speaking, so as not to scare the fish away, and, in the beginning, they manage not to—they wait, casting their lines again when they think they can detect the movement of a fish here or there. The first hour they don't catch anything, and nearly give up—it's the fault of the heat, which rouses those damn flies and puts the fish to sleep. Exasperated, Noah changes his worms every ten minutes: *They don't like those ones.* The fish start biting at around noon, at the same time as the wind rises. Perrine pulls in a bass, or at least that's what they suppose it is, because it could be some other species the sea has brought up from the depths. Louie removes the hook and pounds the creature's head on a stone to kill it. Perrine proudly holds her fish at arm's length before putting it in the basket. *It's a nice one, isn't it?*

They catch a second, then a third, then they have four.

"We'll eat them tonight!" exclaims Noah.

Perrine scratches her ear, puzzled: she doesn't know how to cook them. The scales vaguely remind her of the hen they tried to pluck—pray the scales will come off easily, or that they can leave them on. She doesn't want to have to cut the fish up.

Or maybe they should skewer them, on the barbecue?

The waves lap at the shore, the sky has turned gray again. They observe the clouds. Initially they pay no attention, just enjoying the refreshing cooler air; then the wind begins to swirl around them.

"There's going to be a storm," murmurs Louie.

The others nod, to them this is obvious: in the three weeks since the tidal wave engulfed the earth, there has been one storm after another. And it's not that Louie has noticed any-thing in particular about the vibrations in the air or the way the wind is turning: he has said this instinctively, because the sea is getting choppy and the blazing sun has misted over, he says it and maybe there won't be any storm at all, he simply says it because there could be. But Perrine looks at him as if it were certain.

"A real storm?"

So he nods his head to seem important, his expression solemn.

"I think so."

She is worried.

"Should we stop?"

But Noah wants to go on, the wind in their sweat-sticky hair calms them. Louie studies the horizon. *Five more minutes. Then we go back.* He is giving them a wide margin: Noah is always clumsy at putting away his fishing rod, the line gets tangled, he jabs himself with the hook. A few months ago he got it lodged in his cheek. He has had a clear little mark under his eye since that day, a scar that won't go away, where the skin grew back thinner—the little boy was damned lucky, half an inch higher and he would have lost his eye.

And they'll have to carry the basket with their heavy catch, Louie doesn't want to run, to be heading back through gusts of wind and rain that wrench the door from their hands. He says it again, sniffing the air. *Five minutes.* Noah lets out a cry: the line has gone taut. *The last one!* cries Louie, hurrying over. He brings the fishing net closer while Noah gives some slack, tightens, lets go. Perrine exclaims, watches the sky, then the fish, the sky again, she moves further back on the shore while the horizon fills with black clouds, she blinks suddenly, a raindrop.

"It's raining!"

Noah pulls on his rod—*I'm almost there!* says Louie, kneeling by the water's edge, his net outstretched, and behind them the sea has suddenly risen, like a dragon curling under the waves to toss them skyward, along with the wind, slapping and blowing; Perrine is afraid. The time it takes for her to look again and the heavens are upon them, a cloudbank so low that she thinks it will swallow them up, black monsters with gaping mouths, half concealing the breakers the sea is bowling impatiently toward the shore.

"Let's go, let's go!"

But the boys don't hear her, all attention focused on the fish, which is struggling as they drag it slowly toward them, and that is why she is the only one who sees it, little Perrine, the wave forming out there on the ocean, a wall of water, distant at first, then too near, a thundering sound, Perrine screams in vain, runs back—while Louie senses his sister's movement on one side, hurrying away, and he stands straight, heart pounding, to see what it is she is fleeing from, then a rush all through his body, danger, danger.

"Noah!"

He grabs his brother, tearing away the fishing rod. He leaps away with a roar.

"Perrine, go to the house! The house!"

At the same moment he stumbles, and Noah falls between his legs, *The fish!* The line, the rod: everything has been sucked into the sea. But that isn't what Louie is looking at, his eyes open wide.

It's the wave.

The same one.

No, not the same one.

Not as high, not as strong.

But the fear is the same. The same as on the evening of the great tidal wave. Again Louie sees the water rising dozens of feet above him—how he ran to reach the house, to slam the door behind him. Again he sees Madie's astonished gaze as he clung to her, he sees his own hands, trembling as he tried to explain, and couldn't find the words.

All of that in a few fractions of a second.

And in that moment he knows that he and Noah won't have time, the sea will be upon them before they can get away. He flings himself to the ground behind the hazel bush, dragging Noah down with him. He puts his arms around each side of the bush, grabs his brother's arms. His voice, hoarse and trembling: *We don't let go of each other. Even if you die, you hold onto me. You hear me?*

***

The wave crushes them. Louie counted as he watched it coming—four, five seconds later. He would have liked to be sure Perrine reached the house, to hear the door slamming behind her, hear her steps vanishing into the shelter of the thick walls. But he couldn't. First of all, because he didn't have time; and then because he was incapable of turning away from that wall of gray water bearing down on them, hypnotized by the way it was moving, spouting and swelling, a living thing, of that he is certain, howling, creating the deep trough to take them out into the core of its power; Louie has rolled Noah's sleeves in his hands to grip them tighter.

When the wave flattens them, the impact is so powerful that Louie cannot be sure he has not opened his hands. For several seconds he stops breathing, his belly crushed by the blow. Immediately afterwards, he can feel the water receding, tugging at his body, his torso, his legs, clashing with the hazel bush over them, pulling them out of joint in a rage, maybe he and Noah have already been separated, he doesn't know, he can't see, there is only this terrible painful shaking in his shoulders and arms that makes him hope they are still clinging on and that the bush will withstand the surge. He doesn't feel the blood on his face, doesn't hear Noah calling him, he is blinded, one by one his fingers are pulled back by the prodigious force of the sea, the little boy cries his name, *Louie, Louie!* as the waves turn him on his side like a wisp of straw, twisting his arms, smashing his back against the hazel bush, no, Louie hears none of that, his eyes are closed, his voice is reciting his fierce determination to survive and his refusal to be carried away, this voice that no one can hear, saying, *No, no, no.*

The wave recedes, a few seconds have gone by, ten, fifteen at most—an eternity. It will come back. The wind announces it and precedes it, this wave or the next one, already rumbling in the distance, forming and dissolving, building up anger to return to the shore, to grab hold of anything running, living, and to drag it down to the bottom of the sea, Louie knows he must be quick. Coughing and gasping, he tries to catch his breath, to turn his head toward the sea, which has taken possession of the land, a liquid force incorporating everything, pulling him back again, toward the ocean, toward the vastness and the void, he throws up, he is filled with water, too light, too weak, around him there is nothing left but the roaring of the waves, the whistling of the wind, and the shouts inside his head.

The land is covered with sand and silt, rivulets of water returning to the sea in tiny shining trenches which Louie observes, lying on the ground, his cheek pressed into the abandoned puddles his fingers are still clutching, instinctively, and which he cannot stop. His shoulders and belly are still trembling, his breathing comes fitfully from his throat with a metallic rattle.

Think about nothing.

Fear has taken everything.

Don't look.

So as not to see the catastrophe all around.

Finally, listen: light footsteps on the sodden ground, going *splatch splatch* as they come nearer, little steps first walking, now running, the sound of water being squelched underfoot, that's all, no words, no cries.

Louie tells himself he should turn his head and have a look.

Doesn't move.

Sudden terror: what if he is paralyzed. He moves an arm, rolls to one side. It's okay. He lets out a long sigh. Slowly, the thought that there is nothing left at his fingertips, nothing holding him or clinging to him, works its way into his brain: but for the time being, it doesn't affect him. Emotions have not yet returned, nor has consciousness. Just breathe. Listen.

Louie?

His name.

Louie?

Yes, that's me.

Are you all right, Louie?

He doesn't know. Can't speak. He sticks out his tongue, loosens his frozen jaw, sure that the hoarse, croaking sound that has just come from his throat was a word.

Louie?

I'm here.

Louie . . .

This voice, insisting, a little girl's voice. Perrine?

Louie, are you dead?

A little boy this time.

Then a shiver of immense, wordless joy turns him over onto his back, still with his eyes to the sky, but he sees them, the two figures kneeling next to him, that is what gives him this huge smile, this swallowed sob, he murmurs, *Holy cow.* Perrine leaps up and claps her hands, joyfully.

"You're not dead."

He sits up, cautiously, his body aching. *Guess not.* He gently taps Noah's palm as he holds it out to him.

"So there you are. I thought the sea had carried you off."

The little boy laughs.

"Were you afraid?"

" . . . But you're here."

"I hung on the way you told me."

"When the wave went back out I wasn't holding you anymore."

"I was just next to you, behind the hazel bush. You didn't see me. It's true, I let go of you. But the water went back down just then, good thing, too, otherwise I would've been done for."

Louie nods. The three of them look at the sky, the movement of air, the storm interrupted. *It won't be back,* he says. *Not right away, anyway.*

They head back, taking streaming little steps, shivering despite the soft air. Perrine thinks about the hot chocolate they will heat up on the old stove, exactly the same chocolate that Madie makes when they come home from school or from helping Pata out in the rain in the garden, at the end of the road or of their chores, drenched to the bone, hair clinging in wet strands to their foreheads. When she sees them coming Madie lets out a cry and a laugh, *Oh, just look at those mops, go quick and get changed and then come back!* They run to remove their wet clothes, they toss them in a ball into the laundry basket; they clatter down the stairs and back to the kitchen where Madie has put the milk on to boil and she stirs in the squares of chocolate to make them melt, none of that tasteless readymade chocolate but a sort of magical brew that stays in their mouths and throats with a sweet thickness, and its aroma fills their noses; clicking their tongues they try to keep it at the back of their palates as long as possible. Even on days when something has made them very unhappy it brings consolation. *Yes*, says Perrine, *that's what I'll do.*

Next to her the boys walk like old men, broken and silent. They are thinking of their basket swallowed by the storm, with four, almost five, fish. And it was pointless for the sea to reclaim them, because they'd already killed them, their father had taught them never to let animals suffer, suffocating in the air, and they had done everything as they should—and look what happened. No more basket, no more fish. No more fishing poles, they too went out with the wave, they were surely snapped in two by the wind and the water; and it's not with a branch of hazel bush and a length of yarn, the way their father used to keep Noah happy, that they'll be able to catch anything.

"We could try anyway," whispers Noah.

It annoys Louie when Noah spouts nonsense, he knows very well they don't even have any more hooks. What, they'll just ask the fish to bite the yarn as a gesture of goodwill? Noah hangs his head. *It might work.*

"Yeah, sure," says Louie.

They change into dry clothes, they're still shivering. Perrine has taken the eggs, broken three of them and beaten them with sugar to add to the pan with a pancake. In another saucepan she is heating the milk and a few squares of chocolate, and she orders Noah to stir it slowly. The time it takes to put on a sweater and it already smells of pancakes browning. Their mouths are watering, eyes shining. Eating reconciles them with each other, relaxes them: they talk about the storm, exaggerating slightly, laughing at their bruises and their luck. Not once do they wonder if the sea is about to rise again soon. They look outside, the waves are still rough, the wind is hurling rain through the windows, it makes them jump every time, their hands held up against the gusts of air. Divided between a cozy sentiment of sheltered safety and the fear that a gust will blow the entire house away, they chatter, interrupt each other, go on chattering. The storm worries them, even though its strength is waning; they clench their teeth in silence, listening out for the sound of water and wind and hoping it will all go away. An hour later the sea is almost calm, still they watch, the sea and the detritus it has washed up from the dark depths, bits of wood afloat for months or years and which the underwater eddies have restored to the surface, scattered flotsam drifting on the surface, like dead fish.

The sea is calm and there they are, the three of them, with a strange pain in their chests, on the upper left-hand side. They rub it in vain with the palms of their hands to make it go away, a pain as if they'd been jabbed with a needle and something was pressing it, a sting, an itching, discomfort. Then they know that something else has happened that they don't understand, elsewhere, differently, but which their skin and their guts can sense through this unpleasant tingling, and this something is bound to be bad, they can tell from the impression of emptiness and want and fear that passes over them, they don't speak of it, they gobble down the sweet pancake and lick their chocolate mustaches; it'll go away eventually.

* * *

Eight. That is the number Louie sees on the step, the water licking regularly at the base of the chalk mark, as if it were scoffing at the closed doors, which are powerless to stop anything.

There is no trace of step number seven. Louie sits at the level of number nine, his gaze weary, his chin on his crossed arms. They must have lost eight inches since yesterday. He can't remember his father ever telling them the water had risen that much. Outside, the hazel bush he and Noah had clung to during the storm now has its roots in the water; taking long strides, he measures. Two yards, maybe even three. If the sea keeps encroaching at this rate, in six or seven days even the roof of the house will be underwater.

So he decides: they have to get ready to leave. His feet wet when he comes in from the garden, he tells his siblings.

Leave? murmurs Perrine.

To go where? asks Noah.

To look for higher ground. The only real puzzle is, how?

How? echoes Perrine.

Yes, how? agrees Noah.

"We'll build a boat."

Noah laughs, all excited. Louie frowns because he has already thought of a way, and he really can tell Noah that there's nothing funny about it at all, it's no laughing matter, because there is nothing there to build a boat with.

What if they remove the shutters and doors? The wall of the woodshed?

Louie doesn't know how a boat floats. And anyway none of them would know how to fashion the curves or put a vessel together: he's thinking of a simple raft.

And if there's a storm?

Shush. Shush. Don't even mention it. There won't be.

But if ever . . .

There won't.

He erases the thoughts from his mind.

"So, we're going to build a raft."

Ah, say the younger ones.

"But if there's a storm, will a raft sink?" asks Perrine.

Shush, shush. Don't even mention it. There won't be.

Louie looks elsewhere.

"We'll try, okay?"

No questions.

"Okay," says Noah, conciliatory. "What do we need to build it?"

And Louie doesn't answer right away because he's looking for the words, and they're not at all satisfactory, words that won't frighten them, that won't show how little he knows about what they have to accomplish, how to reply truthfully, not only what first springs to mind and which he tries to translate into something reassuring, but also something besides the obvious fact that spins round and round in his head and keeps him from thinking: *We need something that floats.*

What do you mean, float?

Things that float, I said.

Louie looks at Noah, who looks at him. He articulates, to convince himself.

"We'll find something."

B   ut who would have thought it could be this complicated, this impossible, on an island without electricity, without supplies, without adults to help or show them how? Louie has his face in his hands.

"Can't you do it?" Noah just asked.

And he was tempted, he had to confess, even if his mother would have scolded because it's not nice—but Madie isn't there to give her opinion or give orders or decide what's right or wrong—yes, Louie was tempted to slap his little brother, hard, and scream a terrible insult at him, something which would have brought him some relief, would helped him ease his nerves, allowed him to forget that he doesn't know how to build a raft, and that, indeed, he can't do it.

The simplest thing would be to take the door they'd used to build the watchtower. The door would be the raft. Besides, there was nothing else, no boards they could have put together, other than a few pieces of shipwrecked boat, nothing at all, and yet they did look, because that damned door weighed at least eighty pounds and they would need plenty of imagination to keep not only the door afloat, but also themselves as passengers; it would take a miracle.

So there it was, they had a door, but no floats.

What floats?

Madie always kept her empty plastic bottles. She said you could use them for all sorts of things—watering plants, making iced tea, or dye, you could turn one into a funnel if you cut it, pots for the children to fill with paint, five or six of them, with screams of joy. Empty plastic bottles: there used to be dozens, on shelves and in the barn.

A carpet of bottles strung together under the raft.

But the parents had taken most of the bottles with them; they had left only thirty or so to last until Pata's return.

Empty out the bottles to turn them into floats, and they'd have no more water. It's either or.

Thirty bottles to sail a door?

Louie sighed and looked at the five-gallon jugs his father used to store all sorts of things, and which might have worked—yes, if they'd had the lids. With Perrine and Noah he turned the barn upside down looking for them—upending crates, digging in the drawers of moldy old wardrobes, in boxes of rusty nails, in vain, well, they did find just one, under a pile of newspapers, broken in three pieces; they gave up.

No jugs.

They threw three or four logs into the water, just to see. And they stayed afloat, but as soon as they put their hands on them they sank, and Louie shook his head—if they sink with the pressure of just one finger . . .

What floats, dammit?

The three of them are sitting in the grass in the sun. Before them lies the expanse of sea, without a wrinkle, blue as the sky. They dream of going swimming, of thinking about nothing, it's just that there's this goddamn water that keeps rising and spoiling all their fun, and the days on Perrine's paper are crossed off too slowly, making the parents' return seem improbable, or worse still, pointless. Louie doesn't know whether his siblings realize this, if they too are afraid but don't dare say so, or if it's over their heads and he, Louie, is the only one who suspects the terrible future ahead—in the end, maybe it is better this way.

"And that?"

Noah points to the dozens of bits of wood the storm

brought to shore and which are washing back and forth against the land. Louie sits up and looks. What could they do with those stupid dead branches—but now he remembers. Father used to call them *driftwood*.

Driftwood.

He is thinking out loud.

What if we make a mattress of branches all tied together, and we put the door on that?

"Yes!" shouts Noah.

So they hurry over, bend down, grab, pull. They go all around the island and bring back enough to make a huge pile, and they're a little frightened at the thought they will have to put it all together, a gigantic mattress of gray, twisted wood, like some giant crown of thorns, they hesitate, wonder where to put their hands and how to interlace the branches, which catch and resist being brought together, a tangle of recalcitrant spiny pitch-forks, refusing to be disciplined, ending up in a chaotic cluster. Perrine best expresses their bewilderment when she stands back to gaze at the vaguely rectangular mass, rubbing her chin:

"That?"

Louie bites his lips. But if he runs a rope through, here, here, and here . . . ? Try. It wobbles every which way, it comes together, it comes undone, but he pulls and winds, sends Noah to fetch every last rope, he's making them a sausage, a roast so well trussed that they won't even be able to get a finger in it, it takes time but he is rather proud of the job he's done. The three of them set about tightening the last ropes, the last knots, and Louie wipes his brow, with a smile.

"There we are."

"There we are," echoes Noah.

"Do you think it will hold?" asks Perrine in her clear little voice.

They decide to put the mattress in the water on its own: for a start, it will be a test, and besides, they won't have the strength to lift it once the door is fastened to it. Louie ties a line around a bush so they won't risk losing their strange float. They shove it to the edge of the water.

" . . . two, three!"

They let go.

There's a loud splash.

"Shit," says Noah, as the mattress sinks like a stone.

Louie gazes wide-eyed at the ripples of water, the gray and black hole. He can't believe it: everything has vanished. On the trunk of the nearby shrub, the rope is taut, the leaves rustle. Then suddenly, like some creature emerging from the bowels of the sea, a huge shadow appears all at once, lacking only the powers of speech—and they are convinced they can hear a terrible roar just as the branches that are no longer branches break through the surface, they look as if they are clinging to the waves to stay afloat, and Perrine lets out a shout, or is it Noah, or even Louie, who has his hand in front of his mouth, a monster, yes, it is a monster rising there before them.

"Oh, my, God, that scared me!" shouts Noah, to banish his fear.

Perrine laughs, *It came back up! It's floating!*

They pay no heed to the fact it's cracking and pitching and wobbling, they're too happy, too noisy, as they observe this strange creature-like, almost-living shape, this entanglement swimming on the water like a giant fish, and if they really did look closer, with the critical eye of those who will have to trust the creature and climb on its back, they might see the ropes coming loose, the poorly tightened knots the water is already undoing, yes, they would know how fragile it is, this craft put together by children.

* * *

The three of them are lying side by side at the edge of the grass.

Silence.

Louie and Perrine, their eyes closed, so their tears will not overflow.

Noah gazes at the sky and counts the clouds.

A bit further away on the sea, out of reach, the raft is in the water, half-submerged.

* * *

Come on, come on! shouted Louie, elated, kneeling on the door they had tied to the branches, holding in his hand one of the two boards from which they had removed all the nails so they could be used as oars. *Come on!* And he'd pulled on the line, they'd climbed on board without getting their feet wet; Louie had had to help them, however, because the raft was listing.

Once they were on it, they didn't dare move.

Perrine murmured, *We made it.*

What she didn't mention was the dull fear she felt at the thought of trying to sail anywhere on the thing.

This time she heard the cracking and strange sounds, impossible to identify, which had settled beneath her, in the cluster of branches under the horizontal door. And she wasn't the only one. Louie's smile was unusually wan.

"Shall we take it out?" Noah asked, waving the other oar.

Wait.

He had waited.

Oh, not for long.

First there was a branch that came loose from the float.

Louie was paddling slowly in a circle, not far from shore. He could feel the raft sinking—rather, he could hear it. Gurgling sounds. Sucking noises, a sort of grumbling, the water making its way, sniffing the branches, clinging to the underside of the door. He knew already.

But still, maybe.

Just then he saw Perrine and Noah who, aware of the vanity of their efforts, were in one corner of the raft holding hands, crestfallen, and he cried, *Don't sit there, not on the edge!* But they were already there, and they didn't move, paralyzed by the sensation that, terribly slowly, they were sinking, and right there, the craft had begun to founder.

"Jump!"

Were they were, they could almost touch bottom, it was maybe not quite four feet deep, maybe a bit more. But the fear remained: the cavernous sea, eddies, the black bottomless water. *No, no!* whimpered Perrine, not letting go of Noah's hand.

And what if they were sucked down to the bottom?

Jump!

Finally they had let themselves slide, the edge of the raft nearly leaving them with a long gash to the head or the side. Louie had let go of the rope. Spitting out the water they'd swallowed, they struggled out of the water, slipping on the silty soil of the shore, clinging to tufts of grass. Once all three had managed to reach the top of the hill again, the half-drowned raft drifted further out, lopsided. Louie could have dived in to retrieve it before the current bore it away—he'd done far harder things over the years. But he didn't. Like his brother and sister, he watched the small craft drift away, not lifting a finger, not saying a word.

And after that he lay down and closed his eyes because of the tears—the tears that welled up because he had failed, and the tears of relief that he would never, ever, have to get on that raft again.

It's the water that is driving them mad, Louie is sure of it. He has decided that every morning he will open the door to the staircase and measure the rising of the water level, in addition to the stakes he has been planting in the garden as benchmarks. Every morning his heart begins to beat faster, his hands tremble. He can sense the sea there in front of him, behind him. On either side. He can hear the seepage, sometimes the waves, the faint laughter. He can smell the odor of warm stagnant water on the land, slightly rank, slightly nauseating. Sometimes he is sorry he didn't go after the raft to try and build something better; a split second later he remembers the gurgling sounds and the fear, and he is not sorry at all.

But now this is driving him crazy, this ocean creeping closer, especially at night when no one can see it, at dawn the sea surprises them with its silent waves, ever higher, and the hens squawk because there is hardly anything left to peck at on the last bit of land that is holding out—for a few days the children fed them potato peels but now there's nothing left. They've begun to eat their own eggs, and the children have to collect them earlier and earlier if they want there to be any left.

Louie thinks about the other island, full of potatoes. He could have taken the hens there, they would have found enough to eat—and he could have picked a pile of little potatoes, they could have had golden new potatoes in the pan, just the thought of it sets his stomach to rumbling. An entire island all to themselves, Louie, Perrine, and Noah, which they can neither reach nor eat, because the rubber raft was punctured and they cannot build a wooden one. This makes the older boy all the angrier on those mornings when the sea is licking at the land, ever nearer, and the hens leave the house, complaining. He can't swim that far—or maybe he could, with a board to help him, God knows he's thought about it often enough, but he'd have to be sure there were no storms or currents, and he cannot swear to anything anymore, the weather changes too abruptly and the summer has become treacherous. If one day the sky is an immense blue carpet, should he try his luck?

A panful of potatoes before drowning.

Stupid.

In the end none of that changes anything, the water everywhere around them makes them say foolish things, makes their minds unsteady, and yesterday a red hen ran to the sea, jumped off the shore with a little rustle of feathers, *splish splash*, then swam away with the horizon in her sights, Perrine cupped her hands around her mouth and called, *Where are you going?* The hen didn't turn back, didn't try to come back. They saw no more of her. Louie wishes he too could just leave like that, so that the fear and abandonment would cease. No more feeling the tightness in his throat, his arms dangling by his sides because he's run out of ideas, doesn't know what to do anymore, what to hope for. Let it all go. No, he can't.

He is still here.

All he's good for is wandering around the island in the early morning to see if the red hen has come home.

She hasn't.

Does a hen sink?

—and what if they'd used the hens as floats.

You see how it makes you go crazy.

After a great deal of hesitation, Perrine and Noah again asked him to kill a bird so they could eat it. Perrine and Noah are hungry. But they don't know how to wring a chicken's neck, how to empty out it innards and pluck it. *We have eggs,* barks Louie, yet again. For them it's not enough. They want meat, they want something roasted.

Louie doesn't tell them that he is hoping to keep the hens until Pata's return, to hand his flock over to him like a good shepherd, a good boy.

I'm a shepherd of hens.

And whether he'll make it? He doesn't know.

The parents left nine days ago. Nine days assiduously crossed off on Perrine's sheet of paper, and there should be five or six left—if everything goes to plan. But everything has gone to pieces. His parents' calculations are worthless now, don't mean a thing, not a chance, they're meaningless in light of the storm and the rising waters, the vast floods that are still poisoning the planet, they got it wrong from the get-go, because once there was the huge tidal wave it became obvious that this would never end.

They got it wrong, Madie and Pata, because nine days ago they had to slip away in the middle of the night so as not to be seen.

And because six days from now, with the onslaught of the ocean, there will be no more island and no more house, and there will be no more children.

Louie constantly returns to this thought.

In the beginning, he wanted to cry. Now, he is angry. He tells the others. This time, it is Perrine who cries—it is always fascinating to see her cry with her blind eye weeping like the good one, her white, dead eye you'd think must be all dried up, but it's not, she wipes both eyes, little Perrine.

There will be no more island: he's not sure Noah understands what this means, and Louie explains with rare, chosen words, no abruptness, no rancor. Noah listens and doesn't believe him, he shakes his head. Then Louie shows him the stakes he has been planting every day to mark the spot the sea has reached: stakes standing like little soldiers marching up to the house and past it, flooding the basement, making their way to the top of the hill. One stake equals one day. Louie has his feet in the water and he counts the steps between the most recent stakes and reproduces them on the ground: he puts a pebble at the tip of his big toe.

This is where it will be tomorrow.

And this is the day after tomorrow.

In three days, the sea will be *here*.

"But", says Noah, "that's upstairs in the house."

Louie has his hands behind his back and he gazes thoughtfully out at the horizon.

"So, you see. In three days we'll be sleeping outside, at the top of the hill, and in six days, we'll drown."

ON THE WATER
The same morning, August 19

The mother's heart skips a beat the moment she steps into the boat to leave the island a bit before dawn, with Marion in her arms. She automatically counts the nervous children crowded on the small craft: from one to six. When she reaches six something snaps inside her, something that knows six is not the right number. A surge in Madie's guts to hold back her cry. She sits down, too, trembling all over: hands, legs, her lips that want to say, *seven, eight, nine.*

But don't.

It stops at six.

Madie, in smithereens. She's the one who is leaving. The one who is abandoning.

She faces backward until the very last moment, the fraction of a second when, very precisely, the island disappears into the end of the night. Even her bulging eyes can no longer see.

The little ones look at their mother. Before long, they fall asleep.

Pata, Liam, and Matteo, as taut as animals on the hunt, oars in their hands, deciding whose turn.

She is alone, Madie. Her throat and belly in a knot.

She tells herself she should have jumped. Should have let herself sink into the ocean without a sound, undulating like an eel, or a tired mermaid.

To go back to the island.

Before Louie, Perrine, and Noah wake up, she would have had time to sweep the floor, clean the cooker, and make breakfast. As if it nothing had happened. There would have been the smell of hot pancakes. The glasses filled with orange juice, bright little suns at every plate and bowl.

Madie didn't jump.

She just felt, very faintly, something tearing inside, right to the vibration in her body, part of her on the boat with six children, part of her staying on the island with the other three.

But this is nonsense: nothing stayed on the island, she knows that very well. What is the point of tearing herself apart, tossing her soul onto the shore to protect her little children? There is no point, none at all. To find comfort. To put a bit of balm on her heart, which does nothing to ease either the horror being born inside her, or her silent sobs. In a few hours the children, back there, will find out that they are alone.

* * *

Back to the burning, the one deep in her guts. The little girls woke up with the daylight, the sun already pounding on the sea and the overloaded boat rocking and slowly moving forward. Of course they asked where Louie and Perrine and Noah were. Madie answered. At home, she said. We'll go back and get them afterwards.

"Oh, I see," murmured Emily.

"I'm hungry," whispered Sidonie.

Liam and Matteo, on the other side of the pile of belongings, also heard.

Madie would have liked for someone to worry, to ask questions, to shout. To make Pata turn around, build a tower on the boat, with different levels so they could put the little children everywhere, and she, the mother, would get that torn, painful part of herself back. She'd give the ocean a beating, she'd wave her fists in a threat. Quiet. *Sit*—as if she were giving orders to a dog.

No one asks any questions.

Madie waits, thinks she's about to scream, But aren't you going to ask why? Aren't you going to say you're not okay with this? *I'm not okay with this.*

"What are we going to eat?" says Sidonie again, tugging on her sleeve.

* * *

So she had to resign herself, and stay on the boat, gliding across the sea with six children who don't ask why. Madie has withdrawn into herself. Sometimes she looks around—but there's nothing to see but water, and now that their island has disappeared, there's really nothing, just the ocean as far as the eye can see, no trees, no stones to break the surface, no rooftop to make you think you could hang onto it. Madie supposes they are crossing the plain—*God,* she thinks, *stiffening, we're no further than that, in the car it took less than half an hour.* Tomorrow, when they sail over what used to be the Duens hill, maybe they'll see a little vegetation; for the time being she turns pale imagining the fathoms of water below them, ten or twenty or thirty, bottomless pits, abysses. The eddies she can sometimes sense, when the muddy sea makes ripples, and Pata, with one word, instructs Liam to avoid them.

The boat is so heavy that the water is level with the gunwale when there's a swell. Madie wishes they could go faster, the ocean oppresses her, getting her hands wet, she places them in her lap. Her legs hurt, she turns from left to right to shift her weight. The little girls stand next to her and fidget, feeling numb.

"Careful," says Madie.

"When will we get there?" chimes Lotte.

"I need to have a wee-wee," moans Sidonie.

So the mother takes the little girl and holds her up over the side of the boat, terrified that some clumsiness might make her let go. But the little girl laughs out loud, bare-bottomed, wriggling, chirping and gurgling when a little wave splashes her. *Stop it*, says Madie, panicking, *do you think it's easy to keep hold of you*, the boat leans to one side. And then the others grow impatient.

"Me too, me too!"

And one by one the mother removes their undies, faint with fear, while they giggle and wiggle, *Again!* shouts Sidonie when they've all had a turn, but this time Madie looks at her sternly.

"No, you don't need to go anymore."

They sit back down, time passes slowly when there's nothing to do. Madie brought a deck of Happy Families and for a while they play, sometimes distracted by the movement of the water, or a sound they think they hear. Because Madie is stunned by the silence around them, only the breath of the wind fills the air, and the oars dipping in and out of the water at regular intervals, and the boys' labored breathing—over there beyond their belongings and their supplies, Madie knows from those sounds that they are still pulling hard. From time to time they let the boat drift to rest their arms for a few minutes, and the seepage of the wind wraps itself around them like a frightening mist, a sort of faraway chant, and the mother listens as closely as she can, she's already white, oh she doesn't like this dull whistling, it's not honest, it's not clear.

When Sidonie lets out a cry, she gives a start.

"Look at the fish!"

Madie turns her head, dubious. The long undulating back circling around the boat makes her raise her eyebrows, a huge creature, four or six feet from head to tail, she can feel a shiver run through her arms. They've all seen it, the boys stood up on the other side of their pile of belongings when they heard Sidonie, and the boat rocks, and Pata ordering them to sit back down doesn't help matters, because he too has stood up to have a look, and his eyes meet Madie's, and she whispers, "What is it, what is that thing?"

He shrugs, but goes on rowing. Only the mother notices the slight loss of rhythm to his gestures, a kind of hesitation or precaution, yes, that's it, the father is being careful, eventually he keeps one oar in the air and orders Liam to do likewise. The boat glides soundlessly, slow and solid. Beneath the water, the beast follows, flashing black in their wake. It is following them, that much is sure.

"But what does it want?" cries the mother, trembling, suddenly alarmed.

The father raises his hand imperiously: *Sshh.* Motions to Liam. They give a stroke of the oars, just once. The boat moves forward. The excited children ask questions all at the same time, looking to one side and then the other, searching the surface of the water with their shining eyes, and the mother would like to scold them, to scream *but don't you know it's dangerous?* Yes, to argue with them, very loudly, it would do her good, it would chase away her fear for a few moments.

"Enough!" orders Pata, exasperated.

They sit down, confused. The mother's throat feels as tight as if someone were trying to strangle her. She senses the imperceptible wave of the beast swimming beneath the boat, brushing it with the top of its back and making an infinitesimal twisting motion, it can be nothing else, the sea around them is smooth, not a ripple, just this tiny, terrifying displacement of the water which goes with them and will not leave them; the father does not dare paddle. Gradually the boat slows and stops. *What shall we do,* murmurs the mother. Silence, all of them. Liam, Matteo and the father stare out at the water.

"There it is!" exclaims Matteo.

"*It?*"

"The monster!"

Madie shudders. To her it seems that the boat is rocking harder and harder. And the father is doing nothing! What is the point of standing there motionless if it's just to be food for the fish, you might as well row for all you're worth, maybe the beast will get fed up, maybe it will go back to its lair without disturbing them—but for that to happen, Pata has to regain his wits, instead of this panicky, immobile stare, so Madie suddenly cries out:

"Get a move on, what are you waiting for!"

They all give a start, it is as if she has roused them from a wicked spell, she spreads her arms wide in urgency.

"Row! Row!"

Liam plunges his oar into the water at the same time as his father, twisting his torso in an effort that elicits a grunt. They encourage him, loudly, *Go on, go on*. The inertia of the heavily laden craft is enough to drive the mother crazy, she leans forward as if that could help them pick up speed, her jaws clenched fit to break her teeth, if she had a whip, god knows she would use it right then, and she pulls Lotte and Marion closer, her babies, her treasures. The beast cannot be seen for the strokes of the oars and the waves they make, the spray everywhere, the creature is invisible or has slipped away, the mother begins laughing, it's her nerves, she's laughing with tears in her eyes, and she stammers, "It's gone now, isn't it?"

And then she sees it gliding behind them. Its dark spine is catching up with them, keeping pace by the port side of the boat. The father stops rowing, undecided. At that moment the mother sees in his gaze that he is tempted to strike the animal, to make it flee or to hurt it, she can sense it even in the oar as it trembles for a fraction of a second in the father's hand, at the same time that she realizes how big the animal is and how great the risk; should it get angry, it could surely capsize them with a single lunge—and half rising from her seat, with a shrill cry the mother warns them:

"No!"

In that same instant, Liam and the father thrust their oars into the sea, propelling the boat ever further, ever harder.

Madie loses her balance and almost falls in the water, catching herself on the ropes strung around the gunwale, with Marion in her arms. No one noticed, except Emily and Sidonie, who don't have the reflex to cry out; they are alone in the stern, the mother and her daughters. They are cut off by the pile of supplies and blankets from the rest of the family, from Liam and the father at the oars, and Matteo keeping watch at the bow. If something should happen to them, no one would realize. She's not even sure the sound of them falling overboard would drown out the splashing of the oars. The time to cry out and the beast would be upon them. A few seconds of struggle, red water all around them, and the father would hear too late. The mother sits back down, tries to erase the vision. Swears that if they find an island she will make them all get out so they can move the supplies to the stern of the boat. Never mind, this business of ballast. She feels so far away that her voice would not carry beyond the supplies.

"I think we're all right now," says the father.

The mother stares into the opaque black water, sees no trace of the beast, neither shadow nor movement.

"We're all right," says the father again.

Yes, maybe it went deeper. To follow them without their knowing. To wait for a moment when they're not as vigilant, when they're tired, or night has fallen, there are a thousand ways to outsmart them. The mother thinks again of its strange shape, an animal she has never seen, a stranger to this sea where they have fished all kinds of sea creatures over the years. A beast that the drowned land sent packing, scudded through the water from who knows where, obliged to adapt to an unfamiliar place. Or a little fish, grown gigantic with the miraculous abundance of food and habitat? Matteo is right: a monster. And once again, the mother hopes the father, too, is right, when he says it has gone away.

D uring the night, they dropped anchor so they would not drift. It is so easy to get lost when you have no landmarks either ahead of you or behind you, or any-where. And the oarsmen need to rest, even though Matteo made it possible for the father and Liam to rest for a few hours during the day. He's dead tired, the younger brother, with his eyes as big as the sea, and shadows beneath them seeping into his cheeks. So the mother did not protest when they moored in the middle of nowhere, for Matteo and Liam's sake, because otherwise they won't make it. She examines her boys and they dodge her gaze, they don't want her to see how exhausted the exertion has made them, they're not even hungry, she forces them. She reaches in the first bag for pancakes and hard-boiled eggs; she cooked their entire stock when she knew they were leaving, a whole night spent boiling eggs, fortunately at the time the hens were still laying constantly, she knows the num-ber by heart, there are ninety-two eggs in the bag. She left thirty behind for the little ones abandoned on the hill, the hens will go on laying there, and the children know how to make omelets. She feels a lump in her throat at the sudden thought of Louie, Perrine, and Noah; she reaches abruptly for the knife, cuts up the pancakes, unequal portions as always, she doesn't want the vision of the three children on the island to come to her. How did they react this morning when they awoke and found the house empty? In their panic, did they see the letter? Do they understand that their father will be coming back for them? And what if they did panic? What if they jumped in the water to go after them? *Cut your slices, Madie, shut off your brain, there's nothing good in there.* God, please make sure Perrine manages to cook something. Make it so that Louie will agree to kill his hens one by one, if they get hungry. Maybe they are still at the water's edge, crying, incapable of moving, they'll have lost all will, all three of them—why them? *Yes, why them?* The mother feels the wrenching in her flesh, she knows there were no solutions, it was those three or the others, either way they had to leave someone behind, they are already crammed on this boat worse than sacks of grain, the eight of them. In the falling night, she prays the water level will not rise all of a sudden. That the father will have time to go back. *Stop that, stop right now, otherwise you'll start crying.* Her heart upended with sorrow and rage she peels her eggs, three for the father, two for Liam and Matteo. Just one for everyone else. *Don't eat too fast.* That much she said out loud.

A strange picnic on a boat in the middle of the black waves. They have lit two candles. The little girls want to stretch their legs, to run, to squabble. The mother points to the water: *Where?* They look out at it in silence. Liam and Matteo are already asleep, rolled up in blankets. Emily grumbles.

"There are mosquitoes."

"We'll climb under the sheet," whispers Madie.

"It's too hot . . . "

"During the night it will get cool. You'll see. We'll be glad to have a blanket."

"Where are we going to sleep?"

"Lie down right there. I put a little blanket so it won't be so hard."

"Are we going to put on our jammies?"

"No."

"Are we going to brush our teeth?"

"Not tonight."

"Are you going to sleep there too?"

"Of course I am, where else am I supposed to go?"

The mother glances at the water around them, and touches the ropes on the sides of the boat. Will she manage to sleep? She bets she won't. She's too afraid one of her children will fall overboard. She wishes she could have lashed them all together; but the older ones would have given her an exasperated look, and the little ones would have whined that it bothered them. The father would have said she was crazy.

The father has left a candle burning on the other side of the supplies.

"What are you doing?" murmurs the mother; she cannot see him.

"I'm studying the map."

"Are we lost?"

"No, I have a compass. I'm just looking, for tomorrow."

"Are we headed east?"

"Yes. Always."

"How many miles did we do today?"

"I don't know."

"But roughly?"

"The only thing I know is that that's all we could do."

"We made good progress," says the mother, with conviction.

"It would be better with some wind."

"God forbid."

That is Madie's greatest fear, a storm. Ever since the climate went to the dogs and they've been battered by bad weather, she has been afraid of gusts, of sudden squalls that ambush them with a downpour in a matter of seconds, and more than anything of the wind, the wind that brought the sea to their doorstep, obliging them to flee, the wind that would have them lie flat on the ground if they don't want to be blown away, the wind which on the day of the great tidal wave took the hens from the island. Never before had Madie imagined she would ever see those hens flying away, caught in a wind that whirled them every which way, like wisps of straw that she and Pata never saw again. They would have laughed about it if it hadn't been so tragic, because at the same time the hens were being scooped up from the ground, a section of the barn roof collapsed, crushing everything underneath it. The father wanted to save what he could—tarpaulins, spare bottles of water, and the wood, because it would eventually dry—so he rushed out. He made it ten yards, no further, before he turned around, nearly swept off his feet himself by the gusting wind, left deep down with an indefinable feeling of weakness. Shrubs he knew did not grow on their hill rolled by like tumbleweeds; one of them scratched his leg and he stumbled. He came back in on all fours, his expression wild, his hair clinging to his brow. It was impossible to close the shutter behind him, he was fighting over it with the wind, which kept slamming it against the wall. He gave up. He would never forget the force of the heavens.

Madie does not know that he is praying at least as hard as she is, praying to be spared any storms during their voyage. But the water was still rising when they left their island, and that was a bad sign. The elements continue to brim over; nothing can stop them, nothing can calm them. Hundreds of miles of water with neither rocks nor trees to oppose them. A clear field, open to every gust, every whirlwind. Yes, Pata too knows it's an illusion to believe they can complete the journey without a storm. He just hopes it will come as late as possible, once the former prairies are behind them. He hopes the buttes will still be there, and that they might find refuge for a few hours. At dawn, when he raises the anchor, he looks warily at the sky. There is no hint of anything, just a light, gentle mist, which he doesn't like much either. And with a sinking heart the father senses they won't have to wait for long.

* * *

One day and one entire night. Hours to be afraid and feel the air pressure building. They saw it coming from a long way off, the storm. The clouds gathered on the horizon like a pack of dogs about to spring, growling for hours while they rowed until they were breathless, as if they could outrow the storm, praying that they would find land, while their panicked gazes swept over the sea and found nothing but water and the first waves. Madie can feel the power beneath them, something vast and contained, she knows the storm is strengthening. No matter which way she turns her head, the sky everywhere is yellow and black, and thunder surrounds them. The boat is solitary, tiny and laughable on the angry ocean. The mother looks at Pata with all her might. He is observing the world, he knows, too. He's gauging their chances. They have stowed the oars on the side of the craft, they are useless now. A huge black wall is following them, a mixture of rain and wind, of turbulent waves; when they are inside it—when this gigantic gaping mouth catches up with them and engulfs them—there will be nothing they can do. Lowering his eyes from the heavens, the father's gaze meets the mother's. His lips murmur in silence. *I'm sorry.* And just then, the first waves rock the boat.

What they endure at the eye of the storm will mark them forever. Whenever they think back on it, they will pause mid-gesture, once again; their cries will catch in their throats. The memory, too, of those who—and their hands will squeeze, groping for ropes to catch on to, because that was all the father had time to say, *Hold onto the ropes.*

The waves rock the little craft, playing with it, tilting it up then pitching it down onto the bow, relentlessly. Screams: when it crashes down, it is as if it is headed straight into the bowels of the sea. Leaning into the oars, Pata tries to steer into the currents; in that moment he does believe they will make it.

Wants to believe. He has to. If Liam helps him on the other side—and he opens his mouth to scream above the enraged waves, breathes deep, his eyes stinging with gusts of rain, but nothing comes out, nothing at all, because just as he is about to shout, a huge roller of spray catches him broadside, an ox, a vise, there's nothing he can do, there is only the wave striking him, the water taking him. In a fraction of a second he flips overboard.

At the other end of the boat Madie is on her feet, screaming his name into the wind, his name and then the pain, *No, no, no!* She orders the girls to huddle at the bottom of the boat, to cling to the hooks, which give them some purchase. Tucking Marion tight beneath her coat, she steps over the supplies, caution to the winds, without a thought to the swell which threatens to capsize them, and she falls to her knees at the spot where the father disappeared. *There, there!* roars Liam, pointing his finger. So the mother plunges her arm in, thinking of nothing, neither the storm which is fighting with her for her husband nor the boat which is heeling to one side with her weight, nor even the beast which, beneath them, is just biding its time; it takes all her energy not to yank her hand back when something grips it under the water, ferociously, something holding her arm or tearing it, she's not sure which, she resists whatever it is that is pulling her, gradually; Liam has hold of her on the other side to keep her from slipping, she hears his cries, *Mommy, Mommy!*

She knows she is too heavy for him, but the father, the father!

Mustn't crush Marion at her belly.

She squeezes her fingers in the water, clinging to the rope on the boat, battered by the waves as they tumble, terrifying. It is nighttime in broad daylight. Curtains of rain blind her. Too much pain, as well: she pulls back her hand, with all her strength. The surface of the water is shattered with spray.

There is something at the end of her arm—her arm like a gigantic fishhook, with a shape clinging to it, keeping her leaning dangerously toward the sea, and it won't let go, she opens her eyes wide, suddenly panicking, trying with all her might to sit up straight, her knees propped against the hull of the boat, which is pitching ever more roughly; she is shaken by the waves and this thing that is trying to suck her down. She shouts, refuses, struggles. Like an animal being dragged toward an abyss she snorts, drawing on all her remaining strength to save herself, to pull away from this grasp, she'll sacrifice her hand if she has to, *Dear God, and the children, if I'm not here anymore?*

And then she sees him.

Pata, clinging to her, emerges from the waves as she pulls back with a roar, his face white as death, a ghost, and if he hadn't opened his mouth to breathe as he screamed, the mother would have thought he was dead, there at the end of her arm. A savage joy grips her. Pata! She slaps her other hand onto his.

"Get in!"

But he has no more strength, he has come back from deeper water, where he thought it was all over. On his face the mother reads the traces of the tomb, the horror she wants to pull him from and which has not quite left him, yet, the exhaustion spewed into the water—*Get in, get in!* He shakes his head, depleted. Every time the boat yaws, buffeted by the furious waves, he nearly lets go of the rope he is hanging onto. The boat rears up like an angry horse, hovers for a second, then plunges with a crash, a noise to make you think it will spill all its guts into the sea, and the mother sees the father's fingers slip a little more each time the boat rises, and sees her hope fading. So she leans out again, and grabs his hands. She ties them clumsily, a rope fastened around the one that circles the boat, the same way she would tie a roast, she loops it around three times, a quick knot. The storm can always try and tear her man away, it will have to pull him apart—it doesn't occur to her that if they sink, the father will be pulled under with no way to get free, there is too much wind, too much swell for her to even think about it, just the urgency of keeping him near her; only then does she glance behind her.

And behind her, Lotte is on her feet, crying, arms outstretched. Madie stands up like a madwoman. *No!*

The boat pivots to the left, into foaming white water.

All at the same time Lotte falls into the water and the mother throws herself in with her.

S he bursts out of the water, her hands cling to the side of the boat. She puts an arm through the rope on the gunwale to support herself, coughing and spitting, a sharp wheezing in her lungs, until the air reaches her, she vomits bile. She calls to Liam. Begs him.

Liam.

Her voice so weak it could be a child's.

Liam, I can't hold on.

Her arm through the rope, the mother is tossed by the storm. She clenches her jaw, squeezes her fists. On one side she is holding Marion inside her coat. On the other, she is clutching Lotte by the hood of her jacket. That was all she could grab when the waves took them both, her hood, impossible to strengthen her hold, she prays the little garment will not tear, she holds her arm up high to keep Lotte's face out of the water. The rope is rubbing the inside of her elbow, never mind, she needs both hands to save her daughters, the one pressing against her, who could slip down, and the one being tossed here and there by the waves. On her own, she cannot get them back onto the boat.

"Liam, please, please . . . "

Her vision of Pata is tormenting her, the pair of them clinging to opposite sides of the boat, surely the two older boys are with him, or with Sidonie and Emily who must be trembling with fear, she is convinced that at some point they will realize their mother is no longer there—when they lean over the supplies to tell her something and see the empty space. Then they will cry out and rush to the side of the boat; they will find her, they will haul up Lotte and the baby, and then her, but they'll have to be quick, she can feel her strength ebbing. She won't be able to keep up for long with the boat's maddened cavorting, with each onslaught her fingers edge away from their hold on Lotte's hood, she tugs on Marion who keeps swallowing water and coughing, she can't hear the others, can't see them, perhaps she has already drowned with her two daughters and she can't even tell. The storm, the wind, shouts, the children crying. It has all gone silent in her head. The black clouds above her, the blasts of rain, the boat bouncing on the ruthless water, her eyes widened with horror. Only the buzzing in her ears will not stop, cutting her off from the world, a rumbling roar like an airplane too near, but there is no plane, just something hurting her brow, too great an effort, the pain of it, more than once she has banged her head against the side of the boat, blood mingling with water and she hasn't noticed.

Her arm is going to slip from the rope, she knows it is. She can't take it, tries with her legs to bring Lotte closer, in vain. Paralyzed by the waves and exhaustion, she sees Marion's face held close against her, the face of a baby who has stopped crying, her eyes red, wide open on the storm, Marion spitting out the water that gets into her mouth, saying nothing, her good little baby, her last little soul. The mother huddles on herself with helplessness. Swings her head back, the wind whipping her, her arm slipping, she surrenders, sobbing, oh pray the father makes it, he'll have to look after the other little ones, all on his own, yes, she didn't manage to stay with them.

Liam.

"Mommy!"

The mother screams, eyes wild. Liam, at last. *Take Marion!*

The eldest, and Matteo. From the boat they reach down, grab the baby and pull her from her mother's coat, it feels as if she is being skinned, so tightly have they been bound together, a great chill enters her, suddenly she is shivering, she bites the inside of her cheeks, a few seconds, hang on a few more seconds, if they don't have time to save her, she doesn't care, but Lotte—there! Marion tips into the boat.

"Lotte now, Lotte!" cries the mother, tugging as hard as she can on her arm.

She straightens to bring the little girl closer, she's having visions with the exhaustion, she's so light, Lotte, in her water-logged jacket, she smiles, Liam and Matteo have paused. The mother hesitates, implores.

"Liam?"

Not a vision.

The mother doesn't look. She doesn't need to. From the boys' eyes she can see what has happened. And she stares at them as she murmurs, *No, no, no.*

And screams: *No!*

She holds out her arm. *Take her.*

"Mom," says Liam gently—and for a moment the storm has fallen silent because she hears him, even though he is speaking so quietly, she wishes he would not speak in that tone, with that distress, that sorrow, no.

"Take her!"

So Liam bends over, and from his mother's hands he gently lifts up the empty little jacket.

* * *

The boat moves slowly over the smooth sea. The wind has subsided, the rain has stopped. Of the hours of nightmare, there is nothing left, just a grayness in the sky and the water. Even the soft warm air has returned. A damp air. They are crushed with fatigue.

On the horizon there is an island. That is where Pata is headed.

In the stern, Madie is curled up in a ball. She has left the baby with Emily. She doesn't want to speak, doesn't want to move. To see anybody. She doesn't answer when Matteo calls to her quietly. The mother is a teardrop.

She is holding Lotte's soaked jacket tight to her chest.

Closes her fingers around the sleeves, as if to make sure. But Lotte isn't there. Lotte slipped out. She sank. She drowned.

Doesn't even know where.

Somewhere in the ocean, at some point during the storm. Madie was holding onto a piece of clothing that no longer protected a little girl. Madie did not feel how there was no one left inside.

She let go of Lotte.

She had already fallen in, murmured the father. In any case. Madie, head lowered, sobbing.

"It's my fault."

The father put his arm around her shoulders, shook her chin. No one could have.

"Shut up, go away."

If a mother can no longer protect her little ones. All those times she railed at Pata for being careless, his stupid hopes, his improbable expectations; and she was the one who lost Lotte. It is her mistake. Her tragedy. *Why her?* Like the little ones left behind on the hill: there is no reason. It's just chance that. Oh, the sadness.

She tries to recover Lotte's smell on the jacket, that sweet little child's perfume, laundered by the storm; finds only a smell of silt and damp which makes her cry in silence. Lotte is gone. She doesn't even have a picture of her.

She doesn't have mementos of any of them, that all stayed behind in the house, frames abandoned on shelves, albums stored in cupboards. There was no room on the boat, not for anything; Madie took her children, flesh and blood.

And lost them. *One gone.*

The first, thinks Madie, shivering. In her head it is as if she has been gripped by a strange frenzy, she is reconstituting Lotte's face, the sound of her voice, her crystal-clear laughter. She wants to make her fast deep inside—she knows so well how it fades. When she lost her parents, she thought their age-ing forms were branded forever in her memory. Over the years she has realized she was mistaken. And now this terrifies her: she will forget Lotte. Not her life, not the suffering of her death—but her face and her hazel eyes, her laugh, her little chatter when she was telling stories. All of it will blur, features, sounds. Maybe a day or even two will go by when she won't think of her. A long time from now. If they don't all die during the voyage.

What did she think, Lotte, when the current bore her away? Was she afraid? The mother hopes it went quickly, that she didn't even realize. *Please.*

She doesn't want Pata to try and console her, there is no possible forgiveness. Don't you dare tell me there are eight left. She doesn't care if they need her: it is Lotte she wants. *Give her back to me.* A dream? But the little girl doesn't come back. The world has come apart.

Now there are ten of them on earth.

And the mother lying inconsolable on the bottom of the boat.

She would like to fall asleep and never wake. Or curl up in a hole, a lair, a burrow, and be left alone for good, she deserves no better, hide way at the back, far from a worthless life, as if sleeping, to escape from life, to forget. So the pain will go away, the knives lacerating her womb. Count sheep, she used to tell the little ones, but whatever for, she doesn't care about sheep.

Sleep eludes her, her sorrow is too great. She speaks in silence, her eyes awash with tears, *My little girl . . .*

When the boat makes landfall an hour later she does not get out. There's nothing for it, neither the father nor the five chil-dren—she thinks, *the five children left.* Almost half. Four out of the nine are missing, on the evening of August 21. A carnage.

And an empty place next to her on their small craft as it rocks gently, moored to a pole planted there by those who were there before them, a place for nothing, for no one. After the storm, she almost asked the father to go back to their hill. In two days they can't have gone that far.

But who would they take?

There's only one place.

She cannot bear having to choose anymore. And besides, Pata would not have wanted to. Two days to row back to their island, two days and they'd be back to square one. Lurking squalls. And yet again, who? Madie stifled her question because she knew it was pointless. And so, walled up in silence and boundless sadness, she looks at the useless empty place next to her.

The boat rocks. Madie feels a presence next to her, keeps her eyes closed. To be alone and wretched. She can hear a child breathing, saying nothing. It lasts a long time; she does not have the strength to speak. At one point there is a hand on her arm, stroking her. A little hand. Not Liam, not Matteo. Tender, awkward. The mother shivers, they mustn't make her weep anymore. The gentle rubbing is filling her with too much emotion. *Stop*, she thinks.

No, don't stop.

She opens her eyes. Sidonie is gazing steadily at her.

There you are, thinks the mother.

A pale smile. The little girl smiles back, her hand still stroking.

"Will you come and eat with us?"

"I'm not very hungry . . . "

"Because of Lotte?"

The way she says it. A lump in her throat, the mother replies: *Yes.*

"Are you sad?"

"And aren't you sad?"

"I am, but maybe she'll come back someday."

"I don't think so. She drowned in the sea, you know."

"What does drownded mean?"

"It's when you go all the way down in the water and you can't come back up again, because of the waves or the storm."

"Like fish."

"Not exactly. But a little bit."

"So you see, if she's a fish, she'll come back."

Madie wishes it were true. For hours she has been wondering when, where, Lotte slipped from the jacket she was clinging to. It's pointless, of course. But she can't help it. Trying to find those last seconds, the instant when Lotte was still alive. Her face against the hand that was holding the jacket, her body buffeted by the storm—the mother remembers hearing her cough several times when she swallowed water, or maybe that was Marion, she honestly doesn't know anymore, it all got mixed up in the wind, the only thing for certain was that one second earlier Lotte was still there.

After that, a black hole.

Until Sidonie's clear little voice.

"Are you coming to eat? You have to eat to be strong."

Then the mother's slow wrenching. She feels as if steel slings are holding her to the floor of the boat. It takes her several minutes to sit up, her head is spinning, a mixture of sorrow and exhaustion. Standing next to her, eyes smiling, Sidonie holds out her hand.

She takes it.

When did the days begin to pass so slowly, wonders Madie, shriveled in upon herself as if she were a hundred years old. Since when, her features as ravaged as a drunkard's, her guts and her courage in a tailspin, vanished, null; and how many days? Nine, ten. Who knows. Time slips over her. Lotte's death has woven a strange shell around her. No one else can see it, a transparent web that brings muffled sounds, veiled images. Lights are dim, voices distorted. The mother can't do anything about it, it came all by itself. Sometimes it suits her; sometimes she would like to get away from it, because something inside her is aware that this odd lethargy must not prevail, in the long run, she has to stop it, otherwise she will founder once and for all, which wouldn't bother her all that much, God, but there are the others, after all. She cannot see that her heart is slowly mending, going back and forth along a path toward a kind of healing that will never truly be one, a bandage, perhaps, a compress, pressing hard where it's bleeding, just enough to keep going, to get up in the morning; an ointment for the vanished child.

But Madie wouldn't dare, it's too soon. She cannot imagine that necessity could get the better of pain in such a way, with so much indifference and abnegation. Sorrow devours her and deserts her. If she had time, if she had an inkling to—yes, perhaps, if things had been that way, she would have knelt on the ground and begged, for weeks. But it wasn't like that. There are the five children on the boat, and the three who stayed on the hill. There are currents, and storms, and the beginnings of hunger; there is the beast she sometimes sees behind them, concealed in the boat's wake. There is Pata who is wearing himself out rowing, while Liam and Matteo take turns, the father is white as a ghost, when he lets go of the oars in the evening his hands tremble, they have nothing left to squeeze—everything speaks of urgency and Madie can feel it as strong as her suffering, so she straightened her knees, like a scarecrow kept ramrod tall in his field by a stick, she went back to her place, the mother was once again the mother. Now she observes her family, six ghostly figures—as if they had lost their consistency in the course of these ten days, gradually fading, shadows, dotted lines. The little ones don't even ask to leave the boat when they come upon island hills, more and more frequently, almost every day now, they don't shout, don't throw tantrums. They are enveloped in a sort of torpor, and if she could choose, the mother liked it better when they were insolent, rather than listlessly lapsing into this strange stupor, their gazes drifting on the water, their eyelids swollen with the bites of mosquitos they don't even bother to brush away. That is why she has started talking again, started pointing to grassy patches or clouds, picked up stories where she left off. She is pretending. She murmurs in silence to herself that everything is the way it used to be.

And yet something huge has changed: the number of children on the boat. Madie forces herself not to count. She remembers. One by one, between dreams and delirium, she goes back over the children's names, the memory of each of their nine births, the ones that were difficult, the ones she hardly felt. To pass the time? To lessen the pain of Lotte's death, to bring her back to life, to give birth to her again and again. She spends more time thinking about that particular birth. And it's true, her mind fills with emotions, when she recalls those moments of pain and joy.

With Liam, it lasted twenty-seven hours, yet he wasn't a big baby; then only four for Matteo. At the time she figured she could go on having children, since they came so easily, now that her body was acclimatized. But then for Louie she had suffered again, over a day, and she thought: why have so many children? She and Pata had already decided to have seven or eight, they didn't know why, probably one day they were horsing around and came up with that number, and it stuck in their memory, they didn't discuss it any further, it was self-evident. And the reason was not that either one of them came from a big family—Pata had only two brothers, and Madie one sister and one brother, both younger—nor a shared dream or a challenge or anything like that, it was really just a game, random chance, a lack of imagination, perhaps, and then after Liam, Matteo, and Louie, Madie desperately wanted a girl. So Perrine was born eighteen months later. Pata thought that was a bit too soon. Madie wept with joy. And the birth went well, and quickly, she was in a sort of trance until they put the little girl on her belly, Madie was dying to see what she looked like and wasn't disappointed: the most charming baby on earth. So it had been all that much harder, three years later, when Matteo, playing around with a stick, had blinded Perrine in her left eye, at the hospital the doctors couldn't do a thing, and she became a one-eyed little princess, with her pretty face and her good nature, and now her blank eye—because she didn't want to hide it, she said she wasn't ashamed, just as on the day of the accident she had said it didn't hurt and would they stop talking about it. But in any case, the day of her birth, since that was what Madie was thinking about now, had been a fine day. And it was in part because of it that Madie figured she was game for another round, and she would gladly hatch a few more children, how many exactly she hadn't decided, that would depend—on desire, fatigue, Pata's joyful incursions. And clearly they both went at it heartily, because not eighteen months had gone by when Noah came into the world, ever so calm and weighing less than four pounds; now that they had both boys and girls, Pata and Madie decided to keep the sex of the child a surprise, and it was only on the day of his birth that they became acquainted with the baby they would call Noah. If he had been a girl, they would have called him Emily.

And the mother stuck to her guns: she wanted another daughter now, so that they could name her Emily. The father had sworn he'd give her three more little lads first, but fate proved him wrong yet again: along came Emily two years later. In return for which it hadn't been all that easy, since the baby was in a breech position and refused to turn, it took a long time and Madie, as she put it later, had gone through the mill. It had taken a bit more persuasion on Pata's part to convince her that two out of three births went like clockwork, and that therefore they ought to keep going—which they did, successfully, because Sidonie was born exactly one year and five days after Emily. And while Madie had to concede that the birth really had been easy as pie, she was beginning to drag her feet when it came to heading back out onto the battlefield—the expression was Pata's—and for a while she took a contraceptive, which he tried to hide from her now and again, to give them a chance, so he said, but she didn't find it at all funny.

No one really understood why Madie tossed her pills in the garbage one day. She complained that she'd been putting on weight but, logically, successive pregnancies were more at fault than contraception. She also complained of lethargy, dizziness, nausea—in short, all the poor excuses you come up with when you want to get rid of something, and maybe that was the only reason, Madie wanted to go off the pill without losing face, without admitting that she was wrong, that her fate was that of enthusiastic, disorderly procreation, or at least that was what she thought at the time. In any case, chemistry hadn't caused her organism any harm because she got pregnant immediately afterwards. What no one could have predicted, on the other hand, was how long that subsequent birth ended up taking, or perhaps it was the midwife who got it wrong, thinking that labor had already begun. Forty-eight hours later Madie was still at the hospital, exhausted, and her epidural had gone to waste. When the pain became noticeable, she endured it with courage: *C'mon girl, we'll do it like in the old days.* But in fact the pain quickly got the better of her goodwill, and she ended up screaming so loud that a quaking Pata quickly retreated to the other side of the door. Then they'd had her torn perineum to sew up, because Lotte weighed over eight pounds on the hospital scale.

Thus, it was with great reticence that Madie greeted Pata's joyful outbursts when she came home from the maternity ward, particularly as she refused to take the pill again for the same somewhat obscure reasons she had given before. So they came up with a compromise, which made Pata complain and Madie tremble: during her fertile days, the father would resort to the withdrawal method. He sulked, frustrated. The mother was terrified she might make a mistake, until she got her period and was reassured for two weeks or so. Yet it was because of a miscalculation—unless Pata let something out and didn't say anything—that she found herself pregnant again. And although, once she had digested the news, she accepted the father's pirouettes with good grace up until her eighth month, after Marion's birth she moved her mattress to the other side of the room and decreed that that was it. To be honest, Pata did not protest initially. And by the time he did, Madie had already gotten used to the change and didn't often go back on her decision.

There's no way of knowing whether things would have stayed like that forever, that regular, forced abstinence, but the huge tidal wave, at that very point in their lives, confronted Pata and Madie with far more pressing concerns. The mother deemed that between nine births and a major flood, fifteen years had gone by without a lull. She would have liked to have a moment of rest—but there it was, there were storms, wind, and the ocean constantly devouring their land, chasing them from their home precisely thirteen days after the catastrophe, and life had been nothing but catastrophic ever since.

So there is nothing to thank the heavens or fate or anything for, ruminates Madie. She's had her fill of pain, and if she brought children into the world, it was not so that they would be taken from her. It will be a long while before she's ready to forgive the world. She's filled with spite, is Madie: a week of mourning and fate figures they're even? A likely story. She's hardly had time to come to terms with it. Moreover, Madie plans to get even with the heavens, and she'll start by covering them with scorn. She spits in the water when Pata has his back turned. Makes a vengeful fist, casts a furious gaze. She likes that the heavens would feel hurt. Deep down, she's scared out of her wits. Never mind, she will be brazen. She bets the heavens wouldn't dare come after her twice in a row, not all that soon.

But nothing eases her sorrow. When she has finished thinking about her children, when she has finished imagining what she could do to get even with the heavens, she is crushed with pain all over again. It's like a bad flu, her body aching all over, her throat burning, her head caught in a vise that no one can loosen. Madie puts her hands on her head, tries pressing to make it stop. It doesn't stop.

Leaning over the side, she sees her reflection in the ocean. Recoils. Even in the gray water she can see how pale she is, her features drawn and bruised with grief. She will keep these marks to the very end. She knows: from now on, she will be the mother of a little ghost.

At lunchtime on the tenth day, Emily and Sidonie begin to cry: there isn't enough to eat. The eggs are long gone, the bags are empty; fishhooks stay bare. Neither the father nor the two eldest have the strength to fish once they put down their oars—and besides, they'd have to stop on an island and make a fire to cook the fish, because no matter what Madie says the little girls will not touch raw flesh, she can just picture their noses wrinkling, their disgusted expressions, *It's yucky.* But they will have to make landfall soon: the mother has only a dozen raw potatoes left, so there, too, she needs a fire. In the meanwhile she divides up the last, moldy, pancakes, rather hesitantly; what if it makes them sick. She watches the children nibbling and feels her own stomach rumbling, stirring up emptiness and bile inside, her hand deep in the bag strokes the last two eggs she's hidden from the father, they're for the baby, she'll give them to her when everyone's asleep.

Madie clears her throat.

"If we find an island . . . "

She doesn't finish her sentence. Pata is bound to turn around and ask her.

"You want us to stop?"

"An hour or two, if there's some wood to make a fire. For the potatoes. And if we could try and fish . . . there's nothing left."

The father nods. He doesn't tell her that he's been scanning the water for days and hasn't seen a single fish. Maybe the beast that is still following them off and on is the reason for the penury, devouring or terrifying everything it sees, circling around them as if they will be its last feast, he's sure it's because of the beast. He thinks he can smell its stench of slimy skin and the deep, every morning when they get started again after he has cautiously raised the little anchor that breaks the surface, bringing up the mustiness of the silt. He alone knows that sometimes the beast comes up to rub its back against the boat, testing its resistance; yes, it's like the storm, Pata can tell the animal is getting ready. It's a strange combat they're engaged in, the two of them, muted and mean, and the father wishes he could read the creature's mind, to know what it is planning, to take the measure of his own chances to reach higher ground before it comes to a confrontation, to outpace it; does it know they are getting closer to the mountains?

If only they had a rifle.

Make landfall and stay for days on end, as long as it takes, until the creature grows weary. But with Madie who'd shout that they have to get going . . . with deserted hills where there is nothing to eat, not even roots. The father shudders, scans the horizon. Hopes for an island. They've seen three in two days, a sign they are in an area of higher altitude. He was hoping some of these islands might still be inhabited. Find help, food, a few indications about their route. But the land is dying from salt water and abandonment, people have sought refuge further away. Yesterday they saw the head of a statue above water, incongruous in the middle of the sea, a solitary statue, nothing else.

"Do you think there was a city here?" asked Liam.

Pata nodded. He recognized the stone face of Joseph, he couldn't be sure but it seemed probable, which would mean they were in the region of Vallone, where the statues had been put up twenty years earlier—there should also have been the one of Mary with the child in her arms, but Mary is smaller, so she's surely below the water now, forever, so small, or knocked over—Vallone, thinks the father suddenly, so they must have drifted south, they'll have to change course. Saying nothing, he adjusted his rowing. Behind them, the creature rippled to follow them, the only one who noticed the boat's new direction.

The little girls' restrained tears hover in the air, they sniffle and sob, Madie calms them with a gesture. On land she would have kept them busy with a game. The first one who brings me a. The first one who finds—a blue flower, a round stone, a forked stick. How many flies on that spot of sunlight, how many ricochets on the water when you toss a flat pebble. But what can she give them, here on this boat? Water, water, and more water. The number of planks it took to build the boat, the color of the oars? Who cares. Even the game of Happy Families: they can't stand the sight of it, they're sickened by all the times they've played since leaving home, storms interrupt them. The mother feels as if a drill were piercing through her flesh, this image of the little girls crying, silently, and there's nothing she can do, just ignore them so she won't burst into tears herself, tears of rage, turn away not to see, clench her fists; these cursed days that never end.

"There."

Pata points to something the mother cannot see, a shadow on the horizon, she squints. An island. She says it, to be sure.

"An island?"

He smiles.

"Yes."

The children stir, suddenly excited.

"Are we going there?"

"Are we going to get off?"

"Is there food there?"

Don't know. Matteo, at the oars, rows even harder. *Just pray it isn't a mirage*, thinks the mother, gazing at his tense face.

"When will we be there?" asks Sidonie.

"Another hour."

"Is it long, an hour?"

"Yes," says the mother.

"No," says the father.

But it is Madie who is right: even the final minutes seem to last forever. And for what? A place of loose stones, a sort of callus emerging from the sea. A plateau, several hundred yards square, brambles, dead bushes, then nothing. *I don't believe it*, sighs the father, as he brings the boat gently ashore.

Sidonie, Emily, and Matteo, too: after ten days of rocking on the water, when they step out on land they fall down. They get up, walk unsteadily, fall again. They start laughing.

"I feel dizzy," says Emily, ecstatic.

"It's weird," murmurs Sidonie.

Matteo runs sideways, his arms spread like a bird's wings. His legs stiff and painful. He says, *I've got pins and needles.*

Madie waves to bring them together.

"Come on, let's tour the place."

Tour, honestly? They can see the island from where they are. *We'll count our steps.* The little ones try. Fifty-four, fifty-five. It's hard. In her mother's arms, Marion squirms this way and that to see where they are going. Suddenly they start with surprise. *Blackberries, blackberries!* The brambles are covered with them. Even Pata trots over and gives a cry. They're everywhere. The mother hurriedly rummages for a bowl, while the children stuff themselves with everything they can reach. They are covered in scratches and stains; it doesn't matter.

"Don't eat the red ones, they'll make you sick," warns Pata. "They're not ripe yet."

They eat the red ones.

Madie slaps their hands.

"Leave some, we have to have some for tomorrow."

They don't stop. They laugh. She fills the bowl and keeps them from reaching into it, kicking them away if need be, scolding them halfheartedly. Their mouths and cheeks are purple. Pata has gone to find some dead wood to build a fire, hoping to find other treasures—but the island offers nothing more than a carpet of moss, where they sit and stare at the flames, their bellies happy, their eyes riveted on the potatoes waiting to be buried in the embers; their mouths are already watering.

Afterwards they lie on the ground, astonished not to have to bend their legs or share the space. Madie motions that they should get up but Pata holds her back, the kids are overwhelmed with fatigue, as is he, and the mother.

Let them sleep.

He wants to stay overnight; Madie refuses. She'll be patient, the time it takes for a nap, she looks at their faint smiles, hears their breathing—including the father's, he has collapsed on his side and begins to snore when she stops kicking him gently with her toe, and finally Madie too succumbs, curls around the baby and falls asleep, all seven of them lying in a circle around the dead fire, seven survivors looking like neatly laid out corpses, and the warm gray air lulls them until the end of the afternoon.

B ut they had to go back to sea, and the next day their bellies were just as empty as when they landed on the island; the blackberries were long gone, the potatoes a sad memory. This time, they have nothing left. Madie took some moss and a few twigs, what are you doing, scolded Pata, you're not going to make them eat grass now are you. He is relying on the approaching mountains, imminent landfall—and yet, as far as the eye can see there is nothing but water, and at times he loses heart. He saw one or two hills so far off their route that he didn't say anything; they would have wasted hours. A wager: if there was nothing but loose stones, the father had been right. If there were trees, fruit, berries, his decision to keep going had been disastrous. But he'll never know. It's better this way. No regrets. Just hunger.

And the little girls whining and chanting, *I'm hungry, I'm hungry.* It breaks his heart. He's always been so proud of feeding his family, even during the difficult years, when he lost his job because the factory closed. Madie's little salary had not been enough, and so while waiting for better days, Pata did piecework, never mind what they offered him, field work, gardening, household maintenance, trimming hedges, driving old ladies on errands, which hardly paid for the gas he used, even cleaning house. The eleven of them weren't exactly fat but they managed. They never got the impression they would die of hunger, whereas now . . . A hair's breadth. The father glances at the baby sleeping in her mother's arms. That's good. Marion cried for two solid hours, she doesn't understand, can't accept. So then Emily and Sidonie started up, so what, who could tell whether it was better to shout at them to shut up—it's not as if they were starving them on purpose!—or to let them go on, even join in, because there's no solution, and there's this constant temptation to turn around, but after eleven days it would be madness to turn around. A stupid idea; exhaustion is turning him into a moron. And besides, he knows.

The answer to the mother's question last night, full of resignation: *Why haven't we seen land yet?*

Yes, he knows. He didn't say so, of course. He also thought that with a bit of luck by the tenth day they would start finding islands. They've seen nothing, or virtually. Because the waters are still rising. There's your answer: the sea has covered still more ground and the water level is ever higher. So, should they go home? The father has a lump in his throat. He has no idea what might be left of their hill. He presses his hands on his face not to think of the three little ones left behind, who might have drowned already. For days the word has been drifting through his mind, and comes back when he least expects it. *Murderer.* But he didn't think of it all on his own: it's the word he saw in Madie's eyes when they set off with six children and left the other three on the island, eleven days ago—and it could have been a thousand days ago and it would have made no difference: since that dawn, he has become a murderer. The question remains: how many has he killed? One, two. Four. All of them. He'll find out when he gets there.

The father snivels soundlessly. The baby's silence is wrenching.

But then comes Liam's weary voice.

"There's an island over there."

He sits up straight. For now it's just a dot on the horizon, a dot on their route. Less than an hour off course, at a guess. So the father says, *Let's go.*

"You think there'll be food?"

"I hope so."

"It looks big."

"Yes, fairly big. We're bound to find something."

Madie looks, too. At first she doesn't want to be glad, not to be disappointed. She curbs the unbearable little voice inside her that is already squeaking with joy, she can't believe it, she's sure the island will disappear, a mirage in their tired eyes, in their silent prayers. But the further they go, the bigger the mound becomes. After half an hour they can make out green shapes, bushes or little trees, expanses of grass, woods. And it's true that all of a sudden the island looks like paradise. Madie exclaims, *Oh my lord!* Matteo, Emily, and Sidonie are clutching the gunwale, their eyes feasting on the approaching land. At the same time they keep an eye on the sky, where all the perils have come from, they don't trust it, something worries them.

They're wrong. It's in the sea that the threat is looming, but none of them realizes it just then, absorbed as they are by the clouds, the absence of wind, the outline of the island. Matteo slaps his thighs, *I knew it!* Pata lets out a cry, turns to them, his smile radiant.

"We're saved."

Even the baby, awoken by their exclamations, waves her arms and chirps. *Yes*, says Madie, *we'll go there, we'll find food.* Her hands, white-knuckled, veins bulging, grab the rope around the boat as if to make it go faster, she wants to see, to feel, to be sure of the food they will find there, she's already planning a meal in her mind, picturing them all in a circle around a fire, mouths watering from the aroma of something roasting—what can they roast, for goodness' sake, tubers, forgotten vegetables, a careless bird, some fish at last?

Sidonie stretches her arms out to the island: *Come!* They laugh.

The island is only a few hundred yards away. From the bow Pata thinks he can make out spots of color on the bushes, maybe berries, or fruit, he prays in silence. Feverish agitation overcomes him, he misses the feel of earth beneath his feet, its motionless strength, its warmth. He smiles.

Then his smile fades.

The boat judders to a halt. It has hit something.

He looks at Liam, rowing on the other side, who frowns when he sees the father has stopped. *What is it?* Pata slowly immerses the oar in the water: there's no silt, no resistance, he didn't think there would be, to be honest, no reeds, no rushes to break through the surface here, it's still too deep, it's not land they've scraped against, no. All of a sudden, his terror poorly concealed, the blood drains from his face. Shivers along his skin, like the sudden onset of a raging fever: he knows what they have struck. Turns to Liam.

"Turn around."

Act as if. Pretend. The boat moves a few feet.

"Something stuck on my side," exclaims Liam.

"Try again."

"I can't, it's stuck!"

"It's not stuck. Row."

"I tell you it is!"

Matteo is by his brother and now he leans over and dips his hand into the water to search around the edge of the hull. Pata screams: *No!* And then silence. He looks at Matteo, he looks at all six of them frozen by his cry, sitting straight and motionless, six pairs of eyes glued on him. He shakes his head, looks at Liam.

"Row backwards. We'll move off to the right."

The oars dip into the water, struggling to maneuver the little craft. Slowly, the boat heads again toward the island. *Quick*, breathes Pata. Eighty, a hundred yards. They pick up speed, breathless, look all around not knowing why, only the father, with his eyes scanning the space, his mouth suddenly open—when the wave forms.

"There. There!"

"What do we do?" cries Liam.

They watch the ripple in the water, fascinated by the roller that comes toward them and pushes them away from the shore. Initially they are not afraid, because the wave is round and gentle; until they realize. Everywhere else the sea is flat and smooth. Not a breath of air. No lapping of water. Madie's worried expression: *What is it?* Pata doesn't reply. To say what? To hear his voice trembling when he says, *It's the creature*—no, he goes on rowing, in vain, because the huge invisible body blocks their way, under the water, never mind, he tries again, Liam follows suit. For a few moments they make headway again. Matteo encourages them.

"We're nearly there!"

Yes, but.

Silently the wave forms again. Pushes them back more abruptly, as if annoyed; this time the boat rocks, the mother reaches for her little ones to make them sit on the floor. *It's the creature, isn't it!*

"What is it?" shouts Matteo.

Liam gives a start, holds out his arm.

"It's the monster! It's back!"

It never left, ruminates Pata, biting his lip, feeling the knots in his stomach as he stares at the ripples on the water; the creature is circling around them, shoving them.

"Why is it doing this?" cries Matteo.

To keep us from landing—but the father doesn't say it out loud, too terrified to utter the words, it's just that he's sure, the beast has decided to attack before the water is too shallow for it to follow, before they hurry away, before the father stops being afraid. In a surge of desperation he strikes the water with the edge of his oar, immediately thinks that was a stupid thing to do, but too late, when you picture the size of the thing swimming beneath them, a blow for nothing, for an explosion of anger, a fraction of a second later the waters whirl apart to reveal a gigantic animal. Everyone on the boat screams, mother, father, children, instinctively recoiling, hands raised before them in a useless gesture. Do they see what Pata sees at that moment, the shining gray-black body emerging from the depths, its huge mouth open on razor-sharp teeth, and even more terrifying, its roar—do they hear its hoarse, mournful cry causing the surface of the water to tremble, creasing the air beneath its resonance, petrifying them all in the middle of the boat, tiny and panicked, the little girls crying, hiding their eyes. Liam and his father seize the oars, struggle against the current left by the beast. The shore is a few yards away, Pata could weep for it, he can almost reach out and touch it, jump out, ten breaststrokes beneath the water—and the monster's jaw closing over him, he knows he wouldn't have the time, or the speed.

"It won't let us!" screams Madie.

The boat lurches from left to right, buffeted by waves and troughs. They are lying on the floor, rolling and crashing into the side of the boat as it rises and falls with a sinister cracking sound, they are drenched by the slapping of the water. Liam and Matteo cry out at the same time, there's a leak, the father envisages all the impossible solutions, final seconds, their little boat damaged, the wood giving way, he squeezes the edge with all his strength as if that could hold the boat together, *Don't kill my children*, his head shaking as he roars, *No, no*, and meets Madie's horror-stricken gaze.

"It's going to eat us!" screams Liam.

"No!" But Pata is losing faith and his voice cracks.

He starts to get up, nearly stumbles into the water, bangs into Matteo next to him. He squeezes his shoulder, and sways when he sees the knife in the boy's hand. *Matteo?*

The crazed look on his boy's face.

"If I go for him, you'll have time to land."

"What?"

He reaches out his hand to grab him. The boy leaps away. Jumps overboard, and the father had no time to do a thing. Matteo was there next to him—and a second later, an absence, not even a second went by, nor does he hear the sound of his body hitting the water.

Then Pata's roar, and Madie's, and Liam's. All three of them saw.

The waters swirling, and the foam, suddenly moving away, leaving the half-drowned boat, to plunge a few yards further away. The sun glinting off the flash of the knife blade, and the cries, of the beast, of the boy, the water red around them, all is vain, the father doesn't listen, doesn't look, won't, he has picked up the oars and is rowing like a condemned man toward land.

Only Liam and the father had the strength to drag the beast's body onto the shore, a creature over six feet long, it was stupid but Pata couldn't help figuring its length, that of a bed, roughly, that was it, six feet of power and rage. The mother and the girls are weeping helplessly as they watch them tugging the gray mass, scored with knife wounds, blood still flowing. They don't want to go closer. The father sobs as he slices open the animal's belly and empties it, throwing the guts into the sea. He cuts its head off cautiously, as if its sharp teeth could still tear off his arm. *Fucking monster . . .* Liam is kneeling next to him, his big eyes full of silent tears. His hands curved over the gleaming skin—if he could tear it off, shred upon shred, if the beast were still alive, if it could feel pain the way he does, piercing his heart, a knife wound, a strangling. Pata next to him carves and cuts, slices, skins, a bit more than he needs to, for sure, anger, despair. Liam agrees:

"We'll eat the whole goddamn thing."

He hides his disgust, the nauseating smell, the viscous flesh he is reluctant to touch. The father gestures toward the fire and he skewers hunks of flesh onto wooden stakes and puts them on to roast. Not hungry. And yet. Despite the sorrow, despite the shock which has silenced them all, when the air fills with the smell of fish they go closer, for three days they've been eating the last crumbs of pancakes and potatoes, a few blackberries, and air, they hate themselves, the way their gazes are riveted on the fire, their weak, famished bellies, the saliva at the corners of their lips. Pata goes on slicing, they'll cook the surplus during the night and take it with them the next day, so that it will have served some purpose—to allow them to land, to eat, it had saved them, at last. His hands tremble on the knife blade.

They have not found Matteo's body. Perhaps drifting, perhaps twenty feet under. The father doesn't know. He took the others to shelter on the island, surrounding the keening mother, to keep her from diving in, he murmured in her ear to convince her, and so that the girls would not hear, *He's dead, Madie, he's dead, you have to look after the girls now, you hear me? Jumping in the water won't bring him back.* And she wails with despondency, her suffering greater than the open sky when it rains, her arms straight in front of her. He had to calm her like a little child. Wept with her when she said:

"Another one. Another one."

Pata keeps busy, so as not to think. The fire, the boat turned on its side on the shore to provide shelter for the night, the image of the beast floating on the surface of the water, then carving it up. He goes from one child to the next with a tender word, a smile, a caress.

"I'm hungry," says Sidonie.

"It's almost ready."

When he comes to the mother he hesitates. If she looked up she would see his unsure, questioning, imploring step; but Madie doesn't look up. She has withdrawn into herself, curled around her despair, her eyes hidden behind her palms, and suddenly the father is fascinated by her hands, those of an old woman of forty, with blue, protruding veins, spots on her skin that shine yellow, hands that have been clinging too hard to the boat these last days and which look as if they will never open again, curled like claws. And so he moves on, without making a sound or a gesture, he leans over the baby in Emily's arms, next to the mother, strokes the girl's cheek, let's hope the fish will be good. Liam has begun to pass it around, filling their metal bowls. They eat in silence.

Afterwards the little girls get up. Emily puts the baby in Madie's arms and runs with Sidonie, her legs stiff after so many days, the stop yesterday did not completely revive them. Before long the father hears them laughing. He hurries over— and stops. To say what? What, at the age of five or six, do they understand of death and sorrow? Of course they saw dead animals back on their island, drowned rats, hens the mother was preparing for dinner. But that wasn't death. They only know absence.

Tomorrow they will ask where Matteo is, the way they did with Lotte, and he'll have to keep from shouting at them, how stupid they are, they saw it for themselves, and they were told that Lotte was dead, and now Matteo, too, is dead, dead, DEAD. But they are stubborn. Sidonie insists Lotte is in the sea with the fish. *I'd like to go there too*, she proclaims in her clear, chiming voice. The mother turns pale.

"Be quiet!"

Sidonie looks down, gazes silently at the surface of the water, looking for a familiar shadow, does not know it cannot be, splashes with her hand as if to attract something—what, thinks Pata, corpses, fantasies—miracles. Her innocence appalls and enchants him at the same time: if only they, too, the father and mother, could be content with absence. Take note. Lotte is no longer here, nor is Matteo. Something new is beginning.

But the night lays bare the falsehood, and Pata cannot sleep for grief, with Madie stifling her sobs on the other side of the fire, both of them incapable of speaking or helping each other, a wall between them, for everything they don't want to say to each other in front of the children. Liam has burrowed beneath a blanket so that no one can see him. Ten times the father gets up to go and look at the little girls and find courage there; they have drifted off to sleep, smiling, and their peaceful faces console him for a brief moment, what can be consoled, a balm on a patch of his heart, a soothing breath on a burn. Maybe they are not even unhappy. They cried, earlier, because they were afraid; but sorrow? How will they miss Matteo? Sidonie, as she lies down, says to Emily:

"I like it when Matteo isn't here because that way he can't pester me and yank on my pajamas."

Above all, don't scold them. There is nothing more alive than his little girls, and what could be more right than they are, rooted in the moment, oblivious of the past, unconscious of the future when it goes beyond the next hour or the next meal. He envies their animal spontaneity, the mindless momentum that propels them toward the future come what may, selfish and proud, virgin souls who know nothing of good and evil; his marmots, his little girls. He dozes for an hour or two, his gaze filled with love. If they were not here, he'd be dead already.

At dawn, wandering by the water's edge, he finds Matteo's body.

* * *

Of course, it's only a body. But still.

Pata stepped back once he'd pulled it up on the shore and turned it over to gaze at it. Vomited some bile just there, couldn't help it, it happened too quickly, seeing the boy's face half torn off, his arm missing below the elbow—the right arm, the one that had been holding the knife. Matteo's flesh exhibits the violence of the final moments. The father looks behind him; the others are still sleeping. In a burst of panic he takes his son in his arms and runs to the farthest point on the island to bury him. Madie mustn't see him, not Madie or Liam or the girls, no one, he wants to conceal everything that has damaged Matteo, he wants to keep pure the image of the little boy they had brought up to be a fine lad. But the island is nothing but hard ground and scrabble, and Pata breaks his nails trying to dig a grave, terrified at the thought that Madie might wake, he tries three or four different spots, and fails every time. So he runs to the boat and takes a rope. Picks up the biggest stones and winds the rope first around the stones, then around Matteo, all bound tightly together. When he's sure the rocks will be heavier than his boy he shoves the strange coffin to the edge of the water, but gently, as if it might still have an effect, this infinite care taken by something deep inside him that is not quite dead, murmuring words of comfort, a final caress on the cheek that is intact—he won't look at the other one. One more gesture and Matteo's body slips soundlessly into the sea. For a moment it seems to want to float on the surface, and the father fears it might never sink. Then the water fills the spaces, takes hold, sucks it down, and the boy's ravaged body vanishes beneath the tranquil ripples, no more than a shadow. And then nothing. Pata kneels on the shore, his face in his hands. He stays there for a long time, his mind completely empty, his fingers gripping the fierce pounding in his skull, he huddles over his heaving heart, his insane thoughts. What if he loses them one after the other? Is this his punishment for abandoning Louie, Perrine, and Noah on the island, will three of his children on the boat die now to make him regret his decision, to tell him he shouldn't have chosen those children, but how could he know, how can he be forgiven—nothing is possible anymore, he can only go back to sea and pray he won't finally get there with three empty places, pray that land will appear soon on the horizon, mountains rising up before him, tomorrow, today, in an hour, it is time, they can't take any more of this. Already it is time to get up. In his body Pata feels like an old man.

When Madie wakes, he tells her in a whisper about Matteo. Gives no details, just that he'd been injured, that she wouldn't have wanted to see him. What he did with the stones. Her eyes lowered, the mother nods, says nothing. On her drawn features there is a sort of wretched relief. The father almost adds, *I'm sorry*, but then recalls he has said this already, too often. Silence absorbs them as they ready the boat to leave, Liam at the oars, holding the boat steady against the shore for the girls to climb in. For a moment Pata feels a dull fear in his gut, wondering what the sea has in store for them on this new day, and he looks out, lost, at the vast surface of the water. Then, so what. Does he have any choice, now? He grabs the oar Liam holds out to him. *Are we off?* The boat seems to weigh so heavily in his arms. He forces it away from the stagnant water.

* * *

Emily was the first to see it. What were the others looking at just then, to miss it like that, when they've been looking for it so eagerly for days, when it's been their ultimate goal, their salvation: land. Not an island, not a scrap of ground above the surface of the water in the middle of nowhere the way Pata briefly thought it was, no: real land.

The coast. For hundreds of yards, even miles, like a long curving back above the sea, lost in the mist, a place to stand on, to walk for hours without meeting a barrier of water. For now it is only a very thin line at the far end of the horizon, and Pata rubs his eyes to make sure. It does not vanish.

So there it is. He says so, his voice tremulous:

"Land."

They all turn and strain toward it, as if the wind were driving them all in the same direction, on their knees on the boat's damp floorboards, and Emily claps her hands, *I saw it first*. Madie kisses her, her eyes welling with tears.

"How soon will we be there?"

The father frowns.

"Tonight, tomorrow . . . By noon tomorrow, I'd say."

His eyes meet Madie's, and in the yellow light he can tell they are thinking the same thing: just one day, give or take, and Matteo would have reached the shore, too. They had been so close. They suffer in silence, everything seems vain. They curse the days that have gone before, the day that drowned Lotte, the day that took their boy from them. It does not help. The mother squeezes her clenched fists against her lips. They have to hold out until tomorrow.

Liam on the left, Pata on the right, rowing regularly, for hours. They would like to go faster but their bodies refuse, their muscles seem paralyzed, their bones ready to snap. When the boat can drift all on its own, they let it go, resting their arms, closing their lids on their red, strained eyes, and when they open them again they are blinded by the glare of the sun, and they shield their eyes with the palms of their hands. Shortly before twilight the father motions to lower the oars.

"We won't make it."

The land has expanded before them, it almost seems they could reach out and touch it. A painful illusion, when Pata knows they will need at least several more hours to make landfall, just as this morning they thought the shore was within reach, deluded by the obliteration of distance on the smooth sea and their own desperate gazes, he doesn't want to get lost during the night, he orders Liam to drop the little anchor. While they share some of the fish, the father steals glances at them. Their tired, dirty faces, tangled, filthy brown or blond hair, their clothes and skin smelling of silt and damp—they look like an army of beggars, and he shudders: not the sort of people anyone wants showing up at their door. And as they eat in silence, turned toward that land fading gray with nightfall, the sea rolling under them, Pata wonders what the future has in store, if there is a future, and who will give them a chance, so that his children might never tell him some day that, all things considered, they would have done better to drown back there, on their own island.

All through the short night on the boat Pata is startled awake. He knows that bad luck always strikes at the last moment, just when you think you're home safe at last, when you cry victory too soon, so when the little girls asked him, before they went to sleep, to tell them what life would be like on the new land, he put a finger to his lips. *Sshh.* Above all, when they're so close, mustn't rouse any ghosts or evil spirits, no making light of them until we . . . . A murmur, and a smile to the girls. *We'll find out tomorrow.*

"Yes but what will it be like?" said Sidonie again.

Pata shook his head, not to be moved. *Sshh.*

Sitting at the bow he dozes, opening his eyes abruptly when the swell passes underneath them—but they are only empty waves, currents rebounding from the depths, lullabies. Even though they have come closer, the father can no longer see the land, engulfed by night. He gives a regular tug on the anchor chain to make sure it is still holding; he is haunted by the thought that they might drift, that they might wake up all alone again in the middle of the ocean, just the six of them and the water all around them—and the coast made to vanish by some terrible magic. And of course Pata, on his boat in the middle of the night, could be glad they are about to reach their goal at last, and that tomorrow they will be sure of walking on solid ground, on infinite land, after twelve and a half days of nightmare. But he can't bring himself to be glad, partly out of superstition, and partly because there is no joy left inside him, no triumph to celebrate, he'll have to be glad of the little girls' joy, that's all, and accept that nothing more than that will ever show, just meet Madie's gaze, or Liam's, and carry the knowledge until the end of his life that he is the father who lost five children during the crossing.

Two, he corrects.

Five.

He opens his eyes wide, *Two, two.* The other three, he wasn't the one who lost them, and besides they are not lost—but he knows very well that they are. And in the darkness and the silence, incapable of happiness, Pata feels himself shrinking, his stomach in knots. Not even landed on the coast yet and already he is anticipating the next calamity, the one he will not speak of to Madie, who already thinks he's a bastard, the proof of it being the fact that they fled the island, could it be he was the only one who knew? Was that why he didn't want to sign the note they'd left for their abandoned children?

There is no more island, no more hill, not a chance. If their house is still standing, it is under six feet of water. The level will have risen so much that it was a foregone conclusion before they even set sail: everything would be engulfed. And the father did not leave Louie, Perrine, and Noah only for the time it would take to save the others then go back for them; he doomed them to certain death. Whenever he thinks of it— every day, every night, every hour—he trembles, picturing them back there in their final moments, with no boat, no hope, nothing. And if they are clinging to a piece of wood—what for? For how long? *Stop, stop.* But the mother's gaze is nothing if not truthful when she lets it fall on him with a silent accusation: *Murderer.*

Murderer, yes. He did what he did in full knowledge of the facts. He knew he would never see Louie, Perrine, and Noah again, he chose them, thought for a very long time about the children he had to have with him for the voyage—the eldest—

and the ones Madie would never forgive him for leaving behind because they would not survive without her—the youngest. In the middle of that terrible equation there were three left. And it wasn't because Pata loved them less than the others, whatever Madie might say, or that he thought they were not as good as the others, with their damaged bodies: it was that he had to decide. Either they left all together and died all together, or they saved some of them—and it would not be those three. Of course the father thought about giving up his own place, as did the mother once it became clear to her, before they left the island. But Liam and Matteo wouldn't have been able to take everyone, to deal with the storms, the currents, the hunger, and the monster that had been giving chase right from the start. They would have fought over the food. They would have been frightened when the wind got up, or the waves turned gigantic—they would have capsized, Pata is sure. *They're still children*, he thinks. Corrects himself. *Were*. God.

So there it is. He is the only one who knows, who is carrying this burden: Louie, Perrine, and Noah were doomed the moment the rest of the family took the boat to flee. He also tried to think of a way to cram more of them on board, how to tear doors or shutters from the house and nail them hastily to the boat to make some sort of cabin, but it wouldn't hold, it would be too heavy, it would cause the boat to list, events have proved him right, they would have foundered all together, all dead, what was the point. Since there was no solution.

Pata is on his knees, hands together, at the bow. Lying a few inches from there, Liam is looking at him through his half-open eyes, not a sound, not a gesture. He is not sleeping, either: the feverishness of knowing land is so near makes the blood pound through his veins. Initially he was overcome by exhaustion, slept a few hours, and then his nerves got the better of him, he wishes he could row all night, get closer to the coast so that the mother and the little girls would have a surprise at dawn, to

touch the meadow grass as they hold out their hands, dance a
jig with cries of relief, they're here at last, Liam knows the
father wouldn't want him to say it already but he can't help it,
deep down, they have arrived, at last. The fact that there are six
of them and not eight: Liam puts that aside. There is absence,
there is pain; but something else, too, even more powerful, that
transcends his sorrow.

The joy of rescue.

And at that moment, even if Liam doesn't put it exactly like
this: for the others, tough luck.

No remorse, he's had his share of suffering and fatigue.
Regrets, yes, and sorrow, intense. But tomorrow. For now, only
the ones who are living matter—who are alive, he thinks with
a smile, who are hardy. The fittest. And Pata, you can't really
tell which side he's on, part dead, part alive, all his strength
gone, Liam restrains a surge of tenderness, don't get up, don't
show him you saw him at his weakest, collapsing, just acknowledge that you'll have to take care of him, making landfall doesn't
necessarily mean being rescued.

Pretends to stretch.

"You're not asleep?" murmurs Pata.

"Not anymore."

"Not sleepy?"

"I wish we were already there."

"Yes. Me, too."

"And I'm afraid, too."

"Afraid? Why?"

"Of starting all over. We've got nothing."

"We'll manage."

" . . . don't even have anything to buy food. Where will we
sleep?"

"I don't know. But I'm sure people will help us."

"You think so?"

"I know so."

"Okay."

"But for the time being we have to sleep and get some strength. Tomorrow will be anything but restful."

"We made it, Dad."

"Almost, son. A few more strokes of the oar, and we'll surely be the last ones to have made it to land."

* * *

The next day at eleven the coast guard finds them when they are only two nautical miles from land; they'd spotted them from the harbor. Initially—so they will tell them—they took them for some marine creature, once the alarm had been raised by some people out walking and watching the horizon with a telescope. The blue and white boat cuts its engine as it draws alongside them; the men have rifles. When they see the six wan figures in the boat, they immediately put down their rifles, astonished.

"Who are you? Where are you from?"

The father explains. He wonders if they will believe him.

"Good God, you were at Levet. No one has come from there in days, the few who weren't drowned."

Everyone thought they were dead, the people from Levet and the surrounding area, the land was too low-lying. Everything was inundated the day of the cataclysm, with the exception of the statues in Vallone and a few of the highest hills. Pata listens and begins to tremble: how do they know, how is this possible, he looks at Madie whose eyes are open wide, questioning, shaking her head, and yet, it is so simple. The early days after the tidal wave, the higher ground was overrun by refugees, half-drowned, exhausted, lost. Everything was reorganized to deal with the emergency, improbable shelters were found—sheepfolds, stables, garages; there were injured people to be tended, the dead that people had brought with them, to be buried; and then, very soon afterwards, rescue operations were set in motion to scour the new sea for survivors. With motorboats crisscrossing the flooded territory, they covered hundreds of miles over a star-shaped pattern, methodically, painstakingly sailing back and forth to find a few miraculous survivors, some of whom had gone mad. That is how they knew the statues in Vallone were still above water: they were there two days ago. And just when one of the men exclaims, *But we should have seen you, which way did you go, how did we miss you, you must have drifted miles away*, Madie lets out a wild cry, one hand to her lips, *The children, the children!*

The man in uniform frowns.

"The children?"

"On the island . . . there were three children."

"No, madam, there was nothing."

"Yes, yes! Three children, two boys and a girl! Didn't you find them? Tell me you found them!"

"Madam, I'm sorry. In fact . . . there was no island."

The father reaches out just as the mother collapses, holds onto her with all his strength. To make sure, he says:

"What did you say?"

Madie's mouth is wide open, a huge cry inside her that cannot come out. Pata can feel it throbbing right into his flesh, then she repeats, almost inaudibly:

"What did you say?"

"Everything was flooded, madam. We did find the place where your village used to be, but it was completely covered in water. You say there were still people there?"

But Madie no longer hears them, she has turned to Pata who is still holding her, her eyes glued to him, horrified, *The children*—so the father begins to sob because he has understood, he knew all along, he just hoped his predictions would be wrong, that they would have time to go back. He spent his nights praying that he had been wrong once again, that the water would ease off and give them a chance. But it hadn't. No one ever listens to him.

Softly, not looking at her, he murmurs to Madie, *Sshh, sshh . . .* wipes his own tears from her dirty hair, and when at last she realizes, when her terrifying lament first reaches her throat then bursts out, colossal, enough to cause the people around them to tremble, he buries his face in her neck, petrified by the pain he feels inside, outside, both of them there like ghosts, bags of bones that can barely stand, fragments. The mother feels her heart being torn to shreds, three more—three more gone, all at once, she was so sure she would see them again, Louie, Perrine, and Noah, a matter of one day at the most for a rescue boat, she had been so careful to leave them everything she could so they would not be hungry, honestly, no, she'd never wondered about them in that respect, never imagined she might not see them again, that they might be lost to her forever. Since yesterday when she had seen land she had been planning it, timing it; one hour for the fire department or the police to take charge of them, two hours to listen to their story and grasp the urgency, another hour to launch the boat to go to the island. Six or seven hours to get there. For what?

For a drowned land, and drowned children. Every time she comes up against these words in her mind, Madie lets out a scream, shrinks in upon herself, tears her hair. Later, a doctor will give her a tranquilizer and she will stop screaming. For now there's just Pata holding her hand, saying nothing; he, too, is devastated, Liam is looking after the girls and moving beds into the place they have been allotted, the sun is high in the sky, it is hot, they don't notice.

And that is how their life on the high ground begins, broken hearts and bodies, ravaged like scorched earth, this family who had been ready to repopulate the planet, only six of them left now, half of who they once were, half alive, skinned alive, and when they go to bed that night, in the house which also provides shelter for other refugees, Pata and Madie cannot help but think, separately, that they wish they had died all together, for all the good it has done and will do them, this half-life ahead of them, sometimes it's better not to go on, isn't it, if someone could have told them, if they had known, they would have stopped, laid down their arms—back in the days when they were still happy.

Madie has not gotten up for a week. Liam and the girls have been back in school for two days—as if they'd planned it, they arrived the day before classes started—and Pata has found work in the new port, loading and unloading ships with emergency goods. During the day, Madie and Marion stay alone in the house that had been found and offered them for a very low rent. Everything went very quickly—assistance, care, high school for Liam and primary and nursery school for Emily and Sidonie; a lease, a leg up for Pata so that he could earn their keep right away—he'll see later on if he can find something better. For the time being he is just happy that his children can go to school like everyone else, even if Liam is rebelling—too little freedom, makes him tired, he's been giving these dark looks over the last forty-eight hours, until Pata eventually says, *Yes, son, but*.

Not now. Let us get back on our feet. None of us has the strength to fight, neither me nor your mother, just keeping afloat with each new day, seeing how much is left at the end of the week to buy food and maybe an electric kettle, we can't do anything more for the time being, just light a candle when we listen to the night at our window, and the sea lapping beyond the trees, we're still numb with grief, so we'll talk about it someday, Liam, promise, it's just that. Not now.

What Pata doesn't say is how relieved he is to leave the house in the morning, to go and spend his time with people who shout and laugh, who slap you on the shoulder and spit on the sidewalk, people who are alive, dammit, loud and clear, who make him forget what he has lost for a few hours, and what he finds every evening when he comes home: the mother with her empty gaze and stringy hair, still unwashed, still in bed, the house smelling of despair and the absence of meals, he grabs a few vegetables, a piece of meat, the children come running and surround him. He could be angry with her, Madie, for deserting their life the way she has and leaving him to cope with everything, the return to an ordinary existence, work, the house, the girls' homework, the need for money—and yes, Pata had truly forgotten what life was about during those twelve days on the island and those twelve days on the ocean, the world had become other, a suspended web, the expanse of a nightmare. It leaves him confused, he works overtime in the evening if they ask him to, at the harbor he is both worn out and relieved, and then the time comes when he has to lower his head and go home, and tell himself that he could hold it against her, only he doesn't, he can't, deep down he could easily let himself go and sink down there beside her to sleep and never wake up, and rest, at last.

Sometimes in the evening he takes her hand and tells her about his day, in a low voice as if he were at the hospital, because he has to admit he really feels as if he is, with that inert, silent body next to him, her eyes open on nothing at all, and even if he knows that during the day Madie must get up to take care of Marion, when he sees her empty of everything he wonders if anything will ever come back, if she will get better, if something will begin to resemble their former life. To not think about it, he chatters. Describes the ships, the sounds, the smells, the crane unloading the containers, the seagulls squawking. The construction sites sprouting everywhere to build houses for people like them, who have lost everything, left everything behind, maybe later they'll be able to afford one, once he gets a better job. So, Pata is not angry with Madie, he talks to her. If he followed his inclination, he would even say, *Come with me, missus, come to the bedroom, we'll make some more little ones*, but she's already in the bedroom, and any more little ones are out of the question, because of the sadness that has paralyzed the house for a week or more, every hour, every puff of air. And Pata doesn't know what else he can do.

Often when he is talking with Madie, Liam gives three taps on the door and sticks his head through. A murmur.

"Everything all right?"

"Yes, sure, we're talking."

"Is she talking?"

"Not tonight."

"Did she eat something?"

"A little bit, yes."

"Can I come in?"

"Come in, son."

So Liam sits on the bed across from his father and he takes his mother's other hand. He tidies a lock of hair that has fallen across her face, and he in turn begins chatting, looking at Madie, then Pata, tells them about his day at high school, what he understands, what he doesn't understand, *Your mother could help you*, says his father, he shrugs. He goes along as he sees fit, about the food at the cafeteria, the friends he's beginning to make, how hot it is for early September, they'd feel better outdoors. Pata doesn't interrupt his son, lulled by the rhythm of his voice, it brings some life into the bedroom, he hopes that Madie is looking at them, that she wants to come back to them. But there is nothing. Later, when he stretches out next to her, he doesn't dare touch her, not even for a caress, not even to say goodnight, he remembers the first night on land, her skin as cold as a corpse's, white and stiff, he thinks, Madie is changing. She will end up like a ghost, or a pebble, he is sure of it. It's only a question of days, or months. He waits for her to fall asleep, stretches one finger toward her to touch her, and it has no effect on him, neither on her nor on him, she goes on sleeping, he doesn't shudder, doesn't feel like running his hand any further along her body, and yet God knows they used to have a good time together, the two of them, before, it was joyful, between two babies, that is surely why they had so many. And now, nothing. Madie has become a stranger, he doesn't recognize her. It hurts to feel so far away from her and not to know where to put his goddamn hands at night, they used to rest on her hips or around her belly, it hurts, too, the way she keeps him at a distance through her absence and her furtive glances, he feels sorry for wanting to live, maybe he didn't love his kids enough, no, he did, it's just that it won't bring them back, lying in bed all day long, and besides there are the other four, the last four, they have to watch over them twice as carefully as before to thank them for still being there.

So Pata rolls onto his back and opens his eyes on the night, and thinks of the only pathetic words Madie has been mumbling since they got there, and which lend her gaze an incredible force.

"Have to go and look all the same. Maybe they went to the wrong place."

He knows that in the middle of the night, as she has every night since they got there, she will shake him to say this; and like every time, it will take him hours to calm her down, to explain that the rescuers could not have missed the island, what with maps and the GPS on the boat, it's their job, they're used to it. And anyway Pata already went back to them to make sure that they couldn't have left anything to chance, or missed anything, but the men in uniform shook their heads, so sorry, they crisscrossed the entire former canton to look for people, there was nothing there, they swear, just a few chimney tops still poking through the surface of the water. So you see, Pata did go back to them, because Madie had woken him up with this mad idea of hers which had kept him breathless all the rest of that first night, to the point that by dawn he was almost sure of it himself, full of hope, filled with illusions, and it all came to nothing when the first responders described the sea to him, the bits of houses and belongings floating on the water, an island, yes, there was one, tiny, that would be a summit for a few more hours, with an apple tree at the top—that apple tree, thought Pata, the one that never bore any fruit, above the house. *You see, Madie, they did go that far. They searched everywhere.* But the mother won't listen, she moans, hides her head beneath the pillow—*You said you would go*— and while she gradually drifts off once the father has forced her to take some pills, again she murmurs the unbearable litany:

"Maybe they got it wrong."

Before, Pata would have held her in his arms to console her. Would have tried to make her listen to reason, drying her tears, kissing her hair and her cheeks. Now he looks at this woman who isn't really his wife anymore and he thinks, *This madwoman.* He keeps it to himself, utterly silent so the children won't hear; but there is this disconcerting feeling of loving Madie through thick and thin, the mother of his children, twenty years of happiness even during the difficult times, and now this shame that runs through him when he gazes at this distraught creature, this strange scarecrow, he doesn't want the neighbors to see her, to talk about her behind his back and feel sorry for him, he doesn't want anyone to make fun of her.

In the morning, when she sits lifeless at the window watching the sea as if the dead little children might emerge from it, there is only one thing he feels like doing, and that is shaking her, screaming in her ear, even throwing her out if that's what it takes, so that she'll get a grip on herself, gather her wits. A moment later he dreams of holding her to him and murmuring words of comfort, how much stronger they would be together, *Remember, Madie, how good things were, before*, but he does neither. He waits soundlessly for her to sense his presence and turn to him, tirelessly he smiles at her and murmurs:

"How do you feel today?"

There's no fear of her venting her distress, pouring out the torrents of suffering and ill-being her body displays: she never replies. This is why he asks again, because he knows she will remain silent—he could not stand any more of her pain. And she looks back at him with that gray and black look of hers, berates him in silence and destroys his hopes, does he really think that one morning she will get up and it will be all gone, absence emptiness sorrow, she will toss back the sheets and begin to hum, just like that, as if nothing had happened, as if she'd been healed during that night for no reason, not before, or after: don't even think of it. Madie will not free herself of her sorrow, it is her sorrow that keeps her going. Without her sorrow, she would have already become a puff of air, a shadow, a mote of dust of a mother. She would no longer be here.

And this is what Pata tells himself on the eighth day following their return to land, when he goes into the living room at dawn and Madie is not standing by the window. Initially he pauses, surprised—not because this would be abnormal, but because the thought that occurs to him then is that she was still lying next to him in bed and he simply didn't notice. Perhaps he is the one who is making her so transparent? What if it is his own gaze that no longer knows how to see her? He steps back, silently, his hands running along the walls to find his way through the declining darkness and through the door to the bedroom. Goes in. Cannot see, refrains from switching on the light. A shape under the sheet; he stretches out his arm cautiously, gropes, feels; but it's just the pillow rolled up underneath. He pulls on the blanket: there is no one in the bed.

Something catching in his throat, suddenly. He runs back to the living room.

Madie?

He whispered, his voice hoarse, not to wake the children.

Idiotic, this panic that has suddenly come over him, his thoughts running riot, wondering where she could have . . .

No, not her.

Pata runs out like a madman, around the house toward the tall trees. She wouldn't do that, no. Why did he leave a rope in the shed, why didn't he think of everything. He runs, one hand gripping his sweater. Of course he thought of it. It was two or three days ago, because Madie was staring at the tall, broad-leaved trees with her sad expression. So why didn't he hide that damned rope?

The line of beech trees with their wrinkled bark, turned toward the sky, like lanky, long-haired human shapes. Pata looks. His legs feel like jelly, his arms, his heart. He leans against a tree to catch his breath, coughing and spitting, tears in his eyes.

A hearty laugh.

The mother isn't there.

Not hanged, not dead. He shakes his fist at the clouds.

Sets off again.

Where?

Hears his rapid breathing while he hurries to the house. One by one he opens the doors, to the rooms where the children are still sleeping, to the bathroom, the toilet. She is nowhere to be found. He even pulls back the curtains to make sure she isn't hiding behind them, of course it's stupid, only he's run out of ideas, under the stairs, in the basement, under the bed, even, Madie cannot be found. Gradually the relief he felt on seeing the empty branches of the tall trees is transformed into growing anxiety. No, she can't have vanished into thin air—so, once again, where?

He goes back out to the garden. The shed, the hedge, empty.

The water: the thought goes through him with a shock.

He scrambles down the grassy embankment and suddenly hears voices, down there, by the sea. His heart is pounding, he puts one hand to his temple. He would like to call out, doesn't dare, there's a little group of people by the water's edge, looking at something. His eyes wide with fear, Pata murmurs, *No, not this. Not this.* He is trembling all over.

Please make it not be her.

The same fear as a few minutes ago but this time the trees are no longer involved. The water—why didn't he think of it sooner? The others have seen him. Watch him come running, and it seems to him that they are whispering among themselves, staring at him, at him and then at something where they are, *Please God, no*, they are bending over it, and he comes up to them abruptly and stops and shouts:

"What's going on?"

At the same time he looks all around for—a body, even part of one, a clump of hair, he is prepared for anything.

But this?

The man to his left is staring out to sea, and points to the rope that has been left in an untidy pile on the shore.

"My boat's gone. Someone stole my boat."

L ong after the neighbors have scattered, Pata stays alone by the sea. He did not protest, he did not say it was impossible; and they were sure it was Madie. So maybe. Deep down he knows it's true. Where else could she be, now that he has searched the house and the garden? He promised them he would pay for the boat. Once they were gone, he heard the neighbors quietly voicing their pity.

So now he is looking at the sea and wondering what to do. Later, he will go to the police station to declare his wife's disappearance and they will react exactly as he expected: she is a grown woman, she hasn't endangered anything or stolen anything—the neighbor had assured him he would keep quiet about the stolen boat—it's not a matter for the police. Their advice? Wait. She'll come back. Or not. Maybe she went off with another man, he'd be surprised to learn how often that happens. Pata shakes his head, and so do they. He goes home, disoriented. The children wonder where their mother is. He tells them.

Emily and Sidonie clap their hands: Louie, Perrine, and Noah will be arriving soon! Liam has to explain to them, and then they frown:

"But then why did Mommy go to get them?"

"She made a mistake."

"And when she finds out she's made a mistake will she come back?"

Liam and his father exchange a quick look.

"Yes," says the father.

"Who's going to take care of us?"

"We are, Liam and me."

"And Marion? Who's going to look after her?"

Again that quick glance.

"We'll find someone to help us."

"Who?"

"We don't know yet. We'll look for someone."

Standing by the water that morning, Pata wondered whether someone should go after Madie. But who? There have been too many losses since August, too many departures; he feels as if there are traps everywhere, into which they could fall one after the other, fooled by certainty, rumors, hopes—and the ambushes of nature gone mad, he clenches his fists just to think of it, they've had no storms for quite a while now, so the mother is bound to encounter one on her way, he is sure of it. The neighbor's boat has a little motor, but not enough fuel for more than a few hours, and after that Madie will have to reckon with the oars she took with her, with the craft's greater weight, with the paltry amount of supplies she took. Pata counted a ham, some ewe's cheese, and a big loaf of bread.

What if he followed her.

Leaving Liam, the two little girls, and the baby. He shakes his head. There has been too much abandoning, he can't, not anymore. Save what is left, that's all he can do; and the mother . . . let her go, then, let her break her heart among the drowned houses, go round in circles amid the driftwood, the scraps of plastic, get it through her head once and for all, so there is no more ambiguity, no more useless hope. Basically, Pata doesn't mind, he figures it's the only way for her to turn the page. What does fill him with a different despondency altogether is not knowing whether she'll have the strength to make it back. So he wonders how long it will be before he has to go back to the police station to try and persuade them to equip a small boat and go and get her, or work something out with Gabriel, who also has a good motorboat, even if it would take him weeks to reimburse the fuel, these things Madie makes him do, after all, there are times he could give her a good slap in the face. Pata bites his nails, bleeds a little.

* * *

But Madie knows nothing of the thoughts running through his head, how Pata would gladly slap her just now, his rancor, his urge to scream that *they* are still there, the ones who survived, the ones she should be looking after instead of chasing after phantoms. No, the mother sees only one thing, the boat plowing through the water and taking her closer to their island, she knows the boat will run out of gas long before she gets there, *but this is already a start*, she thinks, with something bubbling inside her for the first time, and she thinks, hope—no, wait, not hope: certainty. This effervescence in her guts, it can't just come out of nowhere, it can't be a simple illusion, she feels it as a sign, she will find them, she doesn't know where or how or why, but she will find them and bring them back. She cannot deny that their little clan has dropped from eleven to nine, she witnessed it herself; but not six. She has not seen them dead, those children, she has not seen them swept away, she doesn't believe in it. Therein lies her strength: unless she comes upon their bodies floating on the surface of the water, she remains convinced they are alive and that she can still save them. She is convinced, too, that it was another house the first responders saw, and this one chance remains, that of error, she just has to seize it, and that is why she is there.

She cannot hear Pata's reproaches, and if she could she wouldn't care. What he does not understand is the breach into which Madie is making her way, the breach that may allow her to forgive herself for letting go of Lotte in the storm, for not grabbing Matteo as he leapt overboard.

Her eyes glued to the GPS, she has set her course straight to Levet. She brought an additional jerry can of fuel that she stole out of the father's shed, and she figures she will have four or five hours on the outboard, during which she hopes to cover nearly three quarters of the distance. Her face is lashed by wind and spray; frowning, she feels ready to confront anything, and she knows she has to keep up the pace. When the motor and the battery give up, she'll have to go back to rowing, to her compass, and to the map.

At 11:20 the outboard begins to sputter.

Madie pinches her lips, says nothing. Just thinks, *Here we go.* This far her escapade has felt like a picnic. She slices a piece of bread, a hunk of cheese, and some dried ham, and wolfs them down while pushing the boat to its last drop of fuel, then she rediscovers silence after the noisy clattering of the motor. At the same time the sea's mute hostility comes back to her.

"On we go," she murmurs, to give herself courage.

She reaches for the oars. She hasn't done a lot of rowing in her life, she left it to Pata, and to the children because they thought it was fun. For a quarter of an hour she struggles with the oars, they swoop up too high or plunge too deep in the water, or get muddled in her hands—this thing that looked so easy when the father and Liam went at it all out. *What an idiot!* she scolds herself, tears welling when she realizes she is going sideways, wasting time, zigzagging despite her efforts, making no headway. Bit by bit the boat gets back on course; she finds it too heavy, and hesitates to dump the outboard into the sea to be rid of its weight, but gives up at the sight of the bolts which keep it in place. Their neighbor must be happy, she thinks with a sigh. She has put on some gloves because of the blisters she knows she will get, but half an hour later, neither the leather around her hands nor the hope that grips her have allowed for the fact that her shoulders, arms, and back are pleading for mercy, already, her face is covered in sweat, her body shakes every time she pulls the oars toward her; Madie's mouth is wide open and suddenly there is doubt, huge doubt all through her.

Slow down.

She shakes her head at the thought, like a stubborn animal.

She hasn't brought enough to eat and drink, if she has to spend two days on the water to reach the island. And yet she has no choice, she resolves to paddle slowly, letting herself ride on the currents which, fortunately, are going her way, moving the boat a little, slightly. From one hour to the next her gestures become more automatic, and she begins to make headway, stiff, breathless. Has she been overambitious? She did not think it would be like this. To her mind, a mother driven by determination to find her children knows neither fatigue nor resignation; the truth is completely different. The truth is that Madie hasn't been eating or sleeping or moving for days. Her body is imploding. Her arms are swelling, her veins are bulging, her blood is pounding against her flesh. And now her heart has begun racing, erratic, refusing to beat steadily, obliging her to stop rowing for several minutes—yes, this is all very different from the irrepressible élan with which she leapt in the boat shortly before dawn, very different from the magical currents that would carry her straight to Levet, or so she thought.

In fact, she reckons she is doing four miles an hour, and according to the map she still has between fifteen and twenty hours ahead of her.

So she'll have to stop for the night.

This reinvigorates Madie, because the thought of spending a night alone on the boat, of feeling the darkness enclose her, deadening her vigilance, her sight, her gestures, makes her so frightened that she has a sudden burst of energy from who knows where. She won't make it to the island but she prays she will find a small hill where she can land and tie up the boat, even if she has to go off course, just not to fall asleep in the middle of the ocean with black shapes swimming underneath her that she cannot see, and waves forming inexplicably, murmuring threats, dull sounds from the depths of the water hatching into growls as they break through to the surface and up the sides of the boat into her ears.

But the thing is, no matter how she struggles and pants and sees strange sparks before her eyes when she closes them, the night has forced her to a halt, and she hasn't found a single island to land on. So she throws the anchor out into the middle of the ocean, terrified by the shaking of the chain which seems to go endlessly down, fathom upon fathom, she tries not to imagine what is down there, waiting for her, sniffing around her. Intermittently drowsy, she wakes with a start whenever the boat moves; her heart, her arms are full of palpitations, slicing her irregular sleep with an exhausting shuddering. Once dawn turns the sky to gray she dreams of a few hours' sleep; the fear of sleeping too long sends her back to her oars, without rest, she feels the fatigue draining her face to the bone, her eyes sinking into the black circles beneath them which she rubs now and again when her vision blurs.

All day long Madie stifles in the never-ending summer heat. The compass on one knee and the GPS on the other, the map open on the floor of the boat, on she rows, sometimes just barely skimming the surface because her body, resistant to deeper water, refuses to fight. With each forward thrust she gives out a moan, bone-tired, in pain, jaws clenched not to give in, with the effort to plow through the sea and hold back her guts which want nothing more than to spill out of her, burning, about to burst, she thinks, she is making so little headway that she cannot understand it when she measures her pace across the water—so she stops looking, her eyelids red from the sun and the silver reflections on the water; her hat is no longer enough to protect her.

At 18:07—Madie will remember this because she checks her watch, an old habit—she crosses the border into the Canton of Levet. It's not because she recognizes the place, everything is still as empty and flooded as one hour or five hours earlier; but the GPS beeps. She had keyed in their address in the field marked "destination," astonished, moved that the little box still knew where their house was. And when the electronic voice calls out, *You have reached your destination. Your destination is on the right*, Madie feels a lump in her throat, she sets down her oars, is overcome by a sudden trembling: she is here, she has made it.

And the trembling grows stronger, but not because she has won. Around her there is nothing left.

On the map, on the GPS screen, this is the place.

In the mother's eyes: a void.

This time she knows there is no mistake. She has circled all around, in ovals, in a spiral, she has crisscrossed the calm ocean, she has gone back and forth in tight rows across the water, like a dog looking for game, always returning to the central point where the house should be.

The boat knocked against something, she leaned over to look at it. A stone. A brick and a piece of metal. This is when she understood. She put her hand in the water and it is as if she could see it with her eyes, she is that familiar with the shape, she remembers it so well, three or four years ago, the little Yagi antenna.

So she is home.

She looks around her, to the left, to the right. Water, everywhere.

Home.

She has no more home.

She does not want to think about what this means, which is

so much more painful: Louie, Perrine, and Noah are dead. For the moment, the words fail her. There is just this awful sensation of her legs refusing to support her, her trembling hands, her heart stopping, and to be honest she doesn't need any words to fall to her knees in the boat, to pull her shirt tight over her chest with pain, to gasp for breath, just a little bit of air, she can't breathe, everything is severed, everything is finished. Yes, because now Madie has seen that she was wrong, against all expectation; she was so sure of the opposite, the conviction was rooted in her flesh, vibrant, but it was worn away as she plowed through the sea, that's it, contrary to every law of nature, Madie is floating above her house and sobbing.

J ust when, hundreds of miles from there, Madie is crying that there has to be a mistake, yet another one, a huge one, Pata comes home from work and it is greeted by the little girls' screams.

Daddy, Daddy!

And it's not an exaggeration to say that his heart skips a beat or two when he hears them shrieking like this, because he has grown accustomed to misfortune, he knows that bad news often takes advantage of absence to surface. Only this time he is wondering: why, what else, what more, is it fated never to end, and he throws his jacket on the ground to run into the house, already crushed, eyes wide. He has time to see Liam, Emily, and Sidonie in the garden downstairs, calling to him, waving their arms, and he turns to them, searching for the baby, his little Marion, where is she if the others are there? Breathless, he arrives with a shout, *What, what?*

But the children are laughing, and Sidonie is clapping her hands and saying, Daddy!, and only then does the father see Marion clinging to Liam's legs. He tells himself he panicked a bit too soon, that nothing has happened at all, but with what life has been throwing at them he has an excuse, after all, at least that is what he thinks immediately afterwards, knuckles white, heart racing, he laughs too, for no reason, tries to steady his voice as he looks at them all:

"Is everyone all right?"

"Look!" exclaims Emily.

She picks Marion up in her arms and walks a few steps away. The baby kicks her legs, beaming, and lets out a delighted cry.

"Marion," says Emily very seriously, "do you see Liam?"

She sets Marion on the ground, holding her with her fingertips.

"Do you see him?"

Liam crouches down and holds out his arms.

And Pata sees his littlest one, his last-born, let go of Emily's hands, and so delicately balanced a single puff of air would blow her over, her eyes riveted on Liam's as he encourages her, she takes tiny steps to reach for her brother's fingers.

Sidonie bursts out laughing.

"She's walking, she's walking!"

Marion collapses against Liam, who picks her up and swings her around, singing, *She's a big girl, not a baby anymore*—and the little girl giggles for all she's worth, radiant, waving her arms to be let down on the ground to do it over again.

"So that's why, so that's why . . . " stammers Pata, still shaken with the fear he felt on coming home. "That's all it was . . . "

Sidonie frowns.

"But it's great!"

"Yes. Yes, of course . . . "

And in front of the squealing, chattering children, all focused on the baby who is no longer quite a baby, Pata slips to the ground, his hands in theirs, with tears on his cheeks because he wishes Madie were there with them, wishes she hadn't missed Marion's first steps and the children's joy in the garden, so she could see that even if there are only six of them, they are still a family, if only she would try, if only she were here; yes. They kiss, cuddle, and tell each other stories, enjoying the soft air for a long while, running their hands through the tickly grass. *Let's have supper out here*, suggests Pata, *I'll go get some ham and cheese, some sausages and fruit*. Emily jumps up:

"I'll come with you."

By the time they return, Liam has gathered some branches and made a fire, despite the heat.

"We'll be glad to have it once it gets dark, otherwise we'll get cold."

"And this way there won't be any mosquitoes," says Sidonie, pointing to her bare arms and going to huddle next to her father, on the other side of Emily, who is holding Marion.

They eat, and jabber away. Pata gave Liam a glass of wine, then another one, and now the eldest's head is spinning and he's laughing at everything. Emily and Sidonie beg to try, too, just a sip, that's all, to see if it does the same to them; when the father gives in at last, they take a swallow and make a face, then burst out laughing a moment later.

"Me too, I feel the same as Liam!" says Sidonie, thrilled.

Liam knows that's impossible, he looks at Pata with a shrug, if they're enjoying it, and the father returns his laughing gaze—*it's fine*. Emily snorts and looks at her sister; they both collapse in inexplicable, uncontrollable laughter, and Liam and Pata cannot resist it, either, even Marion, she doesn't understand why but her clear laugh rises on the evening air, and as he catches his breath Pata listens to them, their high-pitched tones, their voices of babies of children of almost grown-ups, a disorderly joyful clamor, as if echoing a time so recent and so long ago when they were all together, all eleven of them, so some remnant of their strength and complicity is still alive, something lives on, Madie has to come back and see this and begin to live again, with them; that's what he thinks.

* * *

During the few hours of daylight remaining, huddled in the boat, Madie roared at the water, insults and abuse and a promise to destroy the earth if it didn't restore her children to her, she has torn at her face and her clothes, rent the air with her threats, but there's nothing for it, nothing has been restored to her, not even a cry or a mutter.

Now Madie is on her knees but not praying: she is trying to go inside her shattered body. She wants to dissolve, so there will be nothing left to think, nothing to suffer from. To disappear, because all other solutions are illusory. For a few moments she gazes at the water around her and temptation slips by; it would be so easy to tip overboard. But she knows her reflexes and her instincts, and her capacity for struggle; she remembers those twelve days of suffering on the water, her hatred ripening, her fear and anxiety, and that is what keeps her back, in fact, fear—Madie does not want to die in the water.

But she does not want to go back to the place where she failed, either, crushed with shame, disappointment, defeat.

So she reaches her decision: she won't go back.

She won't go home.

She knows what this means: never to see them again. And what is even more certain at this moment: she does not have the strength to see them again. Her sorrow is proportional to her dashed hopes: immense. Madie is inconsolable. And the ocean doesn't give a damn.

There is nothing inside her of a mother anymore, she is like a little fish that the current is rolling endlessly toward the shore, and which has given up on the open ocean, allowing itself to beach on the sand where the lack of water will seal its fate, and it listens to its breathing getting weaker, then stopping, a few instants, one two three, its belly rises and falls a bit more, one two, mouth open, one, nothing moving, zero. She, too, will stop living. On this boat out of gas. Madie throws the last of her supplies overboard. She knows the temptation will be too great, once thirst begins to dry her lips and hunger turns her stomach inside out, she will no longer have the will; so she makes the first move, she takes out the bag with the food, the bottles of water, hesitates. But this is what she wants. She clenches her teeth. In a single gesture she flings it all over the side, as far as possible. She hears the sound it makes as it falls into the water, the sound of life slipping away. She thinks: *that's it.*

She is there in silence.

The moon illuminates her gestures.

Once the sea has swallowed the bread, the cheese, the dried ham, and the bottles, which she uncorked, when the last dish towel has stopped floating at last and darkness has erased every trace, Madie breathes slowly. There are no more solutions, no more alternatives.

She pulls up the anchor, yes, in the middle of the night.

The boat hesitates, rocks back and forth, sways. Gradually a current bears it away, very slowly, imperceptibly. If Madie were standing on the chimney of her drowned house, she would notice that the boat is drifting, whispering, surely going away; but she is lying on the floorboards, and she can't see anything other than the sides of the boat around her and the sky pricked with stars. Eyes wide open she stares at the darkness and the millions of flickering lights.

She knows she won't get up again; this is her final battle.

Madie dozes, wakes, falls asleep again. Whether from exhaustion or emotion, her pain feels as if anesthetized, folded over on one side, buried. She has forgotten that she doesn't want to go home because she has failed; she has forgotten hope, shame, collapse.

She has forgotten that she has a family.

Madie is alone on earth in a boat on the ocean; all that is left of her is a scrawny body empty of all will, of the memory of the children she had, living or dead.

She has been drifting for hours without even looking where she is going. Maybe she turned over, lying on the wooden floorboards which hurt her shoulder; maybe she crawled a few inches to put her head in the shade of the seat when the sun rose and began beating down. She can feel its burning rays on her clothes, the sweat of her body underneath.

She is already thirsty.

Never mind.

A faint, sour smell in her sweat attracts the flies. Madie is afraid. She wishes it were already over, that death had taken her, since that is what she has decided. But deciding wasn't the hardest part: now she has to wait. This body that hasn't wanted food for days, which can no longer stand this burden of woe, her body is still holding out. *Let go, dammit*, murmurs Madie, not opening her lips.

But it won't.

The hot air burns her throat and sinuses—it's not air, to be honest, it's as if she were breathing above a pot of boiling water, she opens her mouth to let it into her lungs, the heat is stifling. Already a dozen times she has been tempted to wet her hair; a shudder, the time to get a hold of herself, no, no, now she just has to get it over with.

The sky is dropping down behind her closed lids, the light is fading. Madie doesn't need to open her eyes, she can tell the clouds are gathering, doesn't need to see to know a storm is brewing, because the wind has picked up a little, caressing her face, and the insects are buzzing around like crazy, after the skin on her face, and she no longer brushes them away. Much later, when she doesn't know if this grayness is from the storm or the falling darkness, when she can no longer swallow because thirst is tearing her throat out, she can hear the rolling of thunder in the distance—it's a storm, she remembers it so well. Just then, she feels a pang inside, because she would like to waste away, tranquil in her boat, as if she were simply falling asleep, but she has a premonition that it won't be completely serene, but still—to die obsti- nately and slowly, that's what she would like, on the water but not drowned, not caught in a whirlpool or a swell, or a storm. A tiny little ball of anger lodged deep in her guts is stirring, she thought it was gone for good, it makes her feel sick and she spits the bile overboard, she gulps, they've won, they have made her open her eyes—the gods, the devils, the bas- tards of this world. And it doesn't make much difference, this opening her eyes, now that darkness has settled over the ocean. If there were land, if there were trees and houses, Madie would see shadows; but all the way to the horizon there is nothing, and the horizon stops where the darkness has engulfed it, just there, only a few yards away. The boat and the mother are rocking from side to side, back and forth, in the middle of the night. The boat doesn't care, but the mother is clinging to the edge: already the wind has disheveled her, she knows the storm is on its way. She cannot tell where it's coming from, or how strong it will be.

Just that it is coming.

For the first time, Madie is alone to confront it. A confrontation so unequal that she laughs—a single, dry little laugh, scornful, masking her terror, she looks like a madwoman with her sweat-soaked hair sticking to her forehead, her big eyes open wide and rolling in their sockets.

But an hour later she isn't laughing, Madie, and she knows that in her entire life she has only ever seen this in books: a magnetic storm. She has watched it coming from far off. The sky torn by bolts of lightning, lines of molten fire plummeting into the waves, accompanied by deafening crackling sounds, it is as if the ocean itself were parting, swaths of phosphorescent green spreading across the surface and illuminating the lower depths, fathom upon fathom. Madie, leaning over the side, in silent stupor, cannot help but observe the drowned world below her when the lightning flashes, the dead outlines of the buildings and trees that were caught in the tidal wave, hulks of cars that haven't had time to rust, illegible signs, turned and twisted. Asphalt streets blistered and split by the violence of the cataclysm; a church steeple. The storm makes them appear intermittently beneath the boat in a bleary yellow and green light, as if they were being photographed in negative, as if the harsh light of a projector was blinding them for a few fractions of a second, and after that, everything returns to obscurity, the mother leans a little further, terrified and tense with waiting, she wants to see more, to rediscover, to revel in this dead world caught in the currents, where everything floats and everything is trapped on the bottom, imprisoned by its own weight.

When a lightning bolt strikes thirty feet from the boat, Madie lies flat on the floorboards. She glances up at the clouds: now the storm is upon her, she can feel her small craft panicking, spinning on itself, the streaks from the sky circling it ever closer. At that moment exactly the mother thinks it is all over, yes, in that fraction of a second when the lightning strikes to her left, then again to her right, and the impact, the vibrations cause the waves to roar, aftershocks coming to ram the boat, and the green light with its charge of electricity stops a few inches from her, a cry, *No!* as she waits for the next flash to hit her, the water is riddled with lightning, a blinding glare, the end of the world.

On the boat Madie sobs among the lightning flashes, her hands over her ears, not to hear anymore; and then she puts them back on the side of the boat to hold on, instinctively, she cannot bring herself to surrender to the storm, to whirl her way down to those drowned lightning-lit landscapes.

She wanted to close her eyes, she couldn't, it was as if they were being forced open to make her see, terror keeping them wide open, incredulous, awestruck, lashed by the spray that is making her weep, but there it is, it's impossible to close her terrified, fascinated eyes, scorched by the lightning which continues to strike with a consuming rage, the bow of the boat is taking on water, Madie holds on, her mouth open in an endless scream.

And then a drop of rain.

She doesn't even feel it.

Another one.

The storm hesitates, but she's not looking.

Not screaming, nothing.

But not dead. Like those soldiers petrified by war who have forgotten how to move.

Her eyes riveted to the floor of the boat.

The storm abandons her just as dawn sketches a gray horizon. Then with no sense of relief, no prayer, Madie bails the water from the bottom of the boat and lies down again, her body drenched, her lips purple with cold and fright. She finds the same position, goes twelve hours back in time, an animal curled in a ball watching the night, then daybreak, out of the corner of its eye, the arrival of the sun, the heat causing steam to rise from her clothes and from the sea. The rowboat glides smoothly, lulled by peaceable currents.

The difference is hunger, thirst, and fear.

And death approaching, holding regrets by the arm.

ON THE ISLAND
August 28

On the ninth day after their parents left, Louie, Perrine, and Noah watched as the sea rose all day. Every hour, they went to inspect the water until it reached the stone Louie had put on the ground, covered it, and moved beyond it. Louie put a new stone a bit higher up, but Noah stopped him with his hand.

"I get it."

The little boy added, as if to reassure himself—as if there was anything left to reassure him about—his eyes moist and his heart beating too fast:

"We have six days left, that's it."

Louie shrugged his shoulders, looking at the top of the hill. *More or less.*

Perrine gazed at the ocean, her hand shielding her eyes. *Pata has to get here.*

And yet there is this strange lack of awareness that makes them chatter as they stride across the island, arguing this way and that, they will die, or they won't, six days or five or seven, where will it flood last, where should they build a hut or put up a tent to keep going until the last moment. It feels unreal, as if death had no consistency—and yet again, their knowledge of that thing was too fleeting for them to be truly afraid of it, they cannot imagine what it means to drown. Right away the idea of a hut distracts them, amuses them; not one of the three tells the others to be quiet because there is danger, because there is urgency. They think. Where can they find wooden poles for the structure of a tent or a roof, what can they use for tarps, which sheets if they have to, how big. What will resist the sun and wind, how much food and water should they take; and the hens, and a mattress for the three of them.

So of course while they are dawdling from place to place on the tiny island, of course when the boat appears on the horizon, a little dark spot melting into the sunlight, they don't even notice it.

Yet it is there, that boat, for the time being it is in the distance, uncertain, but there can be no doubt that it has set its course for their hill—the only land within sight when you are coming the way it is from the northwest, the other islands are on the other side, invisible. On the boat a figure is moving about. It's because of a brusqueness in its movements, an impatience, that an hour later, when Louie springs up all of a sudden with a shout, they will all swear it is Pata on his way back.

The fact that it is far too soon: they don't think of that.

That the high ground is to the east and not the northwest, they've forgotten that.

* * *

Damn water, everywhere, he hasn't seen a patch of land anywhere for days. And for days he's been looking at the sky, after he weathered the storm, well, it passed him by, some ways away, but those huge waves nearly capsized the tub and left it half full of water, damn rotten boat, no wonder he was able to steal it, nobody wanted it anymore. So here he is now, on the sea, he hates the sea—he doesn't even know how to swim—rowing this way and that without a map or a compass, he didn't have time, he knows he's doomed. But as long as there's life, and a rage—so he clenches his fists as he scoops into the water with his oars, he ought to know, it does no good to moan, there's no one there to hear him, no one to help him, *Row, asshole*, that's how he speaks to himself.

He used up his meager supplies two days ago. Just some lukewarm water left at the bottom of a bottle rolling on the floorboards. He left in a hurry maybe a week ago—they were bound to figure out he was the one who'd tortured the old man to make him say where he'd hidden his money; he should've killed that old man, anyway, rather than leave him half dead on the floor of his shack, and now the old man has Ades's face printed on his retina, all he has to do is give his name to the people who came to rescue him and the hunt will be on.

So he left just before.

Didn't think it through.

Where?

Fucking shit. What the fuck does he know, from where he's headed.

It's just that Ades doesn't want to get caught. These days, people make their own justice, and that's bad for him, with all those honest folk who've decided that the earth is too small now to put up with scum like him. They will throw him in the water, not a moment's hesitation, with two fine stones on his feet to make sure he goes down good; he'd been there when Jean and Atta, his old partners in crime, got themselves lynched, and he knows that he isn't any better than them. Only a matter of time: his turn will come.

But he got the hell out of there too fast, that was for sure, and he didn't prepare anything. When he heard the door open downstairs, in the house where a dozen of them were squatting without permission, he got up with a start, grabbed his bag and his jacket, jumped out the window and started running: he knew the way by heart. Escape is burned inside him, viscerally, a spark that can galvanize his entire body in a few fractions of a second, an animal instinct, ageless.

And that was it.

After that, came the old boat—out of gas two days ago, heavy as a tank—and the infinite sea, and the near-certainty that it will all end here.

Unless.

He actually begins to dance, Ades, when he sees the smudge on the horizon. He even barks an oath, narrowing his eyes to be sure he's not dreaming, and hell's bells, no, he's not dreaming, it doesn't move, it doesn't disappear. An hour later he knows it's an island and that he'll reach it before the afternoon is out. He has to get a lot closer before he can make out the outline of the house and nod his head, until it becomes obvious: the island is inhabited. In a way, that reassures him. He'll find something to eat and drink, a roof for his head. But it's bad news, too, because he doesn't know what he'll find on that land, peaceful families or nervous little warriors, and as he runs his tongue over his teeth the way he always does when he's annoyed, he wonders what to expect, and how to present himself. The long knife in his pocket is a comfort. If he looks despondent, he can pass himself off as a man who lost his family in the storm and is trying to find his way back to high ground. They'll put him up for a night or two; then he'll see. It depends on so many things. How many of them there are. What they're like. What they have, and what they tell him. His fierceness is written on his low brow, in the gleam of his yellowish eyes. Some families, when they saw him coming, would offer him what they had in exchange for the promise that he'd be on his way. He loves that mute power, the dull fear his presence inspires. But he hasn't forgotten that people would rather see him dead, that all it takes is one man a smidgen meaner than he is and he'll end up on the ground, felled by the bullet of a rifle or his throat slit by a knife.

But not everyone knows him, of course.

So now he's getting closer to the island, and he's thought through all the possibilities, and decided to show up nice and smiley, and then he'll see. First he'll eat, and sleep. With one eye open, as always. Find out which way to go, hope they have a map. Keep his voice down—unless someone comes looking to start a fight, because he's hot-blooded, is Ades, it doesn't take much to get him worked up. Damnation, he thinks, there was me thinking I'd die on this boat.

He laughs. He can see the island is small, that he shouldn't expect much.

He doesn't care, he's not expecting anything, just some food and a bed. For the rest, he has faith. He is capable of taking everything, stealing everything, killing everything, silently and without remorse. That's his strength, this absence of scruples. His conscience died years ago, in the fire that killed his parents and his sister, an accident the police called it back then, an accident that had tied his father and mother to a chair while someone held burning brands to the curtains. The baby girl was in her cradle next to the fireplace.

No, he didn't do it, it wasn't Ades who set the fire. In those days he was a normal kid. But the father did a fair amount of trafficking; there were threats, his old man was sick of it all, had never believed those threats: proof he should have. He was sure he was untouchable. What Ades learned in that moment was that you were the strongest and the craziest until the day you met someone stronger and crazier than you were—and there was always someone. He owed the fact that he'd lived nearly to the age of forty now to his unrelenting vigilance; mistrust was his bible, and besides, may as well say it, he didn't know what it meant to hesitate, to pity, or to feel.

In a life like his, you're bound to run into strange characters and complicated situations. He's seen it all. Made it through it all. Not that he's come out on top, but then he didn't expect to. All he knows is fighting and thieving—he's good at that, damn sure. And if there's one thing he's learned, it's that with those two gifts you can solve any problem. 'Course he won't tell anyone any of that when he gets to the island. He'll put on his good-boy mask, his stupid smile; sometimes it makes him look even scarier, so he checks his reflection in the water to make sure his jaws aren't clenched and that his features are softer.

Not bad.

Has to remember not to laugh: he looks demented.

Sometimes he thinks he must be crossed with an animal. *Bastard*, he murmurs to himself.

On the shore there are figures moving restlessly. So he's been spotted. His throat tightens: the excitement of something new, maybe dangerous, maybe not, a confrontation with other people, and his life is such a solitary one, this'll be a break, a challenge. In a hushed voice he says, *I'm coming.*

He's ready. Lie low, cross swords, jump out of the boat, run away if anything seems dicey; beg, weep, keep quiet, tell them some story he's made up from beginning to end, once again.

So he is prepared for anything.

Except for the three pairs of wide eyes staring at him when he finally steps on land, disgusted by all that ocean, and ties the boat to a tree next to the drowned jetty.

W hat the hell is this, thinks Ades, looking at them, what sort of welcome, this circus, one kid with a twisted leg, another one knee-high to a grasshopper, and a little girl with a blank eye; he has to refrain from bursting out laughing, this is a freak show, where are the others hiding? There's something disturbing in the eyes of the kids standing there, a special light, like a huge expectation tinged with bitterness, as if they'd been hoping for him with all their might—yes, this is the impression he's getting—and that when he finally stood there before them, everything collapsed. So that's the effect he has on these three brats, a disappointment scarcely concealed by their stunned expressions, their downturned mouths. Ades suddenly gets it: they were expecting someone else.

He hasn't said a word yet.

Nor have they.

He finishes mooring the boat, takes his bag, walking heavily, a few steps. He stands up straight, slowly, feels his back straining after all these days on the water where every movement was made hunched over. The kids watch him. He walks toward them, no hurry. There's no rush—he surveys his surroundings, tries to see whether there could be anyone hiding, he listens carefully. And he doesn't want to frighten them, doesn't want them to go shouting and raising the alarm. He pretends to be walking along an invisible path; when he draws level with them he turns his head toward them. All he says:

"Hey."

The smallest one smiles: *Hey.* The two older ones don't say a thing.

"I'm looking for your parents."

This time, too, only the little boy opens his mouth. *They're not here.*

Ades raises his eyebrow. It's strange how incongruous his answer seems in a place like this, where there's nowhere to go, and the kid saying it as naturally as if he were saying, *They went shopping.* Yes, but where? So Ades lowers his eyebrow in a frown and asks:

"Where are they?"

"They left."

"When are they coming back?"

"In . . . six days." Noah counted on his fingers and glanced questioningly at Louie and Perrine.

Goddamn, thinks Ades, either this kid is a half-wit, or he's making fun of me. But the two next to him don't seem to think it's funny. He decides to be patient.

"Oh," he says. "So who is here on the island?"

"We are."

"And who else?"

"Nobody."

"Are you telling me you live here all alone, the three of you?"

The little boy nods.

"Our parents left with the others, 'cause of the rising water. There wasn't enough room on the boat, so they left us. But Pata is going to come back and get us."

"In six days."

"Yes. But Louie says that in six days there won't be any more island and we'll all be drowned."

Ades surveys the land besieged by the sea. In his opinion the kid's not wrong, and he turns to him.

"You're Louie?"

The bigger boy nods.

"Is there anything to eat here?"

The little girl breaks in:

"There's some but not a lot, otherwise we won't have enough until Pata gets here."

"Let's go check it out. I'm starving."

The little boy follows close on his heels, skipping.

"Do you like eggs? We have eggs."

"That'll do me. I'll have six."

"Six?"

There is surprise on the kid's face but not only. A sort of amazement. In spite of himself, Ades smiles, mechanically counting his steps from the shore to the house, an old habit he hardly notices.

"Who does the cooking?"

"Perrine does. Sometimes Louie helps her, and me too."

"Okay. Perrine, make me six eggs."

The little girl does not abandon her look of surprise, but takes a big frying pan out of a cupboard. Noah adds:

"And we want to eat the hens, but Louie won't let us. And we don't know how to fix them."

"I'll fix them for you, your hens. I haven't had any decent meat in weeks, so if that's all it takes to make you happy . . . "

"Yay!"

Afterwards, Ades cannot recall that he's ever had a meal with three kids sitting around him, not eating, not speaking, just looking at him. In the beginning it bothers him a little; but then deep down he doesn't give a damn about these weird kids with no parents, and he wonders if he should believe their story; yet he sniffed around, kept his ears open, didn't see or hear anything, they really are alone, just the three of them.

The four of them, now.

He feels as if he's some sort of god there among them, as they go on gazing at him. Or maybe he's an ogre, the way he's gobbling down his eggs and pancakes, washing it all down with some bad wine he found in the barn and uncorked with delight: no more having to drink that damned water. But it annoys him to have to eat in front of these brats, are they going to watch him sleeping, too, and he slams his fist on the table:

"That's enough!"

The kids hardly move. They're not afraid.

It hasn't happened often, Ades barging in somewhere so abruptly and inconsiderately, to find opposite him people who aren't trembling.

On the contrary: at times he catches the gazes they exchange among themselves, little stolen sidelong glances at each other with a faint smile, as if they were pleased—yet if they only knew the true nature of his company, for sure their faces would fall, then.

"Where is the bedroom?"

He has asked Noah. He has realized the little one is the least fierce, even if he seems on the slow side now and again—that's still better than the older silent one or the girl who always seems to think before she speaks.

"What bedroom?"

"My bedroom. I have to sleep. I've been on the sea for a week."

"Well . . . "

Noah tries to answer, turning to Louie and Perrine, hesitant.

"There's our parents' room, but—"

"That'll do."

Ades stands up, grabs him by the collar.

"Move it, show me."

He follows him down the corridor, opens the door cautiously, by instinct, what if there is someone behind it—after all this time?

No one.

Ades puts his bags on the floor and sits on the bed. Perfect. He motions to Noah.

"It'll do. Scram."

Once the little boy has left, he gets up to turn the key in the lock, then hesitates. Should he lock the kids up? But where would they go, and who could they warn; he gives a shrug and lies down.

As always, he starts counting to fall asleep. Usually by the time he reaches five, sometimes six, he's out. Eight if something is really bothering him.

Three, four. That will do for today.

* * *

But when he wakes up, Ades isn't pleased, not one bit. For a start, those damn kids made noise this morning, playing, or shouting, or something, while he was still contentedly sleeping between two dreams, until a plate smashed and he sat up with a start. And then nothing was ready. With his hair disheveled, looking like a bad-tempered giant, he walked over to the stove and looked at the little girl.

"Where's the coffee?"

She pointed to a box.

"No," he growled, shaking his head, "hot coffee, shit. Make me a mug."

And he took advantage of the silence caused by his sudden appearance to say, very loudly:

"In fact, next person wakes me up in the morning will get a hiding they'll remember until the day they die. And if that's a problem, death can come real soon. Is that clear?"

No answer. Three pairs of eyes staring at him like frightened mice. Yes, kids, Ades is here now, make it snappy and I won't ask twice. I want my coffee in my cup soon as I get up, and same thing for meals, the minute I snap my fingers.

And I want a map so I can find my way.
Until Noah says in a tiny little voice:
"There's no more map. Pata took them all for their trip."
Crap.
"Are you going to leave?"
Ades isn't listening.
"Will you take us with you?"
This time he looks at the boy, and he hadn't planned it, but it just takes hold of him, he bursts out laughing, a huge, monstrous laugh, he tries to repress it but can't, he was right to think the little brother was a dimwit—as if he would take them. And what else? They can just stay on their island.
"We'll die if we stay here. This morning the water is up to step number ten."
Ades doesn't know what he means and doesn't care. Kids die every day of the week. The only thing on his mind is which way to go and how many days it will take to reach land.
"I need supplies."
"We don't have much."
I'll take it all. But he doesn't say it. He opens the cupboards to make his own inventory. Goddammit, they're right. A dozen eggs, a few pancakes. He looks at Perrine.
"You know how to make pancakes?"
She nods.
"Then get going, use all the flour that's left."
"But . . . then there'll be nothing left for us?"
He doesn't answer.
"And the chickens, we'll kill those chickens and cook them."
Louie looks up all of a sudden.
"I know where there are loads of potatoes. But you need a boat to get there."
Ades stands still.
"Potatoes?"

"A whole field of 'em. Since we don't have a boat anymore, we couldn't go get any. There's enough there to eat for weeks."

Ades thinks. He figures he should leave the island two days from now. That way he should avoid running into the father—and by then the water will cover the land all the way to the second floor of the house, leaving only a few feet of land at the top of the hill. Two days should be more than enough to dig up some spuds and get the little girl to cook them all. If he leaves with forty pounds of cooked potatoes, he'll make it. So he looks at Louie, who is waiting.

"All right. You show me and we'll see when we get there. If they're good, we'll start digging them up."

Perrine and Noah move closer, worried.

"What about us?"

"You stay here."

On his way out Ades adds with an icy guffaw:

"You have to keep watch on the island. You never know, there might be burglars!"

He doesn't see their terrified expressions, and even if he did, he wouldn't give a damn.

But he doesn't see the little black and yellow clouds forming on the horizon, either, or notice that the wind has gotten up, and is bringing those clouds toward them, inexorably.

As he steps foot on the potato island for the first time in days Louie feels a sort of exaltation. And yet the land here, too, has shrunk, eaten away by the water lapping all around the island, but at the moment it doesn't matter, all Louie can think of is showing Ades the patch of potato plants, with a scarcely concealed pride, as if this were his domain, as he comments—*They're not quite ripe but they're fine for sweet little new potatoes, they're really good, and you can eat the skin*—and he fingers the leaves that are beginning to go yellow, and takes the spade from the shed to dig up a plant—*you see, I told you so. They're good potatoes all the same.* Ades is trying to work it out. But he's never had a potato patch.

"How many pounds are there?"

"Where?"

"All together."

"If we harvest them all?"

"Yeah."

"Well . . . I don't really know, it depends on whether all the plants are good or not. Four hundred pounds, maybe?" He chooses the figure quite at random, because Ades seems to be hoping for a considerable amount, and four hundred pounds is huge; he's rather pleased with himself, four hundred pounds is pretty good.

Ades snorts with laughter. *No way.*

"Sure there are."

"Then these two rows here will be enough. Go on, start digging."

"Me?"

Louie is about to say that it will go faster if Ades does it himself, with his strength and endurance, then he sees the way the man is looking at him, the gleam concealed in his vague smile, narrow, chilling, and he swallows his words. Ever since Ades got there, he has sensed something strange—a diffuse, disquieting feeling, not unlike the way the hens react when Ades walks by them, something instinctive: he knows the man is no good.

And he knows that the man has a boat. Even if there's no more fuel, the boat has oars, the means to go forward. He thought about it all night long, was tempted to wake Perrine and Noah before dawn to escape in the little craft, just like his parents did ten days ago, and this time it would be Ades who got left behind, it would be their turn to sail away as fast as they could, to get back to high ground. But he didn't do it. He remembered all of a sudden what Pata had said: the journey would take nearly two weeks.

Two weeks of supplies on the boat. That's what Ades is planning now—for himself alone. The children can't leave without taking something. And they can't start stockpiling food without Ades noticing.

Ades who won't take them with him, ever. He has no intention of doing so, doesn't even think about it. It's not even on purpose: he just doesn't care, that's all. Louie is sure of this, Ades will let them drown, let them die, beyond a shadow of a doubt. He, Louie, doesn't have much time, very little time, to come up with a plan. The potatoes were one way of gaining a day. But he has been pressing on the spade, bringing up earth and potatoes for nearly an hour, and he can't think of anything.

He stands up straight, carefully, his back aching, and wipes his forehead. An instinctive glance, because the sky has imperceptibly changed color. Yes, that is the only thing he can think of: a storm, or at least a good squall. So Louie drops everything, the spade and the potatoes scattered around, and he runs to stand in front of Ades who is smoking a cigarette of dark tobacco, *We gotta go.*

"But you haven't finished."

"There's a storm coming."

Ades shrugs. *So what?*

"If we wait, we won't make it back. I already capsized once. You can't steer the boat through the currents."

Now Ades looks at the sky. *I wouldn't know.*

"We have to go back," insists Louie, and he points to the potatoes scattered in a jumble by the plants he has unearthed: "We'll come and get them later. There's no time now."

The wind is already blowing his hair into his eyes, and there are small waves on the sea; in the distance there are rollers. He shivers, his entire body feels the swell coming.

"You're afraid," says Ades.

"Last time I nearly drowned. And I lost the raft."

"Okay."

He stands up. *Do we have time to get back?*

"Yes."

"Take a few spuds. We can have them tonight."

Louie quickly stuffs his pockets, then runs down to the shore. *Come on!* Ades follows him, taking a last draw on his cigarette. It's as if he's never seen a storm, thinks Louie, or else he suspects me of making it up to stop harvesting the potatoes.

The boat is already dancing on the water.

"Goddamn," says Ades when he sees how it is rocking, and he goes pale.

Ah, so you do see.

"Are you sure it will be alright?"

"There are currents here because it's where the sea divides above the two valleys. We have to get out of here quick."

Idiot, he adds, to himself. *If only you'd hurried a little.*

Ades grabs the oars.

"How long will it take to get back?"

Without even waiting for a reply, Ades pulls hard on the oars, creating so much momentum that Louie stumbles and catches himself on the edge just in time, then bursts out laughing.

"I don't know, maybe ten minutes if we go this fast all the way, or fifteen. That is, if everything goes well."

"It had better go well, because—" But Ades breaks off, and doesn't say why it had better go well, and without knowing why, Louie is still laughing. It helps him to master his fear, because only a few hundred yards from there the sea looks just as he remembers it from the storms he's been through, the last one above all, when they went fishing, with the crests forming and breaking until they're big enough to swallow the surface of the earth.

Louie has stopped laughing. He looks at the clouds and extends his arm.

"That way."

To circumvent the strongest currents.

"Hurry."

Ades grumbles, *I'm doing the best I can.*

Louie knows that if they go to the east of the hill, they will lose six or seven minutes, but they will have the storm at their back for longer. The wind is propelling them, and Ades's straining muscles are like steel chains; Louie looks at him despite himself, fascinated, he has never seen such strength in a man. He'd like to be like that, later—but he will probably look like Pata, who is soft and pudgy, and maybe it's better that way, even if he'll never have the kind of strength that emanates from Ades, magical, almost superhuman, the boat continues to plow straight through the water until they meet the crosscurrents and the waves make the boat pitch and rock, and Ades cries out with rage, *Row, bastard!* and Louie looks at him—it has to be said—with wonder in his gaze, until finally the island appears and they realize Ades has rowed faster than the wind, faster than the storm and the tall waves, the time it takes them to secure the boat, to pick up the potatoes that have fallen from Louie's pockets, and they're on land, and Perrine and Noah are greeting them with rain jackets to protect them. So Louie bursts out laughing again and only stops once he's sitting in the house, his hands trembling, and his voice murmuring, *Incredible, incredible.*

* * *

The next day is like all those strange mornings after a storm, clear and calm, a calm no one can believe in at first, and then it becomes obvious, the wind has gone on its way and the waves have given up, no matter how hard you stare at the horizon there is nothing moving. But it's hard to trust the sky, when you know how quickly it can cloud over, and Ades has been watching for an hour, muttering into the coffee Perrine gave him, his second cup. Fucking country. Fucking water. And fucking children, always in the way when he would like to be alone, running around outside just when he wants to bring them to heel. So he motions with his chin to Perrine:

"Call your brother. The big one."

She runs off. Ades can't make up his mind whether to go back to the potato island. He can still feel the tension from the day before in his aching arms, and he's looking for signs of bad weather. He plunges his hand into the platter of French toast and gobbles down the full day's portion. The kids can just make something else for themselves. Earlier that morning the girl watched him eating all the pancakes, with tears in her eyes, and he almost told her that it was better to eat now before they all ended up drowned, for all the difference it made. But he

JUST AFTER THE WAVE · 217

just barked, *Eat some then, instead of sniveling.* She shook her head. He doesn't like that pale, sad little girl. To be honest, he hates brats of any kind. He really must need Louie, to speak to him in an almost kindly fashion when the boy comes over, breathless.

"Can we go," says Ades.

He doesn't make his words sound like a question. It's a sort of hesitant remark waiting for the decision to come from the boy, a way of reminding him, if things go wrong, that it wasn't his idea, or not completely, anyway. He looks at Louie who is studying the sky now, too, pressing his lips together, and Ades grasps the sheer incongruity of the situation, leaving the matter up to a ten-year-old kid.

"It's okay," says the boy.

"You sure?"

"Sure. There's nothing."

Ades clicks his tongue, puzzled.

"So let's go get the spuds. Get some sacks ready."

And this time, he doesn't take his eyes off the sky, neither all the way there nor on the other island. He doesn't pick up a single tuber, so preoccupied is he by puffs of air and absent clouds, so intent on focusing on the horizon, as if he could repulse any storms by the simple force of his gaze and his will, as if he could drive the winds, astonished and raging, back to where they came from, so that the sea would stay flat, smooth, and motionless.

"There's no danger," says Louie again, leaning over the pile of potatoes he is slowly harvesting, panicked at the thought that Ades will be ready to get away already the very next day, or worse, by the end of today.

A bit later on, the man takes him by the collar and shakes him, *Hey you, you think I don't see you slacking off, you're getting nowhere, get to work, you hear me?* Louie, his eyes welling with tears, thinks of Madie and Pata, his mother because he misses her gentleness, and his father who will be too late to save them, this morning the water had risen even further and the hens sought refuge all the way at the top of the embankment; the hazel bush he clung to with Noah a few days ago is half submerged.

"You can't leave us."

Ades raises his eyebrow. He doesn't turn his head or look at him.

"I can," he says.

Your father is coming. You have to be here.

"What if he doesn't get here in time."

"Anyway there's not enough room on the boat, you can see that, it's a little boat."

"It's little but there's enough room."

Ades shrugs and doesn't answer, takes his eyes from the sky at last to reach for the canvas sacks, and he loads them quickly onto the boat. Three sacks: two for him, one for the kids: he owes them that much. Louie's words went in one ear and out the other, they don't register, he doesn't care. Not the faintest twinge in his throat or his guts anywhere, no hands trembling, not a shiver. In his animal instinct there is no room for love or pity.

"Untie the boat. Let's go."

Louie unties the rope, jumps into the boat next to Ades. He can sense the man's indifference with every pore of his skin, he knows that for Ades they do not exist, not Perrine or him or even Noah, who took to him right away, they are nothing to him, they will not even weigh on his conscience.

During the first minutes in the boat everything opposes them, the little boy and the thief: one who is gradually shrinking, tiny and defeated, and the other filling the air with the rhythm of his powerful, regular breathing, taking the boat to the island, toward salvation, his heart swelling with a fierce joy. This time Louie begs the storm to come, even if it capsizes them, even if they lose their crop, and if he has to lose his life, too, he is prepared to do so; but he cannot watch Ades strip them down to their last egg, their last pancake, and climb into the boat and row away to high ground without them. Louie prays in silence and the sky is still blue, the sun burning his arms and his neck, the sea more polished than a sheet of steel. If he looks straight ahead he can already see their hill, where Perrine and Noah are waiting. If he turns around, he can still see the island where the useless potatoes will rot, and wherever his vision takes him, it is incredulous and petrified, he no longer believes in Pata's return. But this doesn't bother Ades, who is monumental and vile, untouchable Ades getting to his feet, causing the boat to rock, handing Louie the oars.

"Your turn."

Without a word Louie does as he is told, does not try to cry out or protest that he is tired, when he has just dug up three sacks of spuds while Ades sat there smoking by the side of the potato patch—since there's nothing for it, he takes the paddles, settles into the middle of the seat, dips the wood into the water, and pulls with his arms. Ades faces the sea and unbuttons his trousers with a laugh.

Louie hears the stream splashing into the water.

An instinct: he looks.

A flash that makes his heart race. Ades has his back to him.

Don't think. No time. Already his hands are trembling.

On his feet in the split second that follows, with all his might he slams the oar into the man's head.

He drowned," says Louie in a quiet voice.
His siblings look at him, stunned; Louie with his hands still throbbing. He has just landed on the island.

Alone.

They didn't say anything, it was just the way they looked at him. And Louie murmured, *He drowned.*

They wait.

He drowned is not enough. So Louie adds:

"The boat turned all of a sudden. He fell overboard."

Silence courses between the three of them, between their questioning eyes and the words they don't dare to say. Louie won't tell them the rest of the story.

How the bones cracked when the oar hit Ades from behind, half knocking him out and pitching him into the sea, or the sound of the water opening to take in his heavy body, a huge, dull sound, like a rock falling from a cliff, or so it seemed to him. Louie cried out. Ades raised his arm, and as mad as it might seem, at that moment the boy lay across the edge of the boat to hold the oar out as far as he could for the man to grab, to fish him out again, to save him, yes. He even felt the vibration of Ades's fingers on the flat surface of the wood, a long scraping motion, that left a trace on the oar—until he began to splutter and wave his arms, sinking into the water up to his mouth, his eyes rolling backwards in shock and the gash on his head bleeding profusely, until Louie realized that Ades didn't know how to swim, and he scrambled backwards in the boat with a scream.

If he saves Ades, Ades will kill him.

Not for one moment did he think he could ever be the winner in this strange combat. When he hit him, he didn't really believe in it. He was convinced Ades would reach up and stop his gesture; he simply tried.

It was instinctive, as always. To act as quickly as possible so Ades wouldn't have time to sense the movement behind his back—quicker than any intuition of motion in the air, in the rhythm of the oars, in the sound of oars tearing through water.

But even then Louie couldn't believe it. Not with an opponent like Ades.

And then.

And so, gripped by panic, convinced the man was going emerge like a madman from the gray waters to come back to the boat and grab the edge, Louie reached for the oars. And his fear just as he dips them into the water: what if Ades grabs them from beneath the surface, and pulls, and leads him away. Louie rows, then pauses, looks all around him, his heart pounding.

Not pounding: racing, skipping, a little animal gone mad with a fear that has made him breathless, after a few yards he has to stop and sit there without moving, unable to breathe; and what if this is dying.

Wait.

Madness.

He ought to row fit to tear his arms out, to get away, beyond reach.

He can't.

He bends double, begs his heart to start beating again, he can see the ripples, too near. He doesn't know if he'll have the strength to strike again. All he can do is tremble.

Over there, four or five oar lengths away, Ades is still struggling.

Not as violently.

Louie can see his arms waving, his hands reaching out of the sea as if to grab hold of something, but now there is only air, since the boat has moved away, a little air, not enough, and spluttering, hoarse, stifled cries, a lament like that of the horns of ships lost in the fog. Louie wants it to stop, he blocks his ears, weeping.

Gradually they diminish, the eddies, and the foam tossed up by Ades's contortions. Gradually the water grows calmer, engulfing to its depths the big powerful body and the terrible voice.

Closes over completely.

Louie shivers relentlessly in the sun. He murmurs, *I'm sorry, I'm sorry.*

And then his heart starts to beat again.

He waits some more.

What if Ades comes up again from the sea.

After a long while he reaches for the oars and moves away, turning around often to make sure, both sick with remorse and terrified at the thought that Ades's body might be following him, gliding under the water. Until he lands on the island where Perrine and Noah are mute and stunned to see him there alone, he is afraid some shape, some beast will cling to the boat and capsize it.

In his dreams that night, Ades becomes a huge seething wave, tearing after him across the ocean. His cries wake Perrine and Noah. The three of them sit under the tent made of sheets and silently nibble the last of the pancake; fatigue and insomnia are a thousand times better than Louie's screams, which still make their hair stand on the end.

* * *

"We're going to leave," says Louie.

The three of them look at the boat.

"Do you think we'll be strong enough?" asks Perrine.

"There are still some cans of fuel in the barn. We'll get the motor going, that'll mean we can go ten times faster."

"Will we have enough?"

"I don't know. And after that, anyway, we can row."

They look at the boat again.

"I'm scared," says Noah.

"Ades came in this boat, didn't he?"

"I'd rather he were here with us."

"You idiot, don't you understand he was going to leave us here to die?"

The little boy lowers his eyes.

"Come on," says Louie encouragingly, patting him on the shoulder. "We'll take all the supplies we can."

They spend the morning getting ready, somewhat feverishly; what if they forget something important.

Water. Food.

Blankets, even if it's hot, and a tarp for the rain.

Louie looks behind him. He says, *The hens.*

"What?" asks Noah.

"The hens, we can't leave them."

"But . . . the cage will never fit."

"No, no, we'll take them without the cage."

"Like that?"

"Loose, yes. They won't go jumping in the water, will they."

In the meanwhile, they gather all the eggs they can find, and add them to the ones that are left in spite of Ades's appetite: Perrine boils them carefully then places them in a bag, there are sixty or so, which makes them feel better. *I thought there'd be more*, says Louie, nevertheless—but Ades ate so many just himself, and the hens themselves have been picking at them because of their hunger, the surface of the ground is no longer enough, they will have to keep a closer eye on them.

"And what are your hens going to eat on the boat?" asks Noah.

"We'll see."

A twelve-day trip, they recall.

They wrap up the pancakes Ades had set aside for himself.

"Serves him right," murmurs Noah, feeling braver.

The boys take the cans of fuel from the barn and fill the fuel tank.

"Watch out, you're spilling it," says Noah.

Louie groans.

"It's heavy."

The two of them try to get the motor started. Perrine watches them from the shore. They pull on the starter rope, ten times, thirty times, their brows sweating.

"Stupid piece of crap!" shouts Noah.

"There must be something you have to do," grunts Louie, checking the flywheel.

He lowers a lever, turns a knob.

"What's that?" asks Noah.

Louie has no idea. But he's the eldest, after all. So he tries it, he already heard Pata mention it.

"The choke."

"Oh, right," Noah agrees, not knowing what they're talking about either.

Finally, the motor coughs to life, wheezing but regular. Then there's the sound.

"It's working!" shouts Louie.

He slaps Noah's outstretched hand, then immediately switches off the motor. *We have to save fuel for the trip.* In the boat, he lashes down the extra fuel jug, and covers it with a sheet to protect it from the sun.

By noon they're ready, and the boat is full. All that's left is to load the hens, and the three of them, when the moment comes they hesitate, and gaze up at the house, their house, which they're going to leave behind; no one can save it. They are overcome with sorrow, nostalgia for a dying world, the page they must turn on their childhood and their hopes, the island will disappear, and Pata didn't come to get them. Saying nothing to each other, each one of them hopes they will see him on the sea, tonight, tomorrow, in two days' time. If they didn't believe that, they would probably not leave. The ocean frightens them, and the late August storms.

And something else: which way should they go?

A terrible question.

They don't know the way to high ground. They just act as if—and no one talks about it.

Far to the east, Pata used to say. Louie remembers you have to head toward the sun in the morning. But only in the morning, because the stupid star doesn't stay there in the east, it moves, it moves or the earth does, it doesn't matter which one if the result is the same: if you row all day long with the sun on the horizon, by nightfall you'll be back where you started, you'll make a big useless loop, really, an endless journey. So, should you keep the sun on your left or on your right? Louie bites his lips: he has no idea. Maybe it doesn't matter, as long as it's at their back by nightfall.

But maybe it's very important.

He goes over their supplies again, working out how many days they can last, not the twelve days of travel their father talked about, but the extra ones, for the unexpected, what if they get lost, no, they can't, no matter how many times he counts, and plans for the tiniest portions of food, they cannot get lost, otherwise—otherwise what is the point of leaving, what is the point of getting their hopes up, what was the point of leaving Ades to drown after smashing his skull with the same oar Louie will be holding in his hands in just a few hours, or a few moments.

Sitting on a chair in the house, he puts his fingers on the globe and turns it slowly.

Where's the sun, on this stupid globe? There's not even any east. Nothing is indicated on it.

What am I supposed to do?

And anyway the world doesn't look like this anymore. The blue color has swamped everything. With his index finger he traces the region where they are, there it is, to there. But east?

Fuck.

Louie shoves the globe away, exasperated. It hits a bump on the surface of the old oak table and rolls to one side; Louie just has time to stand up but not to reach for it, not to catch it, it lands with a loud, sharp *shlack* on the terra-cotta floor.

A tinkling of glass. The earth is on the ground, the globe shattered to pieces.

Inside, it's hollow.

That's it, they're leaving. It's two in the afternoon. The sun is baking.

"This way," said Louie, when Noah looked at him questioningly.

Twenty-six hens, the rooster, and the three of them on the boat.

But Louie was wrong: when he starts the motor and the old machinery begins to hum, the hens jump in the water. They make it back to the island as best they can, those that jumped in right away. The others stay, the ones that didn't dare, forced to remain once the land is too far away. They pace back and forth in the boat, squawking anxiously, wide-eyed, brushing up against the kids who look at them and wonder if these ones, too, won't eventually make a run for it.

But gradually they calm down, lie down next to each other under the foredeck, where Louie spread some old hay from the chicken coop. They don't like it, and they still squawk from time to time just to make their point. The rooster is there, too; Louie wishes that one had jumped overboard, too.

So now it's eighteen hens and the three of them on the sea.

"Too bad for them," says Noah, facing their island as it shrinks slowly from their field of vision.

The boat doesn't go fast but they're pleased all the same. Louie is holding the tiller, it seems so easy but he can't keep the boat going straight, it zigzags this way and that like a drunken boat, *What are you doing?* says Perrine. Louie gets annoyed: "I'm trying!"

After a few minutes have gone by, he understands that he mustn't try to keep an absolutely straight line, mustn't keep adjusting their heading in order to go east, it makes it worse. They are moving slowly, the motor sometimes acts as if it is out of breath, spluttering, and yet they do seem to be gliding effortlessly over the water, the air on their faces red with sun and excitement. Noah bursts out laughing, drags one hand in the water, making bubbles and foam, he splashes Perrine and she cries out. Louie says nothing, his back to the island that is gradually fading behind them. Sometimes he closes his eyes for two or three seconds, and only opens them again when a sort of dizziness comes over him, he makes sure they are still heading in the right direction, the one he chose when they left, he prays there will be some sort of landmark on the sea sooner or later—another island, a mountain, a concrete pillar—something he can follow without worrying about drifting off course: then he'd be sure and could breathe easy at last. But nothing appears and he dreads the moment when their island will be gone for good, with no new country, no coast or cliff appearing on the other side. The nakedness of the ocean terrifies him. Water as far as the eye can see, not a root to cling to, no grass to look at, a fathomless desert, a liquid abyss. Oddly, this vastness oppresses him. Only their tiny boat, between earth and sky, is an acceptable refuge.

And yet so frail.

Noah would like to try, too, to drive the boat, as he puts it. Louie lets him but stays right by his side. And explains: you have to keep looking at the horizon, relentlessly, stare at a spot in the distance and not let go, otherwise the boat will go around in circles.

"A spot?" says Noah, astonished. "But there's nothing there."

"There is, you have to find something."

"Can I use a cloud?"

"No, clouds move."

After only a few minutes, Louie has to adjust the course his little brother has taken. *You're going too far to the right.* Noah starts to get up, abandons the tiller.

"Here, you can do it."

"You're stopping already?"

"I feel sick."

He crawls over to Perrine, and Louie hears him say again, *I feel sick.* And then Noah leans overboard and throws up, into the ocean. Perrine reaches for a rag in one of the big bags they filled for the journey. Then Noah sits back down and closes his eyes.

"No, don't do that," says Perrine, shaking him; she's the one who always gets carsick. "Look straight ahead otherwise it will start all over again."

"I'm sick," whines Noah.

"You'll get used to it. Remember how when we go on vacation, I'm like that in the beginning, and then after a while it gets better."

The boat chugs along for hours. Noah eventually fell asleep and Perrine put a sheet over his face so he wouldn't get sunburned. She and Louie have tied kerchiefs on their heads, they can feel the heat burning their skin. Of course it would have been better if they could have hung some sort of awning over the boat, but they didn't have time, obsessed by the thought that they had to leave the island as quickly as possible; they simply didn't think. Now they're sorry—even though Louie knows what a struggle it would have been to build some sort of solid shelter, fastened onto nothing, and the first gust of wind would have blown it away, so he pushes up the rag on his brow, convinced he has become some sort of pirate.

The first alarm comes after four or five hours: the motor begins to cough. *Already*, thinks Louie. He shouts:

"More fuel!"

Perrine hands him the fuel can. They don't switch off the burning motor, they're too afraid it won't start again. And it's absolutely vital not to spill any fuel.

"Can it catch fire?" says Noah worriedly, awake now.

"Yes," says Louie.

"Oh no."

They immediately continue on their way, relieved the boat is again moving forward as steadily as an old workhorse. In the can there is a little bit of gas left. Until tomorrow, thinks Louie. After that, we'll have to row.

Shortly before nightfall he lowers the anchor. Perrine opens a bag and takes out eggs and pancakes, and potatoes to the brim, their eyes are shining. She also brought the shriveled little early apples from the apple tree at the top of the island, the one that hasn't yielded anything decent in years; but she took them all the same, Noah went with her, carrying the ladder, she already knew what she wanted. She chops the apples in little pieces to give them to the hens with some grass she cut, hastily, she's not sure that fowl eat grass, actually, but if they're hungry, they'll give it a go.

Once they've peeled their eggs, she takes the shells and crushes them and mixes them with the apples. She has seen Madie do this in winter when the hens didn't have much to eat. Perrine puts half the mix aside, for the next day. She wonders if the hens will go on laying, on the boat. And whether they'll have to leave them their fresh eggs for food.

After they've eaten they curl up in their blankets, their eyes closing already with exhaustion. Around them, millions of stars cast their light in reflections upon the sea, like lanterns on a holiday; there are so many that they can't see the black water below them, stars embroidering a tapestry of tiny suns, and with their heads back they gaze at the echo above them, they play at searching on the water for the constellations they've found above them in the sky, which tremble and blink while they point to them, exclaiming, sorry they don't know them better, fascinated by the glow, the sparkle. When Noah leans over to splash the water with both hands, the world clouds and furrows, the stars blur. It takes a long time for the sea to recover its smooth surface, for the ripples to vanish—no matter, they look at the sky again, motionless despite the trails of satellites. Perrine recognized the Little Dipper and, slightly higher up, the North Star. They fall asleep too soon, fatigue gets the better of them. And if they wake during the night, when the clucking of a dreaming hen disturbs them, they are instantly reassured, lulled by the lights of a world watching over them.

* * *

The next day the difficulties start. Since dawn, when the raw light on the ocean woke them and they started the motor, Louie has been watching the fuel level. For a start he lowered the throttle so it would last longer; at around noon he poured the final drops of fuel into the tank. Now, after spluttering and hiccupping for a few minutes, the motor stalls, stops, no more sound, nothing.

"That's it," says Louie.

"No more gas?" asks Noah.

"Nah."

"Are we almost there?"

Louie looks around him. No way of knowing. He would give anything to see, far far off on the horizon, something that looks like land, but no, and his throat constricts like the night before, the same irrational temptation to turn around and go back to their island, the one that will be submerged in a few days' time, it's stupid, really stupid, he murmurs to himself. How much time have they saved with the motorboat, he has no way of knowing; how long they will have to keep rowing across this monstrous ocean, he doesn't know either. So to forestall any false sense of joy, he says:

"I don't think so."

Noah grumbles.

"There's nothing but water. It's stupid."

"We have to get going, now," says Louie, handing him one of the two oars.

"I don't know how," whines Noah.

"Try."

They paddle unevenly; Noah cannot get into the rhythm, hasn't the strength, he lets the boat turn when Louie sculls on his side, at the age of eight you don't have much in the way of muscles, especially when you're just a little shrimp.

"You have to make an effort," complains Louie, "I can't row by myself for days on end. But hand it over, I'll make a start. When I get tired, you'll help me."

He takes both oars and puts them in the oarlocks, settles onto the seat, and, like Pata, cries out with his first pull, *Heave!* He doesn't like sitting like this, which means his back is to the horizon, which prevents him from seeing where he's going, unless he twists around every two minutes, craning his neck to make sure they're not wandering off course—but what is their course, when the horizon is slack, undetectable, so monotonous you could weep.

Heave, says Louie in his mind, to give himself courage.

Because where courage is concerned, he hasn't got a lot left.

For a long time, the water dripping from the oars between two strokes is the only sound drifting over the sea, slow and regular. Louie's arms are aching, and so is his back; the sweat is stinging his eyelids as it trickles down his brow. He doesn't speak. He doesn't know whether Perrine and Noah have noticed that he is slowing down. He doesn't want Noah to help him yet, the boy is dozing under a cloth for protection from the sun, he can do another hour, anyway, and then the heat will start to decline, and his thoughts decompose, extenuated, there is nothing but water, oars, and the sound of his breathing.

They stop to have a snack, drink something, catch their breath.

"You okay?" asks Noah anxiously.

Louie raises his thumb. *Right as rain.* His brother laughs. In fact, he feels as if his bones are going to snap in two, he is aching so badly. When they set off again after fifteen minutes of rest, Louie's arms feel like metal rods with joints that someone's forgotten to oil, rusty muscles, raw nerves, and everything pounding dully in his forehead and his temples, as steady a beat as the oars in the water, and he often lets the boat glide ahead without rowing at all.

"Let me try."

Perrine has sat down next to him. He looks at her, hands her an oar without saying a word; he hasn't the strength to speak. Just his sunken eyes distorting his face, it feels as if they are pressing right into his head, the sockets sinking into his skull and pulling on his skin and sending a somewhat blurred vision back to him, but maybe it's the sun on the water, anyway he cannot speak, he hands her one of the oars and that's all, he'd like to smile but can only manage an ugly grimace.

"How do I do it?" asks Perrine.

He shows her. Noah is sitting cross-legged on the seat facing them and observes them, nods, *Okay*, tries to remember their movements. Perrine is a quick learner. It's not that the boat is going any faster, but they're sharing the effort, each of them holding their oar with two hands; Louie found them some rags to wrap around the handles, because of the painful blisters that appear on their fingers. And it's not that the prospect of all the days ahead has stopped worrying them, but now they feel a bond, together, indestructible, all three of them paddling as best they can, even when Perrine lets the oar slip and the boat swerves to the side—so then Noah puts in an effort, makes up the difference, helps out, and they begin giggling because it's too hard, because they're dead tired and they can't take it anymore, but they're not alone, and they keep going, letting out wild cries to urge themselves on.

* * *

Early in the morning, Louie goes back to rowing on his own. Deep down, he's not proud of himself. He warns them. *It won't go quickly.* He's aching all over. The other two nod their heads. They'll help later, because just now Noah got out the two little fishing poles he found in the barn before they left, the first ones they ever used, when they were four or five years old, with hooks that have gone a bit rusty. The lines are short, so that they wouldn't catch them in the leaves of the bushes—a precaution that is useless, now, but what can they do, so he skewers pieces of raw potato in the place of worms, and Louie shrugs his shoulders.

"That's the way we used to do it," protests Noah.

"And we used to have freshwater fish behind the house. Now, we have the sea!"

"So?"

"So, you can't catch ocean fish with potatoes."

"If they're hungry, they'll come and eat all the same."

"Yeah, sure," scoffs the older brother.

And yet he will have to concede it wasn't a bad idea, because Perrine and Noah manage to catch three fish in the next hour; not a great catch, but better than nothing, and the fish are a decent size. *Well?* says Noah, showing off. *All right.*

They put them in a bucket of water.

"You'd do better to kill them," says Louie. "It's too hot, they're going to die anyway."

"It's so they'll keep longer, otherwise they'll stink."

"And how are we going to eat them?"

"Eat them . . . ?"

Noah looks out at the empty horizon. *We need an island so we can make a fire and cook them.* He taps Louie on the arm:

"Don't you see any?"

"See for yourself. There's nothing. Just the sea."

"But I wonder if there isn't something," murmurs Perrine.

Of course, it's just an almost invisible shape that could be nothing more than a veil of mist on the water. But you never know. They clamber over to her.

"There," says Perrine.

"I can't see anything," says Noah.

"Maybe," says Louie.

He looks at the sky. If they decide to go in the direction Perrine is pointing to, they will get off course. And they've probably drifted so much already, without knowing it, the boat turning on itself during the night, with its stern to the north when the sun rose, or to the south, or to the west, or who knows where. Is he sure he headed in the right direction every time? And yet he hesitates. If it is an illusion, a fog bank, yes. Should they try? Get closer. He'll give it an hour, a lost hour or an hour on the way to respite, they only left the day before yesterday, and it kind of annoys him, *We can't go stopping already on the third day.* So all of a sudden he makes his decision.

"We're not going."

Perrine gives a start. *We're not?*

"Why should we go?"

Silence. The question surprises the three of them, even Louie who asked it, and they can't find an answer.

"To cook the fish?" says Perrine after a few seconds.

"Just to have a look?" suggests Noah.

"And see what?"

"If there are people there who can help us."

Louie frowns; he is so sure they are the only survivors that he hasn't thought about that. No, the world has become . . . a desert. Emptiness. Nobody. Just the eleven of them, or the three of them, with nothing around them, only water. But if they can find the higher ground, that will change everything. They will see that life has not vanished and there are still thousands and millions of them, on the mountains, and surely they've rebuilt society the way it used to be, before, something he has already almost forgotten about.

"Oh."

Noah laughs.

"You don't think there're any people over there?"

"I don't think so, no."

"So shall we go and see?"

"Okay. Let's go and see."

May as well lug reality around with them: this is what Louie keeps telling himself as he paddles with Perrine, whose eyes are shining, and he cannot understand what it is that is driving her and Noah, their wide grins, this joyful air of theirs, the thought that they might find people they don't know, he cannot help asking himself over and over: what for?

So they won't be alone?

Do they think it will heal the wound of abandonment.

Do they think that through some inexplicable miracle their parents might be there—then that would mean that they, too, failed to find the way to higher ground.

And are they not enough, just the three of them?

Apparently not.

Nothing but bad thoughts in his head, Louie, so he keeps quiet, and rows, and pulls on his arms, heave. A little later, he raises his head to stare gloomily out at the island in the distance.

But there's no more island.

He rises halfway to his feet.

"Hey?"

Looks at the others.

"Where is the island?" asks Noah in a little voice, reaching for Perrine, she's the one who saw it first, so he grabs hold of her as if to a last hope.

And Perrine murmurs:

"I don't see it anymore. There's nothing there now."

L ouie got back on what he thought must be the right course, and now he is rowing again, without haste. Sitting across from him, the two younger ones look dejected. The water is playing tricks on them, creating mirages. Since the vanished island, there was one time they thought they saw a boat, another time the leaves of a tree. And each time, they held out their arms and stamped their feet and cried with excitement, launching into a song of celebration; and each time the boat got closer it banished the images and shapes, and they lowered their heads, pointing to a spot on the sea: *It was there, right there.* Louie, too, has visions. But he knows they're false, and he forces himself to look elsewhere, to ignore the glimmer and the hope; if there was something real, he'd go right by it, for sure, with that way he has of frowning because the sea is playing tricks on them. He'd rather miss an island than head for one all full of joy only to realize, as he sails through it as if it were a fogbank, that it doesn't exist. He'd rather die, yes: he doesn't want to be disappointed. So he carries on, his eyes glued to his hands gripping the oars, and time seems to stretch to infinity, everything the same, hot and slow and painful, today, tomorrow, he can't recall, all he knows is that nights have gone by.

At dawn on the fifth day, the hens cluck and rouse them from sleep. They eat a little, pull up the anchor; the day has begun. Louie, Perrine, and Noah take turns rowing, and the worst is when the two younger ones are at it together. *Leave it,* murmurs Louie, massaging his palms, *I'll row again, we can just stop for fifteen minutes.* The day is spent between the meager meals they have to share with the hens and the boat that has to be propelled relentlessly across the water. After lunch, Perrine and Noah fall asleep, from heat and fatigue, and Louie on his own curses the sun, but not too much, just to let it know, because it's better to burn to a frazzle than to get caught in a storm, which is bound to happen sooner or later. But he complains all the same, because of the sweat stinging his eyes and dripping down his brow, and the feeling he has of being burned all over, suffocating, his throat dry.

Because they're making no headway, and the days that last forever.

Because of his back and his arms, his belly and his legs, all aching.

Because the younger ones are taking naps.

He shouts. *Shit!*

Perrine wakes with a start.

"What's wrong?"

"Nothing. It's just shit."

Shortly before nightfall they stop and drop anchor. They eat, drink, feed the hens, gather the eggs they continue to lay, share them out among the birds and themselves, swallowing them whole and trying not to let anything dribble down their chins. Then they lie down; at last, thinks Louie.

Too hot under the blankets—but with these damned mosquitoes.

Fall asleep like the dead.

And every day it's like this.

How long has it been? They can't agree, is it five days, or six. Seven, said Noah, but Noah will say anything just so you listen to him. Every morning is the same, with the creaking of the anchor being raised, and the soreness in their muscles that make their movements stiff.

Not seven, no, can't be.

"If it's six," says Noah, "then we're over halfway there, especially as in the beginning we had the motor and we went fast. We should be there soon, don't you think?"

Louie shrugs.

"We're not rowing all that fast. We're losing some of the time that we made up."

Noah graciously adjusts his reasoning: *Only halfway?*

But the thing is, all the days are alike—and basically they ought not to complain, thinks Louie, if something were to change, it would mean bad weather, wind and rain.

"Or land," adds Perrine.

"No, it can't be land. Not yet."

Still . . .

Suddenly, all three of them give a start. They look at each other without daring to look up again. Perrine has even closed her eyes tight, murmuring, *It's just another mirage, right?* So Louie turns to the side where the apparition is coming from. He says to Noah:

"Do you see it?"

"Yes."

"What about you, Perrine?"

"I think so."

"Right."

He scratches his head. This is the first time they have all thought they'd seen the same thing. He asks them again, to be sure:

"An island?"

"That's right," says Perrine.

"There it is," says Noah.

"So maybe we should go take a look, then."

An hour later, the island has grown larger. They let the boat glide as they hold onto the gunwale, astonished: this time, it's for real.

"Let's stop!" exclaims Noah.

"And we can make a fire and cook the fish. We have to catch some," says Perrine, already looking forward.

They threw away the first fish they caught long ago, since there was no way to cook them; the hens pecked at them with their tip of their beaks, and they tossed the rest into the sea, because of the smell. This time, Perrine and Noah hastily take up their fishing poles, while Louie returns to his oars.

"How long have we got?"

"Gosh, more than an hour. You have time to catch loads!" Noah laughs, spreading his arms.

"This much?"

"If you can."

And then.

There are times when nothing goes as it should.

Because, for a start, the fish aren't biting. No matter how they bait the hooks with bits of raw potato, and cast to the left, to the right, or let the lines trail behind the boat, all they manage to catch after all that is a tiny little mackerel no bigger than a hand. Noah gets annoyed.

"It's because of the oars, and the noise they make!"

"The other day I was rowing, too, and you caught some," says Louie. "Am I supposed to stop just so you can fish, is that it?"

They don't speak for a few minutes. Noah has pulled in his line, and sits with his arms crossed.

"You're not going to catch any like that," hisses Louie.

"They're not biting, anyway. It's not a good day."

"But look," says Perrine, "we're almost at the island. And . . . oh!"

"What is it?"

She starts whispering suddenly.

"There must be people there, you can see a hut."

"Why are you whispering?" asks Noah.

"We don't know who it is."

"So?"

"What if they're people like Ades?"

Noah stiffens. *You think so?* She doesn't answer. Louie stops rowing. All three squint into the distance, trying to make out something more precise, something to reassure them, a family waving their arms, a dog playing.

"Do you see any people?"

"No. Just a hut."

"Maybe there's no one there."

"Maybe."

"What should we do?"

Louie wrinkles his nose: night is falling, they can't see very well.

"We'll stop here."

"Here?" exclaims Perrine.

She spreads her arms, doesn't need to say any more: to anchor here, only a few hundred yards from the shore, when in fifteen minutes they could have their feet in the sand. Louie shakes his head:

"We don't know."

"But what if there's no one?"

"We don't know. In any case, we don't have any fish. We can fish tomorrow morning and when we've caught some we'll go on to the island, okay?"

Not okay. But it's pointless to say anything.

"You always get to decide," protests Noah.

"Because you two don't even know what you're doing."

"That's not true."

A jab with an elbow, a punch. Perrine raises her hands, *Stop it!* They turn their backs on each other again, until they think they see some slight movement on the island. All three hurry to kneel by the side of the boat, but darkness is falling over them, hiding the little coast with each minute that goes by. So they lie on the floorboards, gazing at the stars, dreaming about tomorrow, and the feeling of warm sand between their toes, and how when at last they can stretch their legs they will run, and there will be grilled fish, and they picture the fruit they will find—some sort of impossible Eden, the kind you imagine one evening until at daybreak you are disillusioned; every time. Sleep comes late; they're too tired, and too excited. The hens have been asleep for a long time, their heads tucked beneath their wings.

Very short night. Very faint nudge against Louie's shoulder. Noah murmurs, Can we start fishing?

"But it's not light out yet," murmurs his older brother, eyes half open as he senses the gray dawn; in the distance, strands of yellow cloud mingle with the rays of the rising sun.

"Yes it is, almost. This is the right time to go fishing."

What does he know, Noah, he's just saying things. But Louie is too sleepy to protest, and he sits up slowly, at the same time as Perrine, who gives a stretch. The rocking of the boat lulls them, a regular cadence, left, right, left, right. Noah doesn't feel seasick anymore.

"Do we have anything to eat?" Louie asks Perrine.

She rummages in the bag, hands each of them an egg.

"Yuck," says Noah. "Eggs again."

The hens look at them with their round eyes, heads tilted, waiting for the shells. Perrine pours them some water in a saucer and strokes the head of one of them.

"You see, they're tame, now."

They gaze fascinated at the sunrise, minute upon minute, second upon second even, as the sphere of light appears from below the horizon. The dazzle of sunlight on the water forces them to close their eyes from time to time, they shield them with their hands, and eventually turn away.

On the other side is the island. They can see it better now. An island with greenery: trees, and thickets. Their stomachs rumble at the thought they might find fruit; they wish they could be there already. They stare avidly at the hut, but there's still no sign of movement anywhere around it. And yet yesterday, they thought there had been.

Illusion.

"Come on," says Louie, "let's try and catch some fish first."

So again they cast their tiny lines, little nylon threads which the sea encloses and strokes, their colorless lures floating and bobbing on the surface. But Noah was wrong: once again the lines remain slack. Sometimes a line dips down and they sit up and pull it towards them—only mirages, every time, the hook is empty and the potato bait remains intact.

"Who cares about the fish," Noah complains after a while.

But Louie is intractable.

"We have to keep trying."

"Never mind," says Perrine. "If we can go cook the potatoes we didn't have time to do before we left, that would already be a good thing."

"Let's wait for a while."

"I'm sick of this," Noah sighs, bringing his fishing pole back on board.

"With you it's just the same as with mushrooms, if there aren't loads of them right away, you get annoyed.

"Yeah, but I don't like mushrooms, anyway."

The boy leans over the edge, toward the anchor chain. *Shall I pull it up?*

"Go ahead," says Louie, exasperated, "we'll keep going for a while."

They hear the familiar creaking, Noah's breathing imitating Pata's and Louie's, *Heave*, he says, and Perrine helps him with the anchor, at that very moment out of the corner of his eye Louie sees something moving by her fishing pole. He shouts and points to it.

"Perrine, your line!"

He stands up suddenly when he sees the line go taut. His

initial reflex, before the others have even realized, is to climb over the seat to grab the pole that is about to flip up and over; but then, once his hands have closed around the wood, he freezes. It's not the weight of the creature on the other end of the hook that worries him, no, even if the line is stretched fit to snap. It's something else, something weird.

He can't explain what it could be.

But it's pulling too hard and the pole has bent down to touch the water.

He cries out.

"That's no fish on the hook!"

"What?" Noah says, alarmed.

Louie hands the pole to Perrine and hurries toward the oars.

"It's shaking too much! It's not a fish!"

"But what is it?"

The older boy doesn't answer. He plunges the oars in the water to move the boat away quickly, he doesn't know why, it's just a danger he can sense around them, underneath them, he screams at Perrine:

"Let go of your pole! Let it go!"

The little girl, leaning over the water to try and hold her pole straight, stands up now, astonished. *Really?* At the same time, emerging from the sea with a gigantic thrust, with a burst of spray clear across the boat, comes an arm, fingers curved, an arm then an upper body, a head with its mouth open as if to roar, streaming, enormous, targeting Perrine for sure, until it falls back in the water a few inches from the terrified little girl.

They scream, all three of them.

"What is it?"

"Get back, get back!" shouts Louie, pulling on the oars as hard as he can.

"A monster, a monster!" Noah shrieks.

No, it's a man.

"Come help me!" Louie shouts again.

Who is after them.

"Come on!"

God, the man is swimming faster than the boat can move.

"But where'd he come from?" says Perrine in a panic.

Louie doesn't answer, terrified. So the island wasn't empty. There's no other explanation—around them, the sea is as smooth as the day before; only the rippling and terrifying spray in their wake, the sound of those huge breaststrokes, brown skin beneath the water. He screams again, *Help me!*

Perrine grabs the second oar. Louie hands his to Noah, bellows, *Row, row!* and hunts under the seat for the emergency oar. There's one on every boat. There has to be.

Not there.

The other seat? With trembling hands and a pounding heart.

He feels it under his fingers at the very moment when the swimmer hoists himself up to their height, grabbing the gunwale with such strength that the small craft heels violently; all three of them are thrown off balance, and the man too, who surely wanted to lean on the gunwale, a fraction of a second, just time enough for Louie to raise the oar and bring it down on him, the way he did with Ades, the image is there before him, with all his strength, smack on the head, yes, exactly the same, except for the piercing scream from Louie's throat, *Noooo!* he doesn't know why he shouted this time, fear, prayer, rage.

And this time too the man tips into the sea. For an instant Louie vibrates with the victorious fear in his guts, the man will wave his arms with cries of rage and terror, he'll sink, that's it, just like Ades, exactly.

No, he won't.

The difference is that when he flipped backwards, either instinctively or with an insane force of will, the swimmer grabbed the oar.

Louie feels it, that he doesn't have time to let go.

The thought goes through him: he's caught already.

Off balance, he falls in the water. All he hears is Perrine's scream and the sound of the water opening to him.

He falls, almost into the arms of the stunned man, who is holding out a hand, an instinctive, animal reaction—grab hold of the kid not to drown. Louie spits out the water from his throat and nose, sees the blood on the man's face, wants to call out, pulls away from the fingertips touching him as they cling to his T-shirt, a cry at last, to Perrine and Noah, petrified on the boat, *Row! Row!* And then the words stop, no more room, all he can see is the fingers like claws groping for him, moving through the sea, he slaps his hands, kicks his feet, the man is after him, grazing him every time, Louie dodges, panicking. His gestures are becoming disjointed, from fear, from a lack of breath, from those arms too near, obsessing him, they're all he can see, those arms and the spray of the sea where they're struggling, the man will catch him, he will, Louie has no more strength. So he thinks of Pata who used to send him after the wild ducks when they went hunting, Pata who didn't want to get another dog when his spaniel died, he said it hurts too much when they leave you, so it was Louie who ran through the swamps and swam out to get the birds, it was a game they played, Pata shooting his rifle and Louie swimming out. Yes, Pata said Louie was the best dog he'd ever had, the fastest to sprint over there and slip into the water, lively and nervous, he always found the ducks, the best, the best.

Swim!

He dives underwater, deeper down, getting away from the man and his shouts as he tries to stay on the surface. He filled his lungs just before, now he has slipped into the sea, his arms close to his sides to be as smooth as a fish, his feet kicking the ocean, three seconds, five seconds, ten. No time, no courage to look behind him, until he surfaces with a hoarse intake of breath, Perrine and Noah are on their feet in the boat, and cry out when they see him.

"Louie! Louie!"

He just manages to grab the stern with a shout, *Row!* Perrine and Noah sit back down at once, grab the oars and try, pull, they're moving, yes, not fast, but enough for the exhausted man to give up on them. With a huge effort Louie presses his elbows then his arms over the transom, for support, he leans on it, kicks his feet as if he could make the boat go faster, as if he could push it, hard, he doesn't want the others to stop rowing and he nods at them, *Keep going*, he constantly looks behind him, oh this horrible sensation that the man is grabbing his feet underwater to drag him down into the depths, but he isn't, he's floating, over there, half alive half dead, thirty feet away now, then sixty, *Go on*, says Louie again.

On the island, several figures have appeared, waving and screaming.

"Who is it?" cries Perrine. "What do they want?"

Louie answers in one breath.

"Our boat. Our supplies."

"But why?"

"Because they haven't got anything left, either. Maybe they want to go to the high ground."

"But who was he?" She points to the man's head still floating above the water: two adolescents are now swimming toward him from the shore.

"I don't know. Their father? Keep rowing, don't look. We have to get out of here, so they don't try to catch us."

"We're too far now."

"Not far enough. Not yet."

And he lets the sea carry him, gazing toward the island behind them, at the man who wanted to take everything from them.

"Do you think he would have killed us?" asks Noah.

Louie doesn't know. The only image he has at the moment is that of the man rising up out of the sea like a monster, a shark, a beast, his arms pressing down on the boat as if to capsize it, oh yes, he was afraid, that the force would take them to the depths of the water, enfold them, suffocate them. Louie's hands squeezing the boat, he trembles just to think of it, he still doesn't understand. Those people laid a trap, they were concealed on the island already last night, of course they'd noticed the boat, they were waiting for first light to take it, and maybe they would have thrown the three of them into the water, Louie, Perrine, and Noah, to let them drown, if they wanted everything, yes, for sure they would have; and right now the three of them would be floating on the surface of the sea, their bellies swollen. Louie shakes his head, the tears stream down his cheeks, salt like the ocean. They won't stop anywhere again, he swears. Ever.

Only after a quarter of an hour has passed does he let the little ones help him back onto the boat. And even then, removing his soaked T-shirt and shorts to let them dry in the sun, he doesn't take his eyes off the island, of course he can no longer make out the figures of the inhabitants, but he can still feel his hair standing on end, he looks at the sea, a few gentle ripples, what if that were another man. He pushes Noah out of the way, takes the oars, and, as if he had the devil at his heels, rows hard toward what he hopes is the east.

And truly he does hope it is, for the sky has turned grayer, the weather seems stormy, he can sense it, and he doesn't know where to go, he looks for the place where the light pierces through the clouds, without being sure that the angle he's trying to follow is the right one, but at least they're getting away from the island, after that there is only guesswork, only pretending, when the little ones ask him, if he believes in it hard enough, it will be the right direction.

They had been expecting it. Louie had told them as much. But until the last minute they prayed the storm would pass them by, would turn back, into their thoughts they drummed the conviction that fate wouldn't do this to them on top of everything else, not after it had almost served them up to a family even more wretched than they were, not after the fright, fate owed them this much, a moment of respite. Well, no.

And yet, when the waves began to form, Noah still thought the storm might trail away any moment now, a false alarm, just bluffing, and he waved his arms as if to shoo it away, spread his arms into the wind to stop it, shouting, *Go away!*

"Idiot," said Louie.

And Noah seemed to shrink, right then and there.

He sat down next to Perrine, clutching the seat, and rolled his eyes, looking out at the surface of the ocean, spotted with whitecaps and spray.

Silence.

They watch.

Try not to notice the gusts of wind mussing their hair and splashing them with spray. They turn their heads every which way, as if an island might appear by magic, they'd force Louie to land, in the end the storm is far more terrifying than the crazed inhabitants of islands.

On the floorboards the hens have begun squawking, coming and going in a confused parade. The children know that the birds, too, can tell bad weather is on its way. They check the ropes along the boat, they'll need to cling to them if it starts pitching too violently. They watch one another, trying to come up with what to say, what to think.

Noah thinks of the sunken worlds underwater.

Perrine thinks of Madie.

Louie wonders if the hens will slide into the water, or if they'll manage to hold on. He decides to spread a tarp across the boat and ties it with string. Noah raises his hand and smiles:

"It's like an umbrella. It will protect us from the rain."

"I hope the wind won't rip it off."

And the impression they get is a very odd one when the storm suddenly wraps itself around them and sets the boat to dancing, because they can't see anything, they're trapped beneath the plastic, but there are just moments when the lightning illuminates the sea—at those moments, it's almost as if the tarp had blown away. And yet a second later it's there again, they can sense it in front of their eyes, they can feel it over their heads. Perrine is frightened: what if they sink. What if they get their legs and arms all twisted in the tarp and can't get free, imprisoned like worms in cocoons that are too tight, drowning without a chance, without a gesture, chrysalises sinking to the bottom of the sea glinting blond and blue.

So she shoves the plastic tarp away without thinking, her eyes wide open, just the words pounding in her head, *I'm scared, I'm scared.*

Louie's shout.

"Are you crazy?"

He yanks the tarp back over them; on the horizon, the light is yellow and pink. He points his finger into the distance.

"It's getting calmer. We're not in the worst of it."

They keep an eye on the far end of the sea, clinging to the gunwale not to be knocked off balance by the waves; their fear doesn't dissipate. For endless minutes the ocean tosses, whips, rolls them, and Louie needs a great deal of conviction to go on believing it's only a little storm, he won't let go, the sky is clearing and the wind growing steadier. The sea terrifies them, however, it has taken over the world, it is so dark that they can no longer make out the boundary between the ocean and the gigantic clouds, there's only a vast black world engulfing them, *It's like being in the belly of a whale*, murmurs Noah, but the others don't hear him.

Then they can again see the shapes of the clouds, gray lights in the sky. Black, somber masses charged with a fierce rain go by on their left.

"Look," says Louie.

They watch the downpours moving past, whirlwinds, and they're at the very edge, pelted only by jagged little bursts of spray that sting their faces; over there the sea is rough, with towering waves that strain skyward.

Pray it doesn't come this far.

Pray the wind will keep the waves away.

They cannot take their eyes off the storm as they move along it, graze past it, helpless to get away or to stop the storm from taking them with it, should the currents change, but they don't think of this, they're too busy clutching the boat, bracing their legs, regaining their balance when they slip.

Not as strong.

It's getting calmer, says Louie again, in a low voice.

Waves slapping on the ocean.

Yes, not as strong.

A tiny burst of joy in their thoughts. *Is it over?* asks Perrine. *Almost.*

Five, ten minutes. No more black. Gray, blue, a little bronzed yellow, as if the sun were trying to break through, to rip open the thick clouds. A single ray of light, unexpected, incongruous, inscribes an arrow of light from the sky to the sea. The boat has stopped shaking them about.

Noah looks up. *And that?*

Then they see it.

Behind them, raised by the elements, a renewed onslaught of waterspouts.

* * *

Before their gaping eyes, the sea has risen again. A sort of nightmare starting over, a bad dream they cannot escape, toying with them, making them believe that—and then.

The boat gesticulates on the sea—that is really the word for it—it twists, distends, a wooden body cracking and contorting, slamming the surface of the water every time it comes down, hemmed in by a pellet spray of lightning all around the children. In the beginning they shouted advice, orders, questions; now there is only a long wailing when the sea buffets them, half capsizing the boat, which rights itself just in time, they can't even bail the water that is gradually making it heavier, it's all they can do to huddle down, cling on, stay on board. The tarp tore away immediately, they saw it fly off into the sky, whirling, descending, heading off again—then they didn't see it again, the storm took it, it's gone; they hold on.

A dozen times, rattled by a breaker, a wave, a dreadful trough, they thought they would let go. Did let go, a hand, a foot, they slipped, by some miracle the three of them are still all in the boat, with the hens, which roll from side to side, beating their wings. The only thing they can feel is that their strength is waning, that the storm will get the better of them, their arms are braced, their aching fingers can no longer close tight enough around the ropes, and sometimes their gazes meet, full of fear, then look away, trying to find some sort of support, a place to hold onto.

Suddenly the wave is there: the one they dreaded.

Broadside, all at once. A terrible sound, as if the boat is being torn apart.

They roll over.

In a sort of a hiccup the boat rights itself then crashes into the trough of the wave, tearing the children's hands from the ropes and the gunwale, sending them crashing against the bow. They cry, scream, no one hears. No one to help. They don't even say to themselves that they are going to die. Words are silenced.

Don't even look at one another.

Everyone for themselves; the world around has vanished. No more thoughts, nothing that is not straining fully toward those clinging hands, those curving fingers, all breath choked by showers of spray.

There is only fear.

And the howling of the wind on the sea, like the terrifying cry of a ghost looking for lost children, parting the walls of storm with great gusts and blasts of rage.

When the wave recedes, they slam together where they have been hurled to the bottom of the boat, their noses bleeding unnoticed, they scratch and graze each other, and the hens in turn lose their balance, slide out from under the seat where even their frenetic beating of wings cannot restrain them. The children hear their squawking and cackling as if from another world; a moment later, the hens come tumbling on top of them, lacerating them with their claws as they struggle to right themselves, wings spread, flapping, hindered by the storm. Several of them roll from one end of the boat to the other, and Louie knows, reaches out, too late—they are catapulted against them, bounce, are projected overboard, they can hear the furious squawking, a few seconds, then nothing more, the children huddle under the seats, terrified by the sea's momentum and how it has taken their hens, nothing more, no, just Perrine's scream.

"My eyes!"

But Louie and Noah don't reply, they don't understand, the storm has petrified them. Bruised from falling, colliding, they cling on, hopelessly, instinctively, it's not anything they can control, their arms are paralyzed. Only Perrine is no longer holding on; her hands are pressed against her face.

But once again, they do not see.

Everyone for themselves.

Not out of selfishness: because they are terrified of death, it fills their minds, absorbs the last of their strength, their last breath.

Perrine is lying to one side.

And this time, the storm recedes.

* * *

Despite the rough waves Louie has crawled on his knees over to his sister, once her moans entered his panicked mind. Wading through the water that has swamped the boat, he shakes her; her hands are still held to her face.

"What is it?"

"The hens . . . they scratched my eyes with their legs . . . I can't see, Louie, Louie I'm blind!"

She has long gashes of open flesh on her face, as if they had been made with a dull needle on which a great deal of pressure has been placed. There is blood everywhere; her eyelids are torn.

"It hurts, it hurts . . . "

"Take your hands away so I can see!"

But Perrine is protecting herself, doesn't want to be touched; her cries are gut-wrenching to Louie and Noah, this never-ending pain they cannot ease. Louie pours some water on a cloth, cleans Perrine's cheeks where she will let him touch her, her forehead, he braces himself against the seat not to slip, with the ongoing tremors, he encourages her in a quiet voice, *Take your hands away, I have to clean it*—and she cries, *No, no, no!*

Noah, holding the water bottle, cries out:

"You want me to make her?"

Louie shakes his head; his gestures jerky with the backwash and the waves, he gives up: he'll only hurt her. He places the cold cloth over Perrine's eyes.

"Just hold it like this, it's cool, it'll feel better."

Her little fingers close around the cloth between two sobs. Louie stays by his sister for a few moments, then slips over to the edge to look out at the sea. Noah kneels beside him.

"She's really unlucky, huh."

"Uh-huh."

"And she already lost one eye."

"Yes."

"You think we're going to die today?"

"Leave me alone with your stupid questions!"

Noah withdraws into himself, goes back to Perrine, who is moaning.

"Does it hurt?"

She doesn't answer. The boy nods.

"Yeah, me too when it hurts I don't feel like talking."

He sits cross-legged, takes her hand.

"You don't have to say anything."

And adds:

"I hope we won't sink."

Later, he'll boast that it was only a little bitty storm—he'll even say, because he'd heard his father use the expression, that they caught the *tail end of the storm*—and Louie will give a shrug:

"You don't know what the hell you're talking about. We were lucky, is all."

Just as the rain stopped all of a sudden, the storm has

subsided. Or did it go elsewhere? They don't know, they know only that the boat is no longer pitching, that the wind is no longer howling, and that the sky, for the few remaining hours of daylight, is clearing. Louie bails with a bowl.

Murmurs: *Incredible.*

Yes, they were lucky.

Except Perrine.

The two boys sit around the girl. Noah raises his eyebrows. "She's been crying for a while."

She doesn't stop.

And the pain, has it stopped?

Noah asks: *Are you all right?*

"Shut up," scolds Louie.

They watch her in despair. Louie spreads his hands as if they could do something—an idea, a miracle; he keeps them open on his lap. Noah blows gently onto his sister's face. It was their mother who taught them to do this, when one of them would fall, or bang himself, or scratch herself, she would blow on the hurt, and the suffering would abate, disappear. He leans closer:

"Does that feel better?"

The little girl shakes her head, does not stop crying; Noah is not Madie. Louie gently lifts off the cloth, soaks it with fresh water, replaces it. Gradually night has fallen and he can no longer see her wounded face. But Perrine's moans haunt them until dawn; she sleeps intermittently—and then Louie can feel his nerves let go, and fatigue gets the better of him. He opens his eyes the moment she starts to sob again. In a quiet voice he says, *I'm here.* And then these stupid, senseless words: *We'll find a doctor for your eyes.*

In the early morning, while Perrine is sleeping, as the cloth has slipped to the floor, he looks—and immediately turns away. Perrine's good eye, the one most damaged by the hens, is swollen and red, oozing a yellowish pus between her lashes.

But Louie does what he can, pours some water to clean it a little; and even though he expected it, he is startled by his sister's cry as she wakes.

"It's all right," he murmurs, "I'm not touching it, it's just water. Here's the cloth. Put it on if you want."

Before they raise the anchor he gets out some breakfast, but Perrine doesn't want anything to eat or to drink, she moans, complains of the heat—*The heat?* says Noah with surprise, for he put on a sweater against the chill from the storm.

Louie puts his hand on her brow, and it is too hot.

He knows this isn't a good sign.

Folded on himself, he holds his head between his elbows. There are too many problems in his head, too many things he cannot deal with, this wound to take care of, the land that isn't there, his little sister's tears piercing him to the bone.

Where are they, now that the storm has turned them every which way, ruining all their efforts, their nonexistent landmarks, the hopes they had raised to keep going?

So Louie reaches for the oars.

Tells Noah: *She has to drink. We have to make her drink.*

And he pulls hard on the oars.

That's all they can do: go forward. He says it to himself all day long, except for the moments when he stops to straighten his back and relax his tetanized arms, when he manages to convince Perrine to eat half an egg, then nothing more, so this is really the only thing he has left, to go on, with his lower lids burning from holding back his own tears, because his sister's tears are breaking his heart, he can't stand it, and he no longer knows the way to the coast.

This void inside him is a chasm spilling out of his body, and the boat, and the sea; a hollow that goes right to the bottom of the world, where even the seabed has vanished, and the rock is hot, so close to the core of the earth. That is where Louie would like to be, curled up in an inaccessible recess, deaf to every lament and every pain, alone if he must be, not to go completely mad, if it's not too late. Alone, and have done with it.

No one left on earth.

So between the drops of sweat that sting his eyes, he looks at Noah kneeling by Perrine, and he wonders if that is not the solution.

Have done with it.

"What?" says Noah.

Louie said it out loud. He bites his lips.

"Nothing."

Knock the two of them out and drown them. Afterwards he will tie himself to the anchor with a rope and let it unwind. He imagines it. Going straight to the bottom.

No more children.

No more suffering.

The thought runs through him like an electric shock.

No.

And suddenly, Noah screaming and turning to him.

T here! There!"
Louie drops the oar with surprise, and it falls with a
bang onto the seat and rebounds against his leg. He
makes a face. Doesn't even hurt.

Noah's face, between exaltation and madness: *You see it?*

So Louie leans closer, all thoughts erased. And yes, he sees it.

"What . . . what is it?"

"Dunno. A rock? A house, maybe?"

"It's little, looks like."

"Can we go there, Louie? Let's row there?"

No.

He looks at Perrine, motionless on the floorboards.

"No noise, then. We don't know who lives there."

Without a word, they reach for the oars. There is renewed
vigor to their gestures, urgency, too, because of the little girl
who has a fever and who has stopped talking, and their
urgency is mixed with apprehension, more than that, a dread
which is twisting Louie's guts—will they find someone on that
island in the distance, someone who will be ready to help them,
or will they be killed for the boat and the food, and the water
and the hens. Louie stops thinking: for now, they are going forward. And yet in his gestures, as they get closer, something is
slowing him, imperceptibly, his fear is too great, there is superstition, too, will their luck see them through. Noah, on the
other hand, is rowing diligently, his eyes staring at the horizon.
The two brothers keep watch on the sea. A sort of latent

instinct reminds them that the sea is all the more treacherous just when they think they might be about to escape, and that the traps are always laid for them just when they think they're home safe. But the storm the night before has cooled the temperature, and, before night turned it gray, the sky wore a sparkling blue. Still, they are wary, they study the water all around them, the eddies, the currents they think they can see. Their hearts and throats constrict whenever they get the impression the sea is changing—uneasy, rising. In spite of their fear, they are so eager to reach the island that the air fills with their hopes and seems to vibrate in their eyes and ears; they want it to bring them luck. They have no choice: they have to save Perrine. Urgency transcends all their hesitancy, their fear, the trembling in their arms. Taking turns, they encourage their sister; she doesn't answer.

"We're nearly there."

"We're going to make you better."

But just when they finally understand what is there ahead on the water, they look at each other, stunned. Noah murmurs,

"Are those . . . houses?"

He doesn't say, *Floating houses*, but that was what sprang to mind. And only one of the houses is still above water, the other two, closer to them, are almost completely engulfed. All that is left of the first one is the roof, and they can see the upstairs windows of the second one.

"Yes," says Louie in a low voice. "Houses."

The third house, the one they can see from behind, and where they are headed, floats above, with a long wooden terrace level with the water, which makes it look as if it is sailing on the ocean. For a few moments they get the impression it is coming toward them, drifting, trundling along, and they pause to take a good look.

There are two figures on the terrace.

Louie and Noah both recoil, instinctively; *What do we do?*

Louie starts to scan the surface of the sea, his heart pounding, looking for a wave, a current betraying some invisible presence, gliding through the water, he is already holding his oar aloft, he feels this throbbing inside him, too insistent.

But then he glances down, the same image as before, little Perrine asleep with the cloth over her eyes, her moans and sobs stifled by fever. And Louie makes up his mind all at once.

"Let's go there. Perrine is really sick."

"What if . . . "

Noah doesn't finish his sentence. Louie nods his head, knowingly.

If it's people who want to get rid of us?

But he hasn't erased from his memory the despair that only minutes before made him imagine a terrifying outcome, a vision that will return to him if they don't find any help, because the fatigue is there, deep inside him, and it's more than fatigue: it's renunciation. If he had to explain to Noah, he would just say that he can't cope anymore. That his thoughts have shut down, that he has no more solutions to suggest, nothing, just emptiness of a kind he's never known, vast and frightening, saturating all the space.

This is why they have to go there.

If it's people who . . . ? We'll see.

And anyway, at this stage . . .

The house looks like a huge wooden skeleton perched on the sea. Louie knows Noah is afraid, and he also feels an unpleasant tingling all over his body.

The two figures have come to the edge of the terrace, their hands on the railing to watch the boat come nearer. Louie narrows his eyes to try and see them better. Suddenly he says:

"Old ladies."

Noah sits up. *What?*

Louie observes them. Yes: *grannies*, Pata used to call them, in the beginning, because they'd never known their grandparents. At the same time as he repeats it to himself, a flood of joy inside him.

Before the tidal wave, there were old ladies in the village. Sometimes on his way to and from school, he would help them carry their shopping, or pick up a scarf they'd dropped, and they would ruffle his hair. Give him some candy. They all had a particular perfume, of face creams and another era, and that faint tremor in their voices—or was it just Louie who couldn't hear them properly, used to the clamor of a family of nine children, where you have to shout to make yourself heard.

And then the wrinkles on their faces, at the corner of their eyes as they looked at you, around their mouth as they smiled at you. It's giving Louie shivers just to see them there now. Madie said all the old ladies had died during the deluge. He's glad to see that it's not altogether true. Noah, who is also looking at them, nudges him with his elbow.

The old ladies wave. Both of them are tiny, or so it looks, reduced by years and as shriveled as the crabapples from that tree they had at the end of the garden. One of them is thin, the other is round. They have identical hair, short and curly, white as snow with blue highlights—*Like the sea*, whispers Noah, fascinated.

The boat comes to bump against a pillar on the terrace and Louie doesn't dare throw them the rope to moor it. In the eyes of the first old lady, who is right there next to him, he can see a terrible weariness, her resignation betrayed by a sigh; and yet, after a few seconds have gone by, she says, *Well hello, children. What on earth are you doing here?*

Louie detects that tremor in her voice, which brings back so many memories.

"My sister is sick."

He adds, with a frown, to look serious:

"Really sick."

He can see the old ladies shifting their gaze to the bottom

of the boat, past the hens and onto Perrine, with the sweat on her brow and the cloth on her face. Their eyes open wide, their mouths forming an "o."

"Goodness, that little girl is in a bad way."

The first old lady, the thin one, turns to the other one:

"If you have the strength, Lucette, bring a towel and a bowl of water, quick. And you, children, come on up here, don't stay there on your boat."

She holds out her arms, feebly. Louie and Noah help Perrine up onto the terrace; the girl is whimpering, and she curls up in a ball on the ground the moment the first granny leans over her, while the other one hurries with tired little steps toward the house. Noah kneels by his sister. Louie, undecided, hesitates between joining him and keeping watch on the boat. Deep down, his wariness has not gone away; he looks at the old ladies out of the corner of his eye, the one who is examining Perrine in spite of the little girl's fingers clutching at her face, and the one who, before long, comes back from the house carrying a basin; he wonders if they too will set a trap—he dreams of lying down and sleeping without fear—fear of water, of men—and his eyes ringed with shadows watch as the old women come and go, watch the things they carry, their furtive glances at him.

"Are you all right, son?" asks Lucette, without pausing in what she is doing.

A timid little nod.

Around them, the elated hens have left the boat and are ferreting, pecking on the terrace, he can hear their *tap tap*, and his head is spinning.

"Adele, there's one last tube of aspirin in the cupboard in the bathroom, if you need it. I can go and get it."

The thin old lady straightens up slowly, looks at the other one, awkward.

"Lucette, you're the one who needs it most."

The round granny brushes this off: *Oh, with the time I've got left . . . don't tell me otherwise, we both know it perfectly well.*

Only then does Louie notice the sweat on Lucette's forehead, the sound of her breathing like a saw cutting into a metal beam, the pale, drawn features on her deceptively round face. Adele lowers her head, hunts for her words.

"Just one, then. For the fever."

"Good. Good."

The old lady seems to be in so much pain when she walks that Louie leaps forward.

"I'll go, if you'd like."

"But you don't know where it is," says Lucette with surprise.

He has caught up with her and puts his arm under hers.

"Then you can show me."

A few minutes that seem like an eternity, the time for Lucette to lead him to the end of the corridor in the house and point to a tiny closed cabinet.

"There. In the white and green tube on the left. You have to take a whole tablet and dissolve it in a glass of water."

When they come back, Adele explains fretfully that she has to prepare a poultice.

"We don't have much left in the way of first aid, but it will do a lot of good. It may seem a bit obsolete, but don't let that fool you, it will work wonders."

Noah and Louie watch her in silence, their eyes open wide: they don't know what obsolete means. It sounds nice. It's bound to work.

Adele bends over Perrine.

"I'm going to put something over your eye to reduce the swelling and remove the infection. Don't worry, it won't hurt, it's just lukewarm. But you have to keep it on, I'll put a bandage over it and you'll look like a pirate. All right?"

Attentive and trembling, Perrine doesn't answer. Noah squeezes her hand: *She's going to make you all better!*

"Tell me, your other eye . . . " says the lady, "is it already blind?"

This time Perrine murmurs almost inaudibly, "Yes."

"Right. Then we'll leave it alone, we have to take care of the other one, which is precious. Here. Drink this glass of water, there's some medication in it, it doesn't taste good but it will make you feel better."

"I've had aspirin," whispers Perrine.

"Perfect. Drink it all down, your fever is very high. Lucette, are you there?"

The round old lady is sitting on a plastic chair behind them. Her voice is no louder than a murmur.

"I'm here."

"I'll leave her to you for a few minutes. Look after her."

As soon as she is out of earshot Noah goes over to Lucette.

"Are you sick, too?"

"Noah!" says Louie.

The old lady smiles, wipes the sweat from her temples with an embroidered blue handkerchief.

"He is right to ask. Yes, I'm a little bit sick and a little bit old. But it's not too serious."

"And Adele, is she your daughter? She helps you?"

This time Lucette seems momentarily taken aback—Louie kicked his brother, but too late, he can see very well that the two old ladies are the same age, so he cries out to apologize for his brother:

"He doesn't know about . . . he doesn't understand—"

"Adele's my neighbor," says Lucette slowly. "She can be difficult but she's a good person at heart. I used to live in that house over there, you see?"

"No," says Perrine.

"Yes," says Noah.

Louie looks at the house that is no more than a roof.

"The water went all the way upstairs and flooded everything," explains Lucette, for Perrine's sake. "So I came to live with Adele. But even here . . . we're starting to have water around our ankles."

"And the other house?" asks Noah.

"Oh, that one. It was our third neighbor, Valerie-Rose. We don't know what happened. Since the sea rose all of a sudden, we think she must have gotten stuck there at night and drowned. We haven't seen her in six days . . . she must have died."

The little boy opens his eyes wide.

"Is that why you're sick? Are you sad?"

Lucette thinks for a moment.

"Oh, no. She wasn't a good neighbor, she was always fussing. But maybe if there were three of us we'd have more fun. It's a bit boring around here."

Louie raises his hand the way he does at school when he wants to say something, then lowers it abruptly when he realizes.

"Why are you here the two of you? Isn't there anyone else?"

"The people who lived here and who survived the great tidal wave decided to leave—I suppose it was the same where you're from. But we didn't want to leave. You know, I was born here, and I'm eighty-three years old. Adele is eighty-six. We didn't want to go anywhere else. It's too late for us to start a new life."

"But you're going to be drowned, too."

Like us.

Lucette's gaze mists over, thoughtful and sad, yes, that's it, thinks Louie, there's a sadness about her.

"That could be," murmurs the old lady.

"For sure," insists Noah.

"Anyway, we don't have a boat."

"But we do. We can take you."

Lucette smiles: *That's kind of you*—and Adele's voice suddenly, behind them, makes them turn their heads.

"It's ready."

Perrine starts to cry.

"No, no, it won't burn, or sting, at all. It's just a bit warm at first."

Louie has to take Perrine's hand and squeeze it, quietly reassuring her, *Come on*, but even so it does not stop her from struggling when she senses the poultice, first of all the smell in her nose, and she protests, *No, no*, and then the heat on her eye, she doesn't even know if it hurts but, instinctively, she lashes out behind her and hits Louie in the jaw; he cries out. A moment later Adele is winding a bandage around her head, and it's over. Perrine is still crying, one hand on the bandage.

"Tomorrow," says the old lady, "when I take off the bandage, I bet you'll be able to open your eye and you'll start seeing again. They're so pretty, your blue eyes, even the white part; it would be a pity not to use them anymore."

* * *

During the night, Louie tosses and turns. A strange restlessness prevents him from sleeping, a restlessness that followed the relief of knowing they are safe—for a few days, a few hours, just so long as there is some respite. But in spite of himself he wonders which one of the three of them is bringing them bad luck, causing the days to go by with neither sweetness nor light, never leaving them the time to regain hope between two tragedies, or even catch their breath, just a little gasp, an intake that is too short and too fearful.

Because there is an evil spell on them, on them or on one of them—which one? And how long before their mere presence will make Adele's house sink to the bottom of the sea?

The house will not capsize.

Because of Perrine and her blind eye—there used to be an old woman in the village who, whenever she saw her go by, would cry out and cross herself: *The eye of the devil!* It used to make them laugh. But now?

No, no.

Noah, who forgot to grow up?

The house is strong, resisting the onslaught of the waves, the way you cling to a rock, it's the world around that's moving, not the house, the house is standing, the house doesn't tremble.

Or he himself, Louie, with his game leg.

The waves smashing to bits against the walls.

Or all three of them together, because that's a heap of deformities if you put them side by side, it's enough to make you laugh, if it weren't so sad, you'd hardly notice, maybe someday someone would say, yes, there's something weird about those three, nature or fate needn't have bothered—isn't that the reason why they were left behind on the island and not the others, not Liam or Matteo, not Emily or Sidonie, not Lotte or Marion, just those three, the gimp, the dwarf, and the one-eyed wonder?

Three runty little pigs.

I'll huff and I'll puff and I'll blow your house down.

The next morning Adele and Lucette open their shutters onto a sea of glass. The children slept on mattresses on the floor, exhausted. It rained during the night, and the wind had been gusting, Adele tells them, but the children didn't see or hear a thing, not even the lightning that usually wakes them with a start. Louie, who thought he'd been awake from nightfall to dawn, can't get over it, and yet, the puddles of water on the terrace and the steam here and there on the windows and walls indicate the passage of the storm. Louie runs his palm over the sea: so smooth and silent, contemplative, the wind is calm, the sky as blue as Perrine's eye. So he sighs, as if he had been keeping the waves at arm's length all night long, watching the gray line of the horizon and the vanished waves.

And that next day, as Adele had predicted, beneath the poultice there was a surprise waiting: Perrine's eye, almost normal, still a bit swollen, her eyelid torn, but clean, with a red circle below it like a strange bruise. *It's looking good*, whispers the old lady, pleased. The fever has gone down, too; Perrine's forehead is dry and warm, but still too warm for Lucette's liking, and saying nothing she goes to fetch a second aspirin in the bathroom and hands it to Adele. Once again, Adele frowns and hesitates.

"How many left?"

"A dozen or so."

They exchange glances and they both know that Lucette is

lying, but the ailing old lady tosses the tablet into a glass of water and gives a shrug:

"Now she'll have to drink it."

Adele slowly cleans Perrine's face, even though the girl cries out. Bit by bit the wounded eye blinks, flickers, finally opens not completely but halfway, sitting nearby Louie and Noah can see the blue of her iris. So Perrine gives a start and recoils suddenly, and Adele leans over, then smiles as she straightens up.

"So there you are, you can see me today, can't you?"

Perrine nods without speaking, her lips trembling.

"I'm the one who looked after you yesterday," says Adele. "I'm an old lady. Didn't your brothers tell you? In a few years I'll be a hundred. Don't be afraid, they're right here." She takes Noah by the arm and stands him in front of Perrine: *You see? Everyone's here.*

She changes the bandage, while Lucette hums. They share their food among the five of them, the hens' eggs and potatoes from the children, and canned food and smoked fish from the old ladies. *Hmm*, exclaims Noah, *this is good.*

Yes, now all is well, from Perrine who has regained a bit of appetite to Louie who has left off his wariness. Until Lucette asks him the question. Louie frowns. But she was bound to ask, because the two grandmothers don't exactly run into three children adrift on the sea every day, and Lucette is clearly the more curious one, in spite of her illness and fatigue, so there it is, she asks the question they already heard yesterday, an innocuous little question, and yet it is huge, with everything it implies:

"So what are the three of you doing on that boat all alone?"

Perrine's eyes are bandaged again, but if she had opened them, she would no doubt have done the same thing as Noah: look at Louie. And like Noah she remains silent, waiting for her older brother to reply, and at last he murmurs:

"We're headed toward the high ground."

Adele looks puzzled.

"But . . . just the three of you?"

"Our parents left before us. We have to meet up with them."

"And they let you go to sea all by yourselves?"

"Um, in fact . . . they left with the others but there was no more room for us. We were waiting for them on our island but the water was rising. So—"

Noah breaks in.

"Then there was Ades, and he wanted to steal everything we had to eat. And he drowned, and we took his boat. That's why we have a boat."

Adele rubs her eyes—*I'm not sure I understand.* They explain it again, the children, even Perrine from behind her bandage, it gets all muddled up, and it takes all the old ladies' patience to get the story straight, patience and common sense—and after that they are silent for a long time, their fingers on their lips, eyebrows raised over their wrinkled eyes. Adele clears her throat.

" . . . so you're going to the high ground?"

"Yes," says Louie.

"And you've come from Levet."

"Yes," says Noah.

"Do you know where we are, here?"

"No," says Perrine.

"In Tanat."

Silence. So Adele looks at them and continues.

"That doesn't mean anything to you."

And as it's not a question, they don't answer.

"Tanat," explains Lucette, speaking in turn, "is about ten miles from where you lived."

Louie suddenly turns pale. He understands.

His siblings, no.

Adele looks at him. She smiles at him. She says, *it doesn't matter.*

And Louie, in trembling voice, *Yes, it does matter.*

"What's wrong?" says Perrine, worriedly.

Three, four, ten seconds. His sister murmurs, *Louie?* And Louie, almost in tears, suddenly exclaims, pale and unsteady:

"We got lost. We went backwards!"

* * *

They show him on a map. A map from a time still so recent, when there were roads and real villages, not three half-drowned houses where chickens peck looking for insects and parasites, and a despondent boy, his hands ravaged from days of rowing, is talking to two old ladies, next to a blind little girl and a tiny shrimp of a boy. And no matter how Louie peers and points to the roads the old ladies show him, the calculation always comes out the same, between Levet and Tenet there are just over ten miles, and that is how far they've gone in eight days, two of them with the motor, hardly more than a mile a day, *Oh no*, thinks Louie, *we went for miles, dozens and dozens of miles, how could.*

They did get lost, indeed.

They went round in circles.

A fine arc of a circle; they headed east the way they should, and then because of the sun, and daylight, or the lack of it, and the wind, and fate, and storms, and misfortune, and their parents who had abandoned them, and rain, and hens, and fear—they drifted south, and then random chance brought them back up, in a perfect and terrifying loop, and that's it, from Levet to Tanat, they rowed fifty or sixty miles to end up with ten, and there they are, in a house that is taking on water, with two woebegone old ladies who are trying to console them.

"The main thing," says Adele, "is that you're all alive."

But Louie shakes his head:

"All of that for nothing . . . "

"It's never for nothing."

And yet. Days of fear and suffering, watching the sea, trembling at the thought of storms, hands bleeding from the oars he had to hold from morning to night, the traps that might come their way, right down to men who hide underwater or the claws of terrified chickens. Days of sleeping badly and getting no rest, wondering if the weight of the anchor won't pull them down with it when they lower or raise it. Days of waiting for the morning light, of rowing despite the fatigue that was like a dagger in his gut and his back. Days of doubting, silently weeping, not to frighten the others. Days that lasted for centuries: this morning, Louie is one hundred years old.

Do they know, Adele and Lucette, how they have stifled their terror and despair, do they realize, too, that the children no longer have enough food to leave again, or enough hope to believe that this time they will find their way, without a map or a compass? Louie hid his face in his hands so no one would see his distress. In his inner eye, as if indelibly, the map shows him again how they went astray, and his thoughts come tumbling, throbbing: what are they going to do now?

He wants to live, he doesn't want to let himself die on an island, or in a house once the waters have risen, he doesn't want to become resigned, even if everything seems to be conspiring against him, even if there are not enough supplies or water, even if they have to choose between having the eggs and eating the hens, even if it takes ten more days to reach the high ground. And that is exactly what comes out of him when he pounds his fist on the terrace, his eyes welling with tears:

"I want to live!"

Just tell him what to do, and he'll do it.

It might be superhuman. It might be impossible.

He's game.

But give him a second chance.

Perrine gropes with her hand, closes her fingers around his.

Noah comes, too. They sit there in silence. They don't know what else to do, other than to cling to each other, to show their love.

The old ladies have slipped away, soundlessly. They closed the door to the house behind them.

* * *

For a few days they fashion a strange existence together, the children and the grandmothers, made of bandages and care, waiting, impatience. Perrine's eye is gradually getting better, Adele gives her half an aspirin when it hurts too much; after three days, Perrine removes her bandage. The sun still dazzles her, never mind, she can see. Sitting at the edge of the terrace, her feet in the water when the heat is stifling, she chirps the songs that Lucette hums when she's not's in too much pain— in those moments of pain, the old lady withdraws, they don't know where, somewhere in the house where no one can see her or hear her, and then she reappears a few hours later, her features still drawn, but wearing that smile that makes their hearts leap, they run up to her but don't hug her, not to knock her over, they take her hand and sit down next to her. Afterward, Noah looks out to sea.

"When are we leaving?"

Louie feels a lump in his throat every time he hears the question. Leave, yes, but he doesn't know where. The old ladies have promised to point him in the right direction. Even to give him their compass; they'll never need it again. But in spite of this he's afraid. He's lost his faith. And he already went astray once, so . . .

"I dunno," he says.

"Here too, the water is rising. The terrace will be flooded soon."

"Of course if the water is rising here, it's rising everywhere."

"Do you think our house still exists?"

"I don't think so, no. It was flooded a long time ago."

"But when are we leaving?" insists Noah.

"When Perrine is all better."

"I'm better," says Perrine.

"Not quite."

A day or two more of respite—a sad respite, to be honest, because Louie feels a dull dread gnawing away at his guts, and every sunny morning is spoiled by the fear of the voyage they must undertake, the impossibility of finding landmarks once they're alone again in the middle of the ocean; at the thought of the boundless blue-gray expanse Louie loses his appetite, cannot drink, a sort of bile simmers inside him, burning his flesh, Lucette ruffles his hair the way Madie used to and he turns his head the way a kitten does to heighten a caress, he's upset, and lost, they have to help him, he doesn't want to be the one who has to answer for everything, he doesn't want to be the big brother.

L ouie takes his fishing pole over to Noah and kneels once again at the edge of the terrace. They've been there for nearly three hours. Just behind them he can see shadows fluttering over the old ladies' faces from the uneven torchlight. It reassures him to know that Adele and Lucette are sitting behind them; the night doesn't seem as dark.

And yet: when he looks up, there is no moon. An ink-black night.

Perfect, said Adele happily a while ago.

Because they need fish, lots of fish.

"We tried," said Noah when they started. "They don't bite anymore. There aren't any more fish."

"But were you trying to fish in the daylight?" asked Lucette.

"In daylight?"

"Aha. So you do have a few things to learn."

Yes, loads of fish, because they need to feed all five of them, Adele, Lucette, Noah, Perrine, and Louie, on the boat for days—they don't know exactly how many. And since there aren't enough hens anymore, and they have to be fed too, there won't be enough eggs.

Thousands of fish, agreed Noah with a laugh, when they cast their lines.

Because they are going to leave together.

No, it wasn't what they planned.

Yes, now, it's decided.

They will go all five of them to the higher ground, that's what the old ladies promised when they came out of the house this morning. You could see that the decision pained Adele; Louie looked at her on the sly and he could tell she was in a bad mood, he could tell that Lucette must have cornered her between the four walls of that room where they had heard their voices raised shortly before dawn, and she wouldn't let her leave the room until she got her way. Louie knows this because Lucette whispered the secret to him, yesterday.

She didn't picture it like this, the end of her life. She thought she would be on her own, a peaceful decline, until one day she would fall asleep and simply not wake up. And besides, she was sure it would go quickly. But instead, she is in pain, Lucette, her entire body radiates with a word that Louie can't remember and that makes her cringe over her joints, she says, it feels as if everything inside her is shrinking and gradually drawing her in, and if this goes on, she won't be able to bend her arms or her legs, you just can't imagine how painful it is, this feeling of being sucked inward, it takes her breath away.

Louie didn't say anything. He frowned; he understood that something was wrong but that Lucette was right when she said he could have no idea what she was going through, and he refrained from turning his head to ask where the others were, whether they had started the meal, whether the hens were all there. Then she murmured something about a sort of impossible battle, convincing Adele to leave, all together on the little boat, and at last Louie looked her right in the eyes:

"Really?"

Oh, such immense hope in those eyes, Lucette found it hard to look away. In a low voice she said, *Yes.*

But it won't be easy.

This she did not say, not to dim the glow in the wild gaze

there before her. Convincing Adele to go with the three children who arrived on the wave. And go back to die among her family, on solid ground, not the one gradually shrinking away beneath her own feet. Lucette also has another idea behind all that: to put an end to her suffering. There are times when the simple vibration of Noah's steps running toward her on the terrace is enough to make her wince with pain. And it's not the few remaining aspirins that reassure her, when she shakes the tube, not to see how many days are left; then what, the absence of relief, Adele's poultices: on her, they don't work.

Lucette's day, yesterday, went by in a sort of indecision, between the pain in her body and the excitement of her promise. A thousand times she opened her mouth to speak to Adele; a thousand times her courage failed her. *Last chance*, she thought, at midnight, when they said good night after a cup of lime-blossom tea—and she let the last chance slip. It gave her an odd palpitation in her heart, made her breathless for no reason. Adele finally noticed and asked her if she was all right.

"Yes," replied Lucette in a meek voice, inwardly cursing herself.

They went to bed, each in her own room, soundlessly, by candlelight, and Lucette still hadn't said anything. Perhaps she didn't sleep all night long, or maybe it was just an impression, but at six thirty she heard Adele moving around on the other side of the wall and this time, she went to knock at the door, even if it would mean her heart stopping for good.

So of course it's because of her if Adele is in a bad mood today. But she doesn't care.

She got her way.

She said as much to Louie, exactly like this: *I got my way.*

And the little boy began laughing and crying at the same time.

Today, Lucette feels almost no pain. She rubbed the tube of aspirin and thought of how now there'd be enough for an extra day that with a bit of luck she'd make it to high ground, she wouldn't disappear before then, dragged down by her shrinking body; and it is her wildest desire, to see for herself that somewhere there is land as far as the eye can see, to forget this maddening ocean that blinds her in the sun and worries her when the wind gets up.

What she had to do in order to get Adele to comply, she'll forget about that, too. How she moaned and wept and went down on one knee despite the terrible pain. She'd have thrown herself in the ocean if she'd had to.

All that just to go and die somewhere else, she thinks, taking a fish from Noah's line.

For a moment she stands still: maybe she won't die yet, if they can treat her, *there*?

As for Louie, he stopped counting when they pulled the fiftieth fish from the sea. He doesn't know what part of the night it is, the beginning, the middle, he just knows that Noah can't keep his eyes open, now, and he has to keep nudging him in the ribs to keep him awake. Perrine can't help them, but she has removed her bandage to watch. Every time Louie or Noah catches a fish she takes it to the old ladies for them to kill. The buckets are nearly full.

Right at the edge of the terrace are two torches, burning with a raw, yellow light, and they attract the creatures, fish and insects, like tiny lighthouses, everyone bustling around them, mosquitos and flies, kids, old ladies holding out empty fish-hooks to be cast back in the water, buckets filling with dead fish. Sometimes tiny moths fly too near the torches and their wings make the sound of rustling paper; a little flame in the air, sometimes a mere puff of smoke, the rest plummets. Louie goes on pulling out fish, Noah has stopped shouting whenever one bites. They spent the afternoon preparing their bait with corn and pieces of potato—*Double or nothing*, murmured Adele gravely.

It's a winner.

Like Lucette.

Tomorrow they will smoke the fish, so they'll keep for the length of the journey, and they'll filter the water to fill the empty bottles. They'll inventory the last potatoes, and the last cans in the larder, they'll check for hiding places where the hens might have laid eggs. They'll picture how to arrange the boat to hold the five of them, with cushions for the grannies' old bones—this was their request. But for now they still need a few more fish, until Adele finally gets up and stops Noah and Louie as they're about to cast their lines for the hundredth time. Very precisely, she puts her hands on their shoulders and says:

"I think we have enough, now. Time to get some sleep, to build up your strength."

And everything stops.

Time doesn't go by; that's what they are thinking the next day, as they make endless preparations for the voyage. The water, more than anything, is slowing them down, taking so long to filter, but Adele won't have it any other way, she wants to fill their thirty-four bottles and not a single one less. Under the baking sun Lucette explains to Louie and Noah how to rig poles in the boat on which to stretch a canvas. They are afraid it will blow away with the first gust of wind, like their tarp during the storm: never mind, says the old lady, it will last as long as it lasts. And besides, in September the spring tides are over, the storms less frequent. Even if the seasons have gone haywire.

The two boys exchange glances. Their memory is of storms coming one on top of the other.

Maybe they were the last of the season.

But maybe not.

Lucette hums a tune they don't know, a song her grandmother used to sing, she explains, a long time ago. She and Adele have been up since dawn, cutting the fish and preparing the fillets: by the time the children woke, they had lit the fire and already extinguished it again so that only smoke remained. No flames or embers; and yet you had to keep it going underneath, otherwise it would all go out, and the fish would never get smoked. They showed Louie how to keep an eye on the hearth. The first fillets had been carefully arranged on a grill.

"It stinks," said Noah, "it makes me feel sick."

So he went to get the boat ready.

Perrine stayed with the old ladies.

Hours of waiting, clenching their fists to urge the fish to cure and the water to flow more quickly, and accept the fact that it wouldn't help at all to blow on the fish or to stir the water to filter it—an entire day, a wasted day, according to the children; they chafe at the bit, they wish they were already on their way, to have it behind them, because in reality one day more or less makes no difference, but, when the children see how Adele and Lucette gaze at the houses—what's left of them—and sigh, and lower their heads as they come back inside, walking slowly, they're afraid one of them might get cold feet.

And they are right to be afraid.

Oh, until the end of the afternoon, nothing alarming.

And then.

When they'd finished filling the water bottles and placing the fish filets in plastic containers, separated by sheets of paper, when everything had been readied in the house for the next day, except for the hens, which they'll have to catch at the last minute, belongings on one side, food on the other, and they were sitting on the sofa staring at the black television screen, counting the hours until departure, at seven in the morning, since before then it's still dark out: that's when the argument started.

Initially they didn't hear it, or paid no attention, Adele and Lucette were in the bedroom, talking, on the other side of the thick walls.

But their voices were raised: that's why the children started listening.

"Do you understand?" murmured Louie faintly to the other two.

Perrine and Noah shook their heads.

"What can they be saying?" said Noah, worried.

No time to share their questions any further: a door slams, Adele comes into the room, three pairs of eyes instantly riveted on her, Lucette follows right behind, waving her arms with such intensity that if her rheumatism weren't restraining her those arms would enfold the entire living room.

"No, you won't stay!"

"Yes, I will."

"I won't leave you here."

"Of course not. Go ahead and try."

"We won't leave without you!"

"What?" exclaims Louie.

The old ladies freeze. As if seeing the children for the first time, as if they are about to frown and wonder who they are, that's how far away they seem, but then something lights up in their gaze, they acknowledge them, and fall silent, embarrassed. So Lucette turns to the children:

"Adele doesn't want to leave anymore."

"Huh?" says Noah.

"Who?" says Perrine.

Adele purses her lips:

"I helped get everything ready for the trip, I've done my bit. But I'm staying here."

"But why?" asks Louie, stunned. "The sea is rising, and you'll die."

"Never mind. I no longer have the strength."

"We're the ones who'll be rowing!"

" . . . to live somewhere new. I'm afraid of leaving. I'm afraid of being all alone in a foreign place."

"I'm here," protests Lucette.

Adele spreads her arms in a gesture of resignation. A faint smile.

"It's not enough."

Louie looks at her. He doesn't understand. Or only just an inkling, because there are three of them, Louie, Perrine, and

Noah, until they find their entire world—which will mean all eleven of them, Pata and Madie and their six brothers and sisters who left before them on the sea. If they were alone, would they feel the same? Who is waiting for Adele? Maybe no one. If he had no one, thinks Louie, would he confront the sea?

Yes he would, dammit. Because of drowning. Feeling the sea rising until there's nothing left under your feet on which to climb any higher. Having to resist, and keep on resisting until you have no more strength. And then giving in. To Louie there can be nothing more frightening—not even setting out for a second time on the gray, menacing water in a leaky old boat.

The thought of being drowned in her house: she must have realized, Adele, she can't not care. The vain struggle against the water, against fear and asphyxiation. Has she ever experienced anything as awful as the waves submerging you, and the water filling your throat all the way to your guts, and the fear taking your breath away, paralyzing your arms and legs, when you're just a dead weight hanging on your heart—that's what happened to him when the man on the island toppled him into the water and tried to cling onto him, then went after him, and he only got away at the last moment, hanging onto the boat like a fish on a hook, he was, and he is sure that if Adele had ever experienced anything like that, she wouldn't want to stay here, in this house that is about to be engulfed.

But he doesn't say anything.

He just looks at her.

In fact, there is no solution.

No one has one.

And that is what is suddenly driving Lucette half-crazy, this helplessness, because none of them can convince Adele, none of them can oblige her—to be sure, if Lucette were strong enough, she'd grab hold of her and drag her onto the boat, they'd all leave the island together and speak of it no more, that is what Lucette is thinking, but she is only too well-acquainted with her flabby arms and aching back, how every morning she has to roll over to the edge of the bed to get up without it hurting too much.

And still: she shouts, Lucette, and weeps, too, she doesn't want Adele to die, and she flings her hands about as if she were about to move, to let the sorrow out, to hit her, of course she won't hit her, but she will vent all her anger and sadness and despair. Adele gets annoyed, *Hush, stop it!* Then Lucette takes her by the shoulders and shakes her.

"Do you realize what you are doing? Do you realize? The scene we are making in front of these children? How selfish you are being? What a coward? And me, have you thought about me? I'm all alone, too!"

Furious, Adele shoves her aside with her outstretched arm. But Lucette hangs on, this time: she grabs her by the sleeve, and yanks hard—too hard, and both of them suddenly lose their balance. For a moment they look weightless, tilted in an impossible position like two old trees twisted by the wind, and Louie springs up, because he can see what is about to happen, he opens his mouth to shout and nothing comes out, and nothing would help, anyway, Adele and Lucette are reeling, tilting and unsteady before the eyes of the three petrified children, they are no longer arguing, there is just this look of astonishment in their eyes, and some fear, too, and then time moves forward again and the trajectory of their bodies speeds up, they take a step, stumble, that's it, they're entwined, entangled, and they fall to the floor.

There is the sound of something hitting the wood, a dull crack.

A moan that is silenced.

At last, Louie hurries over to them.

No one speaks, on the boat. Gripped with fear, per-haps, or tense with the effort and attention required to travel by night: Louie has a candle next to him, lighting the compass on the seat. Sometimes he meets Noah's gaze. They remain silent.

Put distance behind them.

Don't think about—

At the stern of the boat, Lucette is bundled in a blanket.

Perrine is sleeping next to the hens, defeated by weariness and emotion. She rowed the first hour with Louie.

Louie tries not to think about anything.

"It will be fine," murmurs Lucette.

He prays it is true. Focuses on the compass, on the east they never found, before, and toward which he is now heading with the steady determination of a bloodhound, the compass placed on the map, which is open wide, to be sure. This curdling feeling in his throat, in his guts: he pays no attention to it, frowning, he channels all the fierceness into his arms as he rows with Noah.

Again the brothers exchange glances. The little boy whis-pers as quietly as he can:

"Do you think she's dead?"

Louie replies in a similar tone: *No. No, no.*

They wish there was more noise coming from the stern, where Lucette is lying huddled.

Adele is lying on a blanket; Lucette regularly wipes a damp cloth over her face.

"Do you think this was a good idea?" says Noah.

"I dunno," murmurs Louie.

* * *

To leave just as night was falling, hastily cramming their supplies onto the boat, chasing down the hens to the end of the terrace; slowly lifting Adele's inert body, as Lucette cried out, *Watch out for her head, to the left, a bit more to the right, careful, now, careful!* Getting her settled as comfortably as they could. Looking at each other, all of them: and casting off with one deep, long breath.

"We won't get a second chance," said Lucette, when she told them they had to leave right after the accident. "We'll never be able to take Adele with us by force. It's a sign, all this, so let's go before she comes to."

"Is it serious?" asked Perrine.

Lucette didn't really reply. She shook her head:

"She's sturdy."

But how sturdy, wonders Louie. A little bit; very. Very sturdy, but for an old lady. That's not as much as an adult like Madie or Pata. It's enough for her to wake up, yes; he wants her to. He can feel it. There's a stirring in his belly as it arches to row faster, and an empty echo in his ears as he listens out toward the stern. Adele saved Perrine, so he can think of only one thing: to help her in return. Revive her, take her with them to the high ground—she can live with them if she wants to, his parents are bound to welcome this old lady who helped their daughter. She won't be alone, ever. And if she doesn't want to live with them, he can build her a house of her own, with a bed of planks and a lopsided table, that, yes, he could do. That much yes, really he could.

Louie savors the suspended time of the night, the boat moving under its own momentum, the absence of noise. Maybe something can begin again.

Maybe, yes . . . then suddenly he feels the boat hit against something, and he sits up with a start.

Bump.

It's an impact that has caused it, *Bump.* All of a sudden, striking them dumb. He felt the tremor, the dull thump.

The boat comes to a sudden halt.

Against what?

They look at each other, pale. Restored to their fear of an ocean where they control nothing. Once again they realize: it is the middle of the night, they have stopped rowing and the boat is drifting.

"What is it?" says Noah.

He gropes his way together with Louie to the bow of the boat, where the impact was.

A rubbing sound.

There's something there. A boat, bigger than their sorry skiff, and the hull is banging into it with this stubborn thumping, to the rhythm of the waves, *thock thock thock*—so it's a boat, and inside it they can hear hoarse breathing.

Noah reaches for his brother's hand. He won't admit he's scared.

But damn, is he scared.

* * *

Madie, too, felt the impact. But she doesn't care. She's not sure she fully understands, either, because she has been drifting in and out of consciousness for hours. She's not even sure this boat where she has decided to die really has struck something, since she has been delirious for god knows how long now, yesterday, this morning; the end soon.

She cannot swallow, she has no more saliva. Her lips are dry, as if dead: when she opens her mouth, the skin cracks.

She licks the blood, instinctively.

The impact, then voices.

Is she raving?

Madie opens her eyes onto the night, thinks she is blind. She stretches out her hand along the floorboards to be sure. Yes, she's still here.

So.

Voices again, children's voices. To hurt her, to remind her of her lost little loves, Noah and Perrine and Louie crying, abandoned on their sunken island. Madie recognizes those voices.

An aberration.

She's losing it.

And yet, the sound doesn't go away. It's even coming closer.

She swore she would not get up again.

Besides, she has no strength.

A little girl's voice asking what is going on.

Little girl?

Madie trembles.

The boat is rubbing against something. Yes there *really is* something there.

A shout.

Not a shout: a scream. Of fear, but not only: there is joy there, too. So Madie tries. She has nothing to lose, after all. With a start she tears herself away, if she can just steal one last image of her vanished children, never mind if it's not true, a mirage, a hallucination held out to her by death, laughing at her, playing with her just a little longer.

It's as if her skin is glued to the boards of the boat.

There, she's sitting up. Oh, such an immense, terrible effort. Her head is spinning but her eyes are wide open.

And she sees them.

Her children.